GONE FISHIN':

Crime Takes a Holiday,
The Eighth Guppy Anthology

Previous Guppy Chapter Anthologies

Fish Tales (2011)
Fish Nets (2013)
Fish or Cut Bait (2015)
Fish Out of Water (2017)
Fishy Business (2019)
The Fish That Got Away (2021)
Hook, Line, and Sinker (2023)

GONE FISHIN':

Crime Takes a Holiday, *The Eighth Guppy Anthology*

Edited by James M. Jackson

First Edition
Trade Paperback Edition: January 2025

Wolf's Echo Press
PO Box 54
Amasa, MI 49903
www.WolfsEchoPress.com

This is a work of fiction. Any references to real places, real people, real organizations, or historical events are used fictitiously. Other names, characters, organizations, places, or events are the product of the authors' imaginations.

Cover design by Emwryn Murphy. Cover images are used under licenses from istockphoto.com and shutterstock.com. Individual image credits are: Goldfish: ChrisGorgio, Beach Background: HAPPY-LUCKY, Beach Chair, Umbrella, and Picnic Basket: IGORdeyka.

ISBN-13 Trade Paperback: 978-1-943166-48-0
ISBN-13 e-book: 978-1-943166-49-7
Library of Congress Control Number: 2024947586

Printed in the United States of America
10 9 8 7 6 5 4 3 2 1

CONTENT WARNING:

Sisters in Crime is committed to creating safe and welcoming environments at all gatherings, in its communications, and in its publications. This includes being sensitive to topics which may cause emotional or physiological distress in readers, listeners, and/or viewers.

In providing this content warning for *Gone Fishin': Crime Takes a Holiday, The Eighth Guppy Anthology*, the Guppy Chapter of Sisters in Crime is intentionally creating an inclusive space that respects the myriad lived experiences of the many individuals engaging with our chapter. Please note that this book includes the following instances of sensitive content:

Ageism
Alcohol use or intoxication
Blood
Child abduction and exploitation (nonsexual in nature)
Child endangerment
Death or dying
Dementia
Disappearance or death of a child
Eating disorders
Infidelity
Kidnapping and abduction
Mental illness and ableism
Murder or attempted murder
Self-harm and threatened suicide
Selling drugs
Sexism and misogyny
Stalking (physically or on social media)

Swearing or curses
Theft and robbery
Use of deadly weapons including firearms, knives, and toxic substances
Violence (verbal and physical)

If any of these topics would compromise your health, well-being, and self-care, please do not read beyond this page.

Table of Contents

INTRODUCTION

CONNIE BERRY

Ah, vacations—time to relax and put your feet up, read a good book, spend time with family or friends, explore new horizons. Doctors and psychologists tell us that escaping from life's routines, even for a few days, can significantly lower our stress levels, reducing the risk of serious disease and improving our overall mental health.

Unless something goes badly wrong, of course.

Whatever your idea of vacation may be—chilling out on a sandy beach, sightseeing in foreign locales, camping in the woods, or an adventurous road trip—the reality often falls short of the dream. Delays, detours, and disasters are ever-present, lurking behind our carefully curated itineraries. Flights are cancelled. Bookings are mishandled. That recommended five-star hotel has bedbugs. Sometimes we're to blame ourselves. I remember one European vacation I screwed up by forgetting that March has thirty-one days.

In *Gone Fishin': Crime Takes a Holiday, the Eighth Guppy Anthology,* the stress of missing a flight or the pain of falling victim to pickpockets is only the beginning. From a creepy holiday cottage and an ill-fated cruise to a romantic getaway turned deadly, twenty-three short-story writers from the Guppy Chapter of Sisters in Crime explore the devious twists and turns of crime-on-holiday. Guppies is the largest and only online chapter of Sisters in Crime, with more than 1,100 members from all over North America and beyond. The Guppy Steering Committee and I are especially pleased that a significant number of our anthology authors are published here for the first time.

My deepest thanks go to the eight independent and highly qualified judges who read and scored the submissions; to our editor, former Guppy Jim Jackson; to our cover artist, Emwryn Murphy; and to our Anthology Coordinator, Grace Topping, whose diligence and attention to detail kept us on track and on schedule.

We hope you enjoy these twenty-three stories of crime-on-holiday. Perhaps you'll read them while relaxing on the beach or toasting marshmallows beside the campfire on your next safe, serene, and (of course) crime-free vacation.

Connie Berry
President, Guppy Chapter of Sisters in Crime

POSTCARDS FROM LOON LAKE

SUSAN DALY

Loon Lake nr North Bay, Mon 26 Aug, 1935
My dear Julius . . .

I SAT ON THE SPACIOUS verandah of Loon Lake Lodge with the other women, all of them engaged in the various ladylike activities encouraged by their husbands. Knitting, exchanging anecdotes about their respective children and grandchildren and various church activities, writing postcards . . .

That's how it is in the Lake Nipissing area, and every other hunting and fishing lodge in Ontario. The men come here to indulge in their manly activities. They go out and have a good time canoeing and killing things, and leave their women at the Lodge all day, knitting and gossiping, enlivened by rounds of bridge in the afternoon. The men come back around teatime (also known as opening time), filled with tales of overpowering wily fish—*I tell you, he put up one heck of a fight, but I landed him at last*—and shooting ferocious bears—*Then, just when he reared up and prepared to attack, I dropped him with one clean shot right through the heart.*

The lodge and its activities haven't changed much since it opened in 1884—except, perhaps, to re-cover the worn cushions on the sturdy rustic couches in the big common room with the huge stone fireplace and replace the ancient moose head over the fireplace when it became moth-eaten.

Even the postcards are vintage. Hand-tinted pictures of moose and Mounties and local native guides holding strings of enormous fish. Women wearing skirts that haven't been that long since before The Great War.

The only new postcards are of the local miracle.

The Dionne Quintuplets, five identical baby girls, all born alive and now kicking, have been making headlines around the world for the past 15 months. And—astoundingly—this miracle occurred in the village of Callander, barely five miles from Loon Lake Lodge. Nearer, as the crow flies.

I looked down at my postcard. What to say that was new? Not that it mattered. I suspected Julius of paying little attention to the content of my postcards over the past thirty-one years, other than to glance at the picture of a bull moose posing on a high rocky outcrop, and say with a grin, "Right. Sounds like she's okay."

Julius is a criminal lawyer. I'm proud of him and his work, but too often, like now, he becomes tied up in Toronto for weeks defending either the guilty or the innocent. More often the guilty, since they present a gratifying challenge. That's when I often head to my favourite northern retreat, Loon Lake Lodge, run by my old friend Marian Tweed.

Julius's case was wrapping up, and he hoped to join me at the end of the week for a well-deserved rest.

I picked up my pen and expanded on *Dear Julius* . . .

The days have been calm and relaxing—

I looked up at the sound of someone pounding up the steps at the far end of the verandah. Young Jim McAllister appeared in his hunting gear. He ground to a halt, panting, clearly big with news.

"One of the Quintuplets has been kidnapped!"

The ladies dropped their knitting, their grandchildren's photographs, their bridge hands (I later heard—twice—Mrs. Pargeter was holding the makings of a Grand Slam) and rose as one to pull young Jim into their midst.

The questions flew at him. *What happened? When? Who did it? How'd you hear it?*

He filled us in as best he could. Just before lunch. No, they didn't know who'd done it. Frank Bigcanoe had a shortwave radio at his cabin. He'd passed it on to his wife's nephew. And so on . . . At some point, it had reached the Loon Lake Lodge hunting party, just returning from their day in the wild.

"Which one?" I asked.

All the buzzing stopped at once, and they stared at me.

"Which *one?*" Jim echoed, as if I'd asked him to name a star in the Big Dipper.

"Which girl was kidnapped? You *do* know they are five individual children, not a litter of kittens? Annette, Cécile, Émilie, Marie and—"

"How should I know?" he snapped. (Thank goodness, because darned if I could remember the fifth girl's name.) "Sorry, Mrs. Delany. They didn't say."

"Yvonne," Marian Tweed said from the inside doorway of the verandah. "The radio says it's Yvonne."

The verandah was now awash with men, as the various hunting and fishing groups showed up and began explaining their ideas, opinions, and plans. It was clear through the deep rumble of men with a mission that every one of them intended to form search parties, to go out tramping through the woods and manfully rescue the helpless little girl from whatever evil had befallen her.

Fortunately, Marian could deliver a piercing whistle through her fingers, and she did so. The din died to a murmur. Marian took charge with her no-nonsense voice.

"Okay, men, I know you're all anxious to help out. Here's what's happening. I just had a call from Sergeant Béliveau of the North Bay Provincial Police detachment. He's on his way over to organize search parties. Anyone who wants to volunteer can head to the dining room and wait for him there."

This news produced a general air of cheerful, manly purpose. The men began to jostle each other to squeeze through the inner doorway.

Marian again silenced them with a whistle.

"Sergeant Béliveau says *No guns.* So, every one of you has to store your hunting gear safely away first."

This dictum was less happily received, but they grumbled their way off the verandah, and we ladies remained in the peace they left behind. The others shared their shock and worry over this turn of events, and speculated on what might have happened.

Then the murmurs of *wasn't there that other little girl . . . last year?*

I hadn't heard about it, but now the details came out fast and conflicting.

Four years old. Kidnapped. Wandered off. Abandoned by her mother. Murdered.

They agreed on one thing. Her little body had been found in the woods. Days after her disappearance.

Marian nudged me. "Come on, Evelyn, let's go have a drink."

I was glad to escape to her office, reflecting I'd have plenty to tell Julius now. Marian poured us each a generous shot of Northern Spirit Rye, then shook her head with a sigh.

"Ever since that five-ring circus came to town last year, things have been a little crazy around here."

"Lots of tourist traffic? Isn't that good for business?"

"Not this kind. Since those kids were made Wards of the Crown and removed from their parents' care, they've been holed up in that purpose-built combination nursery, prison, and fish tank, courtesy of the Province of Ontario." She paused for fortification from her glass.

"So now there's a steady stream of government busybodies, attention-seeking movie stars, and hundreds of rubbernecking tourists arriving day and night. All looking for places to stay. There's new hotels and auto-courts going up, and lots of private homes offering accommodation. Well, good for them. But what I don't need is the overflow sniffing out my place. I run a hunting and fishing lodge with exactly the amenities my regular guests expect, and nothing more. I don't have the time or the room for a bunch of last-minute one-night stands."

"So now what's going to happen?"

"Well, I couldn't say no when the Provincial Police asked to use my dining room as their centre of operations. Especially after what happened last year, poor little kid. That means we'll have the big shot OPP guys showing up, along with men from the government. Not to mention the reporters and newsreel crowds hanging round. Again."

A knock at the door. Marian admitted a six-foot-something wall of dark uniform and introduced us. Sergeant Béliveau impressed me as a strong-minded, no-nonsense kind of guy. He sat down and accepted a shot of rye.

"Well, Sergeant," Marian said, "Anything my friend and I can do to help? Although, you've got all those outdoorsy men eager to go out and find little Yvonne."

He nodded with a smile that implied skepticism. "I've handed that particular search detail to one of my constables. We want to keep those men doing what they *think* is useful and prevent them from running around the woods in a dozen different directions."

"Wise of you," I said. "I notice you disarmed them too."

He smiled again. "*Bien sûr.* We've got our own men doing the serious searching in the immediate area in and around the compound."

He filled us in on what they knew.

The Quintland Compound included the so-called hospital where the girls lived, a staff house for the nurses and other attendants, and a separate area known as their "playground," where multitudes of tourists could observe the girls three times daily through one-way glass. A seven-foot-high barbed-wire fence surrounded the whole affair.

To keep the public out, or the girls in? I wondered.

Even so, with all this security, just after they'd been on display in their play area, staff had escorted them back to their living quarters for lunch. That's when they'd realized one of the girls was missing. For a minute, everyone assumed she and her escort were just dawdling along the pathway, but soon it became clear that little Yvonne was nowhere to be found.

Everything had exploded from there.

"So now," Sergeant Béliveau said, "everyone is getting involved. All the way up to Premier Mitch Hepburn, because the girls are wards of the Crown. So he is sending a man from the Public Guardian's office to, well, throw his weight about."

The government man wanted to keep clear of the waves of tourists who were now a fact of life in Callander, along with the inevitable reporters, so if Mrs. Tweed could put him up at the lodge . . . ? He was arriving shortly on a private flight from Toronto. And if Mrs. Tweed could send someone to collect him? Because, let's be honest, the police had more important things to do.

That someone turned out to be me.

LEANING AGAINST MARIAN'S DODGE TRUCK parked at the Trout Lake Air

Harbour, I watched the seaplane come to a standstill by the dock. A millionaire fan of the Dionnes had offered his private plane to bring in the Premier's man.

A fiftyish man in an expensive-looking brown suit manoeuvred his way from plane to dock. He had senior civil servant written all over him—well-groomed, well-nourished, and well-entitled. Mr. Aylwin Ford, from the Office of the Public Guardian.

I explained who I was and where we were going.

It was an hour's drive to the Quintland Compound, where Mr. Ford would make his first stop. No doubt, as Sergeant Béliveau had suggested, to throw his weight around. Because, frankly, there wasn't a thing he could do to help find the child.

"Well, Mrs. Delany," Mr. Ford began, "I hope you can appreciate the seriousness of this situation. Premier Hepburn has sent me to ensure that no stone is left unturned in finding this missing child."

"That's very good of him—and you—to be so concerned, Mr. Ford. And yes, I do appreciate how serious it is. A child has vanished from her home." If you could call such a place home. "But I'm wondering if the Premier would be so concerned about the disappearance of just any child, if she wasn't also part of a massive commercial venture that's been pouring money into the provincial coffers."

Out of the corner of my eye, I noticed Mr. Ford turn a delicate shade of purple. Well, I had no axe to grind with him personally, but I couldn't help thinking about the little girl who'd gone missing last year—and had not been found until it was too late.

He cleared his throat and rallied.

"You may not be aware, Mrs. Delany, that it was, ah, essential for the Province to step in for the good of the children, when we discovered the father had signed a contract with the, ah, Chicago World's Fair to put the quintuplets on display to the whole world. Of course he couldn't be allowed to, ah, exploit the girls for *money*."

I made a non-committal *hmmm* . . .

"Which is why Premier Hepburn took the step of making the girls wards of the Crown. To save these defenseless babies from commercial exploitation at the hands of their father."

His story sounded well-practised.

I didn't repeat my contention that it seemed to be just fine, however, for the government to make money from them.

I LEFT MR. FORD AT Quintland, and headed back to the lodge, with instructions to pick him up later that night. It wasn't my idea of how to spend my holiday, but anything I could do to ease the pressure on Marian was all right.

Come early evening, with the late summer light still shimmering off the lake through the trees, I relaxed on the verandah, vaguely wondering what I'd done with the postcard I'd started—how long ago? It seemed like days.

There'd been an early supper for the returning men. This allowed more time for anyone who wanted to go out again before the light faded. Some had called it a day, while a few determined souls were prepared to keep on all night.

Most of the guests, men and women, had decamped to the main lounge with coffee or nightcaps.

I leaned back in the chaise longue, enjoying the evening as the light faded and the haunting call of a loon echoed over the water.

"Mrs. Delany . . . ?"

I started at the quiet voice and looked up to see Jim McAllister looking nervous, unsure, like he hoped I could make things all right.

"Jim?" I was whispering too. "What's happened?"

He glanced along the deserted verandah. "Can you come with me? Please? Down to the lake?"

My heart sank. What had he found?

"Of course. What is it?"

He put his finger to his lips, and I followed him down the steps. We took the path through the woods to a stretch of shore out of sight of the lodge.

Sitting on a rock was a young woman, looking both terrified and relieved. In her arms, wrapped in a blanket, was a sleeping child. A girl of just over a year old. There was no mistaking that adorable, world-famous child.

Yvonne Dionne.

I waited for Jim to speak, since I couldn't find a word.

"Louise, this is Mrs. Delany. She's going to help you. I hope?" He turned to me for confirmation.

"Jim, I can't. I don't know what. . ."

"It's like this . . . I went back out after supper. By myself. A lot of the guys had given up, but I was ready to keep on. Even that constable in charge didn't know I'd gone. I was wandering along the edge of the lake . . ."

He'd heard a noise in the woods. That's when he'd found this young woman. Louise. With the missing child.

Louise got to her feet. She was barely more than a girl herself, perhaps sixteen. She looked straight at me, held out the sleeping child, and said, "Please. Take her. Take her home to her mother— No, they already took her away from her mother."

I accepted her. She was warm and solid. She barely moved as she settled into my arms with a sweet baby sigh.

"Louise, you have to come with us. You need to tell everyone what happened. There are hundreds of people out looking for her. They're worried sick—"

"Well, imagine that. *You* take her back. Not me."

Jim looked torn, as if he just wanted to get this over with.

"Louise, please," he said. "It'll be okay. They'll be so glad to have her back—"

"No! I'm not coming. If you force me to, well, I won't. If you tell them it was me, I'll—I'll drown myself in the lake." From her look, now all anger and fear, I could believe her. "And that will break my mother's heart all over again. After Michelle . . ."

Now she broke into tears.

"Michelle . . . ?"

Jim took a deep breath. "There was another little girl. Last year. She wandered off and was found, uh, in the woods."

He didn't say "dead," but I remembered the outcome.

Louise wiped her tears away and found her anger again. "Yes! My little sister. You know who finally found her? Me. Because no one else but our family and people from the church looked for her. The police didn't care. They had more important things to do, protecting those five newborn babies from the tourists, and there was all the crowds of reporters and famous people and complete craziness going on, and no one had a moment to spare for a little girl who needed help. Who died cold and hungry, lost in the woods.

"And the newspapers didn't even care. It was on page five—a single paragraph about the missing child found dead after four days. Because the rest of the paper was taken up with those precious Quints."

She lost her energy and gazed at Yvonne. "Yes, she is sweet, sleeping like that."

"But Louise . . . why take her?" And how, I wondered.

"I got a job at the compound last month, nursery maid-in-training. No one recognized my name, because no one ever paid any attention to us. There was plenty of supervision, you can believe me, and I learned my job well. I watched and waited and planned for the right time."

"How did you get her out?" Jim asked.

"I created a secret exit at the far end of the compound." She gave us a bitter smile. "That fence isn't nearly as strong as they think."

"But why?" I repeated.

"Why?" She paused, as though finding the words to make us understand. "Because . . . I wanted to show how different it would be for the pampered darling, one who was born to a poor family just like Michelle, but because she happened to have four identical sisters, people everywhere went crazy about them and crowned them little princesses. They gave them a life a thousand times more than any child could want. I wanted to show that when *she* went missing, the police and the province, and the whole world would move heaven and earth to find her."

Exactly the accusation I'd thrown at Mr. Aylwin Ford this afternoon.

"Come back to the lodge with us, Louise," Jim said. "It will be better if you turn yourself in." He paused. "Honest, it will."

She held her defiant look for a few moments, then seemed to lose her fight. "They will crucify me, won't they?"

We walked back up the path to the lodge. Holding the million-dollar baby in my arms, I could only imagine how right she might be about that.

"I took good care of her, you know. Better than they did at that prison where they keep those girls. But you know what? The people may want to punish me for taking their darling away. But the law will persecute me for something different."

"I know," I said. "The province made those girls wards of the Crown not to ensure their well-being, but to create the biggest tourist attraction in Ontario next to Niagara Falls. And you stole their valuable commodity."

She paused on the path and stared at me. "You understand, don't you?"

I nodded. "Yes. And I promise I'll do whatever I can to help you."

THE FOLLOWING DAY, I DID my best to avoid the predictable sound and fury arising from the recovery of little Yvonne. To evade the reporters—and believe me, they were after me in droves—I took refuge in a deck chair by a little secluded bay Marian told me about.

Once again, I was composing a postcard to Julius. I tucked away my first two attempts and selected a new card, one with a picture of the Dionnes.

My Dear Julius,

Don't get too ready to relax. Have I got a case for you.

Just Chillin'

KM Rockwood

FORTUNATELY, MARTHA HALEY NOTICED THE dust rising at the foot of the winding driveway and spotted the sheriff's patrol car climbing the hill.

She wasn't sure if her nephew, Josiah, was down in the basement or not, but she wasn't taking any chances and rushed over to the stairs to holler a warning. Then she glanced in the full-length mirror on the outside of the bathroom door to make sure she looked presentable.

Appearances were important.

Yes. She was fully, appropriately clothed. She patted down her hair to smooth it, opened the front door, and stepped onto the porch.

The unpainted boards felt rough on her feet.

Shoes! How could she have forgotten to put her shoes on this morning?

Maybe no one would notice. Maybe they would think she didn't wear shoes in the house.

Two deputies climbed out of the car. Martha didn't recognize the driver. The other was Deputy Rollington, an old acquaintance.

He approached the porch, but the other deputy wandered around, looking behind and under the pieces of old farm equipment that stood rusting in the weeds next to the driveway.

Martha steadied herself on the doorframe and cleared her throat. Except for that shout down the stairs, she hadn't spoken at all today, and she didn't want her voice to catch.

Maybe she should get a drink of water.

Not enough time.

"Good morning, Mrs. Haley." Deputy Rollington touched the brim of his uniform cap. "How are you today?"

"Well, thank you." Martha's voice sounded strong to her ears. She dared to venture more. "Would you like to come in and have a cup of tea?"

"No thank you." Deputy Rollington stopped at the foot of the porch steps, his thumbs hooked into his duty belt.

"Speak up, please." Martha cupped a hand behind her ear. "I'm afraid I don't hear as well as I used to."

That wasn't true. Her hearing was as sharp as ever. But she had learned people expected old folks to be hard of hearing. If she got confused and said something nonsensical, she could claim she hadn't heard properly. Everyone would just sigh and repeat things louder.

Much better than admitting that her mind might be going. "Mild cognitive impairment," the doctor had told her. He'd questioned her closely about her living arrangements. She had assured him that she lived with her nephew, Josiah, who had driven her to the appointment and now sat in the waiting room.

She hadn't made a follow-up appointment and figured she would never go back. No one would be likely to notice.

That was before all the turmoil, when the sheriff and his deputies had descended on the property and removed all Josiah's supplies and equipment from the barn.

Josiah called it his "business workings." The sheriff called it a "meth lab." Something to do with illegal drugs.

Which didn't surprise Martha. She couldn't say she approved, but how much different could it be than the moonshine still her grandfather had kept?

She'd had her suspicions that Josiah'd been involved in something unhealthy. Never a big person, he had become skinnier and skinnier until his cheekbones jutted out like cliffs beneath his sunken eyes. And his nose ran constantly.

When the deputies had arrived for the raid, Josiah and his friends had not been around.

Thank goodness.

The sheriff had flashed a piece of paper in her face, saying it was a search warrant. They had gone through the house, the outbuildings, and the entire property, guns drawn, with flashlights and dogs, confiscating some things and leaving a mess behind them.

Martha knew better than to try to stop them, but she had let herself get a bit hysterical.

Mistake. That had triggered a visit from a social worker.

Deputy Rollington asked loudly, "Have you seen or heard from your nephew lately?"

"Not since the last time you asked." That wasn't exactly true, either. Josiah had been around some. Mostly he was down at the shore, he'd told her. Fishing on a friend's boat. He'd brought her some nice fresh fish, although he hadn't cleaned them before he gave them to her, the way a good fisherman should.

When he was here, he kept out of sight. Martha couldn't blame him. She was pretty sure they wanted to arrest him.

"Didn't I tell you he was on vacation?" she said. "Fishing down at the shore? You could look for him there." But that was in Maryland, not West Virginia. Out of reach of the sheriff and his deputies.

"Yes, ma'am. You did. I just wondered if he'd called or anything."

"Too busy, I imagine. You know how these youngsters are. Never think about the old folks back at home."

"Yes, ma'am. Do you mind if we check in the barn?"

She narrowed her eyes. "Do you have a warrant?"

"Not this time," Deputy Rollington admitted. "I'm asking for permission. I can't look unless you consent."

Martha knew that if she said no, he would reckon she had something to hide. He could go get a warrant if he wanted to.

She gestured toward the lane that led to the barn. "Go ahead."

"Thank you, ma'am. I just want to make sure none of those people have come back. They might be dangerous."

Probably not as dangerous as a trigger-happy deputy.

"I would've seen if anybody'd been around." Or smelled the heavy ammonia scent that Josiah's "business" gave off.

"Thank you, ma'am," he said again. He glanced over to the barn, its doors latched.

The other deputy was peering behind a stack of rotting wood pallets. Martha hoped a rattlesnake might be hiding there and strike out.

No such luck.

Deputy Rollington waved to the other deputy to join him.

He lowered his voice and turned away from Martha. "She gave us permission to search. She can't hear good, but I bet she can lip-read. So turn this way and talk softly."

His partner nodded and faced the barn. "Do you really think anybody'd set up here again? After last time?"

"That type of shake-and-bake operation is pretty portable. And they might think this was a safe place, since we'd already raided it once." He glanced at Martha.

She heard them, but stared off into the woods and composed her face into a vaguely confused expression.

Keeping his voice low, Deputy Rollington said, "If the kid's gone down to the shore 'fishing,' you can bet he's not chilling out on some vacation. He's on a boat picking up shipments out at sea. And bringing them back here. Probably fentanyl."

The partner nodded. "Likely."

The deputies had to struggle with the heavy latch on the barn door. Martha found that her arthritic hands made it almost impossible for her to open it herself anymore, so she couldn't be a hundred percent sure what was in there.

She was relieved when the two officers exited the barn empty-handed, relatched the door, and came back to the porch.

"Do you need to search the house?" Martha asked. If she offered, they were less likely to think there was something to interest them.

Besides, if he had been in the basement, Josiah'd had plenty of time to slip out the rear door and into the woods and they didn't have the dog to track him. Or sniff for drugs.

Raising his voice, Deputy Rollington said, "Thank you, no, Mrs. Haley. You'll call if you hear from Josiah, won't you?"

Did they expect her to turn in her own kin? "Certainly," she answered.

"Addiction is a disease. We'll get him into treatment if he needs it, ma'am."

Sure they would.

Deputy Rollington looked around. "It's kind of lonely out here. Do you want me to send somebody from the local Aging Agency? I'm sure a social worker would be happy to come out to see if you need anything."

Heavens no. Last time, Martha'd had the devil of a time convincing that nosy busybody that, although she'd been very upset, she'd calmed down and was quite capable of taking care of herself.

She should reassure them. "Not necessary. They set up the Meals on Wheels for me. A lady brings food out a few times a week. She'd report if anything happened."

He nodded. "That's good."

Martha hadn't wanted to accept that service, but if she didn't, the social worker might have taken steps to remove her from the isolated old farmhouse. As it was, she had come to appreciate the food, even though it was often pretty tasteless and tended to be mushy. It saved her needing to cook, and it didn't cost anything. She ate what she wanted and put the rest in the chest freezer in the basement. If she ever got snowed in or something, she would have plenty to eat.

The deputies got back in the patrol car. She watched it wind down the driveway, the dust trail ending when it reached the road. Taking a deep breath, she pushed off the doorframe.

A wave of vertigo swept over her. She stubbed her toe on the threshold. Stumbling inside, she sat down and closed her eyes.

When the dizziness passed, she thought about the visit from the deputies. That had just been today, hadn't it? Her hearing might be fine, but her memory was not as good as it used to be, and time could get all muddled up in her thinking.

She'd handled it well, she thought. Cooperative enough to calm their suspicions but giving nothing away.

No irrational babbling, no burst of uncontrollable anger. And, clutching the doorframe, she'd hidden her precarious physical balance. It wouldn't do to fall in front of them.

They may not have noticed her lack of shoes. At least they hadn't mentioned it.

With any luck, they would not be back for a while. They were unlikely to send a social worker, at least this time.

If Josiah had been around, he'd escaped their notice.

She couldn't quite remember the last time she'd seen him. Had it been when they'd had that huge shouting match over him bringing the law to her property?

Of course, when she passed, it would be his property. They were the last of their clan.

The shouting had progressed to shoving. Martha remembered Josiah giving her a strong push that left her teetering at the top of the steep basement stairs.

But he hadn't meant any harm. He'd grabbed her arm and swung her back into the kitchen before she fell, putting himself between her and the stairs. She'd clutched onto the edge of the old stone sink and regained her balance.

Was that the last time he'd been here? She couldn't remember him bringing any fish lately.

If he were here, he'd stick to the basement or the barn. He wouldn't want anyone to notice he was around.

Martha had trouble keeping track of the days when the Meals on Wheels lady came. It was getting late. If she were coming today, she'd have been here by now.

Lots of food in the freezer for supper. All she had to do was bring some upstairs and let it thaw. She didn't mind eating it cold.

Holding tight to the railing, Martha eased down the stairs, making sure she placed both feet on a step before taking the next one. Walking to the freezer, the basement floor felt cool to her feet. When had she taken off her shoes? She opened the chest freezer and peered in.

Ah, yes. Josiah had been here the whole time. He lay sleeping in the freezer, snuggled in among some of the fish he'd brought her. She'd been careful to tuck the food packages around him so they wouldn't weigh him down.

The Follower

Erin Jori

THE TOWN WAS NESTLED ALONG the eastern shore of Green Bay beneath towering limestone cliffs to the north and rocky beaches to the south. Shops and restaurants dotted the main street, where tourists milled about buying t-shirts, bottles of cherry wine, and everything else under the sun imprinted with the name "Ellis Bay, Wisconsin." What better setting for a fictional murder than among a never-ending supply of curious tourists, quirky locals, and breathtaking scenery?

But before I could draft my next bestseller, I needed to recharge. I had confided in my friend Maria that by book seventeen of my mystery series, I felt my work was getting stale. Maria suggested I take a much-needed trip to clear my mind and find my muse and generously offered her vacation rental home as my retreat. Spending time in an idyllic setting like Ellis Bay could help me re-evaluate my writing and give my work a fresh start.

That's how I found myself relaxing outside a tavern by the bay, enjoying a cool glass of rosé as the sun began its descent over the western shore. Seagulls hovered above a fishing boat, trying to nip the day's catch.

After watching the birds dive-bomb the boat for a few minutes, I took a selfie and uploaded it to Instagram. Social media was new to me, but to the delight of my agent, it worked. I had amassed thousands of followers and received hundreds of comments. After years of obscurity, I enjoyed the newfound attention. People liked my books, but they also liked me or who they imagined me to be under my pen name, T. L. Washburne. The persona I created on social media as T.L. was a world apart from Louise Landreski, the awkward, shy, lonely girl I had been since birth. T.L. was the one who enjoyed a glass of wine along the bay before heading to her friend's lake house for a week of reading, relaxing, and brainstorming ideas for her next story. Louise merely came along for the ride.

"Here you go. One Caesar salad with grilled shrimp." My server, a nice college kid named Rae, set the plate before me. I sat at one of several outdoor tables. Couples or small groups occupied the others. I was the only loner. Despite my thousands of followers, some things never changed.

"Need a refill on the wine?" Rae asked.

"Not yet," I said as I set down my phone. I had dined at the tavern twice on my trip and had encountered Rae both times. She was pleasant and hardworking and helped me connect to the tavern's Wi-Fi to check my email and social media accounts. She might have been angling for a larger tip, but I didn't mind the assistance. Heaven knows my middle-aged self could use help when it came to technology.

"Uploading more big-shot author selfies?"

"Just one. I thought I'd give my favorite new restaurant some free advertising."

Rae grinned. She had short brown hair, blue eyes, a nose ring, and a smile that could quickly smooth over any wrong order.

"Why don't I take one of you? I'll even get our sign in the shot. Can't do that with a selfie."

Before I could stop her, she grabbed my phone, took a pic, then handed it back to me.

"There you go," she said, pleased with her work. "Now you'll have something to show your fans besides selfies."

Maybe she was right. In the last twenty-four hours, I had posted five photos, all taken by me with my arm outstretched. I thought they turned out fine, but there was that one "up my nose" shot. Rae's photo might spice things up.

"You never know," she added, "if your post brings in a crowd, my boss might comp you tomorrow's dinner."

"If that happens, I'll become a regular."

Rae laughed, then left me to enjoy my salad and rosé as she checked on her other tables. After posting Rae's best pic with the hashtag #EllisBayTavern, I spent the next half hour enjoying my meal and watching passersby. After I ate all the greens I could stomach, I opened my Instagram to check on my post's progress.

In only thirty minutes, I had ninety-one likes and three comments. One was from Maria, who commented on everything; another came from a crime blogger called Spine Tingling Books; and one came from a fan and included only an emoji of two large eyes.

I wasn't sure what the eyes meant. I clicked on the fan's profile—ThrillrTeachr—but it was set to private.

Rae's sudden reappearance startled me. I was a little jumpy after seeing the post.

"Sorry, I didn't mean to alarm you. Can I get you anything else?"

"Just the check and maybe an answer to a question?" I held up my phone. "What do you think this means?"

Rae's brows arched when she saw the emoji. "It could mean someone's interested in you. Do you know them?"

I shook my head. "They must be a new fan. I've never seen them comment before."

"My guess? They're trying to grab your attention."

I closed the app and set down my phone. "If they are, using an emoji isn't the way to do it. Words I understand. Not tiny pictures I can barely see."

Rae took my bill from her pocket and placed it on the table. "Insta can be great, but be careful. There are some real whackos online. I should know. I'm one of them."

Rae grinned as she took my plate.

"Thanks for the advice." I placed a fifty on the table. "I doubt it's anything to worry about. With fans all over the world, I've only met a few here and there at book signings and conferences. I doubt I'll ever meet ThrillrTeachr in real life."

"You mean 'IRL.' That's short for—"

"Rae, I know what it means. I might be an old fogey, but I'm not *that* out of touch." I placed my purse strap over my shoulder and stood. "As you youngsters say, LOL."

* * *

THE RIDE FROM TOWN THAT evening was as magical as it had been the day I first arrived. The road hugged the shoreline and cut through dense birches and pines winding past extravagant homes and smaller ones that looked like they hadn't been fixed up in a hundred years. As the sunset splashed across the sky like watercolors on a canvas, my phone buzzed with text messages. A few years ago, after nearly veering into oncoming traffic while glancing at my screen, I vowed never to check my phone under any circumstances while driving. Whoever it was would have to wait.

If I hadn't switched on my headlights when I did, I would have missed the sign for Agatha Lane, which was obscured by dusk's shadows. When Maria had searched for a vacation home, she couldn't pass up one built on a road named after her favorite author. She called it destiny.

I followed Agatha Lane to the end, turned onto the sandy driveway, and drove until the lake house's natural cedar shake siding and white windows came into view. The house had three bedrooms and an expansive deck overlooking the lake. The property also had a small, secluded dock where Maria kept her and her rental guests' favorite toy: a 19-foot sailboat appropriately named *The Christie*. As I took it all in, I realized once again that Maria was right: this was the ideal getaway and possibly the perfect setting for my next novel.

After parking, I grabbed my phone and found three texts from Maria and one from an unknown number, probably spam.

As I climbed out of the car, I thumbed through her messages.

Hey, girlfriend! Love the pics! Glad ur having a great time in town. Remind me again why I didn't join you? LOL

LOL. At least having Maria as my friend taught me the basics of texting lingo.

BTW, what's up with the creepy dude standing in the window of the bar? Talk about a photobomb!

Creepy dude? What creepy dude? I didn't see anyone else in Rae's photo.

OK, seriously, Louise. What is up with the freaky guy? Why is he in ALL your Insta photos? Are you pranking your fans? If so, BRILLIANT!

I re-read the last text twice before replying.

I'm not pranking anyone. What creepy dude?

I hit send and walked up the steps to the front door and expected to hear back immediately, since Maria was always glued to her phone. But as I punched in the door code, I received a "message not sent" reply.

Maria had warned me about sketchy cell service given my provider. She said I might have to venture closer to town to make calls, send texts, and check my email, which is why she had switched carriers after buying the house.

I opened the door, stepped inside, and flicked on the light. A breeze swept across the living room into the foyer.

That was strange. I didn't remember leaving a window open.

I tossed my purse and keys on a small table in the foyer and walked into the living room. White curtains billowed from the open window like ghosts.

I crossed the room and looked out the screenless window. I could have sworn it had one earlier. Lights flickered across the bay and the air coming off the water made me shiver. As I shut the window, locked it, and closed the curtains, an uneasy feeling snaked through my stomach.

I removed my phone from my pocket and tapped the screen. Without data, I couldn't access Instagram, but I could view the photos stored on my phone. I opened the app and started with Rae's most recent pic at the tavern. I looked relaxed as I sat under a red umbrella with my glass of wine. Rae made sure to fit the tavern's sign in the frame.

What was Maria talking about? I sat in front of a window and couldn't see anyone inside except—

Wait a second. What was in the window? It appeared to be more of a shadow than a person. Were those eyes peering out from the darkness, reflected in my phone's flash, or lights from behind the bar?

I swiped to a selfie I had taken in town. Dozens of people roamed the sidewalks, popping in and out of shops. I scanned the background. In the lower-left corner, standing beside an older couple with two brown shopping bags, stood a skinny guy in jeans and a black hoodie with his hood pulled over his head. He wore sunglasses and appeared to be the same size as the shadow in Rae's photo.

Who was this guy? Was he following me?

I swiped again. The next selfie I had snapped while walking on the beach in the late morning. Sunbathers and families were setting up canopies and staking umbrellas in the sand. Behind me, a couple of children chased seagulls, and two teenagers sat side-by-side staring at their phones.

I spread my fingers to enlarge the picture and scrutinized it. My stomach twisted when I spotted him. He stood on the beach, his body facing the water, but his black hoodie-draped head turned sideways as he stared at me through dark sunglasses.

My hands started shaking so badly that I accidentally scrolled to a photo I had taken on my book tour. My last stop on the tour was at a reading and signing at Laura's Bookshop in Chicago. I always took a few pics at every bookstore I visited to remember my experiences. I loved to take at least one shot of the audience. Those Instagram posts always gathered great responses.

We'd had a good turnout that night with a standing-room-only crowd. I zoomed in and checked their smiles, waves, and excitement.

I knew I was being paranoid, but I looked anyway. Surely, the guy in the hoodie wasn't at the book signing, was he?

My legs gave out and I collapsed into a chair. There he was, lurking in the back of the shot, wearing his signature hoodie and sunglasses, giving me that same icy stare.

He was following me. Not just here in Ellis Bay, but everywhere I went.

As I swiped through more photos and searched for Creepy Hoodie Guy, something crashed upstairs. Did I leave another window open, and something blew over? Or was someone in the freakin' house?

My heart throbbed in my chest. Unlike a character in a horror movie, I knew better than to head upstairs and come face-to-face with a mass murderer with an axe. I wasn't that stupid.

I glanced at my phone, hoping it had miraculously found cell service. No luck, but I did notice the icon telling me I had one unread text that had already downloaded. I tapped it open. There was a picture attached. It wouldn't download without data, but I could read the text.

My dear T.L., you really should lock your windows.

As Rae might say, *WTF?*

Who sent this, and how did they get my number? No one except my agent and Maria knew I was T.L. To everyone else who had this number, I was simply Louise.

The floor creaked overhead. *That* was not the wind.

I hurried toward the foyer to grab my keys and purse and get the hell out of here. My purse was still there, but my keys were gone. I grabbed my purse and rifled through it but didn't hear any jingling. I scanned the floor in case I had dropped them. No keys. Had I left them in the car when I checked Maria's messages?

If they weren't and I had to run to the road and flag down a car, I would. I raced to the door and tried to turn the doorknob. The door wouldn't open. The deadbolt wouldn't budge, either. How could I be locked in from the inside? If I had cell service, I could text Maria and ask her to open the doors with the app she uses to remotely lock them or turn down the heat for guests who forget at the end of their stay. Panic swelled in my chest as my fingers frantically tried to get the lock to turn.

The ceiling creaked again before footsteps rapidly pattered across the second floor.

I ran down the hall into the kitchen with its French doors that opened to the porch and yanked the doors' handles. They. Would. Not. Turn. I stepped back and slammed into the doors with my shoulder, but it was no use. They wouldn't open. I grabbed a chair to break the glass, forgetting Maria had furnished the kitchen with lightweight plastic stools that were more likely to bounce off the doors than break them.

As I turned to head back to the living room, thinking I could climb out the window, footsteps thumped down the stairs. Damn it, I would have to pass whoever was coming downstairs to get to the living room. He had me trapped. I had to hide.

Grabbing a carving knife from a drawer, I raced to the pantry, which was in the other direction. I flung open the pantry door and wedged myself beneath the lowest shelf. Then I closed the door and waited.

My pulse pounded in my ears as I tried not to hyperventilate.

Several seconds later, footsteps padded across the tile floor.

"Come out, come out, wherever you are," the intruder whispered.

I peered through the slats in the door. The figure wore a black hoodie, just like the guy in the photos. If he had a weapon, I couldn't see it from where I crouched. At least I had a knife. The problem was that I had never carved a turkey, let alone a human being.

The figure slowly turned to face the pantry. I swallowed hard. The knife shook in my hands, and I broke into a cold sweat.

"Are you afraid, T.L.? I hope so. Now that you know what fear really feels like, maybe you'll write better books."

The figure stepped forward and placed his hand on the knob. My chest ached from nearly hyperventilating, and my heart pumped with adrenaline. I looked down at the knife in my hands and thought for a moment that I was looking at someone else's hands holding it.

The door flung open. I closed my eyes, lunged forward with all my strength, and plunged the knife into his bare flesh just beneath his hoodie.

I opened my eyes to find him grabbing the knife as he slumped to the ground.

"Louise," he whispered.

He knew my real name.

The intruder's head lolled toward the French doors, his delicate features now visible in the moonlight.

I gasped.

"Maria?"

I SIT AT THE TABLE, pen in hand, ready to sign a copy of my latest novel, *Death on the Lake.* The next person in line, a young woman, timidly approaches.

"Ms. Washburne, it's an honor to meet you." Her smile is tentative, and she brushes a strand of long blond hair from her eyes as she hands me her book.

"What's your name?" I ask.

"Leslee, with three e's," she says. "I love all your books, but this is my favorite."

"Why is that?" I ask as I inscribe it.

"I'm not sure. It just seems so much more . . . *realistic* than your other ones. What changed between this book and your last?"

I hand her the book and smile. "Let's just say I did my homework for this one."

She gives me a sideways glance and smirks. "You didn't actually murder someone, did you?"

I look past her down the line of fans that stretches across the room. For a moment, I think I see a shadowy figure standing next to a display. I close my eyes briefly, and it's gone.

"Of course not. If I was a murderer, I'd be behind bars, not here signing your book."

Leslee smiles and nods as another fan steps forward. I greet them and take their book. As I open the cover, I see the dedication.

To my dear M. The one who taught me everything.

Maria was a good friend. She knew that for me to truly understand fear, I had to experience it firsthand. She didn't tell me what she had planned; it wouldn't have worked if she had. What she hadn't counted on was also teaching me what it felt like to kill someone and hide the body.

I also learned that being a mystery writer has its hidden benefits. I knew how to get away with murder.

With gloved hands, I had wrapped Maria's body in the living room curtains before cleaning up the mess in the kitchen. Then I searched the premises for Maria's car, which she hid behind the shed at the far end of the property. On the front seat, I found her purse, a duffel bag containing a change of clothes and toiletries, her cell phone, and what I guessed was a burner phone—the one she used when she texted me as ThrillrTeachr. I placed all of them except the burner phone in one of the spare bedrooms. That, I'd dispose with her body.

Fortunately, the property on Agatha Lane was secluded enough that no one could see me creeping around the dock under the moonlight. After I unfastened the boat's mainsail, started the outboard motor, and loosened its dock lines, I secured the tiller and pointed the bow toward the bay. One shove later and I watched *The Christie* float across the water like fog.

The next morning, I called the Coast Guard and reported Maria missing. I explained that she had arrived the previous night to join me on my vacation. She had set out on a solitary moonlit cruise. I didn't accompany her because I was tired, and Maria didn't take her phone because she was afraid she'd drop it in the lake. I hadn't seen her off, so I had no idea if she had been wearing a life jacket.

Later that day, the search team found the boat adrift all the way north near Escanaba where it ran out of gas.

I guess the lake house was my destiny, since Maria left it to me in her will. I immediately took it off the rental market and hung a "no trespassing" sign at the end of Agatha Lane. No one will ever know that beneath the soft pine needles covering the south end of the property lies the most loyal friend a writer could have.

I regularly visit Maria's grave at sunset. Just yesterday, I took a picture of the spot as reds and oranges and pinks streaked across the sky. It looked just like the night Maria taught me her final lesson. Too bad I couldn't post it. I knew the perfect hashtag.

#RIP.

THE CABINS AT HIDEAWAY LAKE

TRACY FALENWOLFE

"I'M SORRY, I'M SORRY, I'M sorry," Jennifer Fuller said to her poor car. The sporty convertible had already shuttled her seventeen hundred miles from her home in Miami, Florida over the past three days, and she didn't want to piss it off. What would she do here in the middle of the wilderness if she popped a tire or something?

She should have gone to a spa.

"This can't be it." She'd followed her friend Steph's directions exactly, but as she bumped past a ramshackle lean-to on what had to be the literal road to nowhere, she figured one of them had made a mistake.

Since Steph had so graciously offered her the use of the cabin, Jennifer pressed ahead, wincing every time she hit a rut. She'd been hoping to see snow. The little patches of dirty slush scattered beneath the trees were a disappointment.

She drove on, regretting her rash decision to get away from it all, until finally, Hideaway Lake materialized in front of her. The road evened out, and five sturdy log cabins popped into view. Lined up at the water's edge, they looked like fairy tale cottages. Steph had put Jennifer in cabin two. "It has the best view and the biggest bed," she'd said. "The key will be under the mat."

Jennifer was surprised to see another car on the property. Steph had said she'd be the only one there since it was the off season. They would see each other tomorrow. Jennifer needed a shoulder to cry on. She had not been the one to request a trial separation. She had been happy in her marriage.

She thought Evan was, too. Now she needed time alone to figure things out.

The other car, a white sedan with a pink and purple sunflower decal in the back window, was parked behind cabin three. Steph had mentioned needing to hire housekeepers. Maybe she had.

Jennifer's cabin was unexpectedly luxurious. Steph had left a note explaining how to use the gas fireplace and the high-end shower. She'd stocked the fridge with wine and cheese. She noted the Wi-Fi password, but warned it was iffy, and that cell reception was spotty. That was okay. What Jennifer needed most was time to think.

She went out onto the porch. The sun was a golden orb, sinking behind the frozen lake. It was peaceful until a man and a woman burst out of cabin three, running and laughing and shrieking with delight. Not housekeepers.

When they caught sight of Jennifer, she lifted her hand in a wave. The man, wearing a fluorescent green ski hat with a pom-pom on top, smiled and waved back. The woman, with red hair in a long, fat braid that hung to her waist, offered a stone-faced stare.

Unsettled, Jennifer turned back to watch the sunset, but a haze had rolled in, veiling the sun, and dulling the daylight. She went back into her cabin and locked the door. Her phone rang.

"You made it." It was Steph.

"I just got in," Jennifer said. "I'm glad you talked me into coming."

"Did you find everything? Blankets, towels, wineglasses?"

She'd looked for none of those things, but she wasn't worried about it. "I'll be fine."

"Good. My flight gets into Bangor tomorrow morning. I'll get to the cabin by ten."

"Awesome," Jennifer said. "Hey, I thought you said I'd be the only one here."

"You are."

"I'm not. There's a couple in cabin three. I just saw them. And there's a car here. I assume it's theirs."

"You're kidding me." Steph sighed. "Okay. Let me talk to Bill and make sure he didn't book anyone. If he didn't, I'll give the sheriff a call, and he'll come around and roust them."

"You don't sound especially concerned."

"We get squatters from time to time during the off season. It happens. We found it's best to let the sheriff deal with them."

Jennifer heard an announcement over the loudspeaker wherever Steph was.

"I gotta go," Steph said. "I almost forgot to tell you, you're supposed to get snow tonight. If it's a lot, just sit tight. Our guy Hal will come around in the morning to plow."

Cool! Maybe she'd get to see some snow after all.

She settled in for the evening with a plate of cheese and olives, a glass of Pinot Grigio, and a book. But she couldn't relax. She wondered about the people in cabin three. Were they squatters? If so, they'd know she was the one to rat them out when the sheriff showed up. She popped an olive and went to the window. The couple was outside, sitting in front of a campfire. It looked like they were roasting marshmallows. The man's fluorescent green hat made him visible in the dark. As Jennifer watched, the couple moved closer together and began to kiss. Maybe Steph's husband, Bill, had booked a couple of honeymooners.

She read for an hour before her phone buzzed with a text from Steph. *Bill didn't book anyone into cabin three. Sheriff will be around in the morning. See you tomorrow.*

Okay then. If Steph wasn't more concerned, neither was Jennifer. She went back to her book, but must have nodded off, because she woke around midnight to the sound of loud buzzing in the distance.

She looked outside and marveled at the blanket of white. Snow! She opened the door, and her cozy snow fantasy abruptly ended. On television, big fat flakes floated down and landed on people's heads while they smiled and sipped hot chocolate. This snow was fine and icy. It swirled around and pelted Jennifer in the face like a thousand tiny needles. Still, she grabbed her phone to video the snow for her friends back home.

While she was recording, she spotted two lights out on the lake where the buzzing noise was coming from. Headlights, she guessed. She zoomed in and could make out the fluorescent green hat and a yellow craft that she assumed was a snowmobile. Steph had mentioned they had snowmobile trails nearby.

Back inside, Jennifer posted the video and tagged the Hideaway Homestead Cabins page—word of mouth for Steph and Bill's business and all. Since she had Wi-Fi at the moment, she scrolled through social media, her email, and the national news. A story about a bank robbery in Virginia caught her eye. The FBI had posted pictures of the two suspects, a man, and a woman with a long, red braid. The article said they'd killed the guard.

A tingle crept up Jennifer's spine.

She texted a link to the article to Steph.

Her phone buzzed. *Message not sent.* Damn. She tried again with the same result.

Jennifer looked outside again. The snow wasn't falling, it was swirling. The wind was whipping so hard she couldn't see anything but white. Her instinct was to flee. To get away from the dangerous criminals in the next cabin. But there was no way she could drive her car anywhere in this. She'd have to hunker down.

After making sure the door and all the windows were locked, she armed herself with a kitchen knife. She sat next to the fire to call the FBI tip line. *No signal.* She couldn't even make an emergency call to 911.

Now she felt isolated. The only comforting fact was that the couple next door didn't know she knew who they were. Her lame, Pollyanna, "howdy neighbor" wave had proven that.

THE NEXT THING JENNIFER KNEW, Steph was shaking her awake.

She jumped up, baffled by the daylight.

"Easy." Steph stumbled back. "Did you sleep in the chair?"

She had, and she couldn't believe it. "Did my text finally go through?"

"What text?"

A man ducked in the front door and stamped his snowy boots on the mat. He nodded to Jennifer. "Morning."

"Jenn, this is Hal. He plowed the road and the parking lot for us." Hal was a Paul Bunyan type dressed in green and black flannel.

"What about your squatters?" he asked. "Need help with them before I go? The sheriff is going to be awhile."

"About that . . ." Steph turned to Jennifer. "You said there was a car?"

"They're not squatters," Jennifer said. "They're bank robbers. That's what I was texting you about."

"Bank robbers?" Hal did a double take. "That's a new one on me."

"How do you know?" Steph asked.

"I saw a news article about them. The FBI set up a tip line, but I didn't have any service."

"Well, there's no car out there now," Hal said.

"They must have left." Jennifer breathed a sigh of relief.

Steph cast a wary glance toward cabin three. "I'd like to be sure."

"Come on," Hal said to Steph. "I'll go with you to check it out."

"Shouldn't you call the police first?" Jennifer asked.

"If we find something, we will," Steph said. "Law enforcement is stretched thin up here, and the sheriff is already planning to stop over."

The three of them trudged over to the cabin. "No footprints," Hal said. "Although drifting snow could have covered them."

Steph peered through the window. "Looks empty." She stamped her feet on the porch and pulled a set of keys out of her pocket.

Jennifer pointed to a spot in the yard with less snow. "They had a fire there last night. And they were out on the lake with a snowmobile."

"That was stupid," Hal said. "The ice isn't thick enough. I wouldn't even walk on it. We've had too much thawing and refreezing this year."

Steph looked around inside the cabin. The place smelled like lemon-scented cleaner. Throw pillows were neatly arranged on the couch, and vacuum marks lined the rug in front of the fire. She checked out the bedroom and the bathroom. "It looks exactly like I left it."

"But I saw them," Jennifer said.

"I'm sure you did," Hal said. "They probably took pictures with their cell phones so they could cover their tracks really well. Didn't want anyone to know they were here."

But Jennifer knew they were there. And they'd seen her. They all knew it. She could see the apprehension on Steph and Hal's faces.

"You've been through a lot this week," Steph said. "And you had a long, exhausting drive."

"You're right."

"The sheriff is going to have to handle this. But right now, I'm starving. Why don't we have lunch while we wait for him?"

"All I have is granola bars," Jennifer said sheepishly. She'd eaten all the cheese and olives last night.

"You were going to live on granola bars for a week?" Hal asked.

It was more that she hadn't expected the cabins to be quite so secluded. "I guess you don't get pizza delivery here."

"Come on," Steph said. "Let's head into town. We can grab some lunch, stop at the grocery store for supplies. Want to join us, Hal?"

"Can't. Gotta lotta plowing yet to do."

Jennifer and Steph went to the only pub in town and caught up over burgers and fries. "I think he's seeing someone else," Jennifer said of Evan.

Steph looked down at her plate.

"What?" Jennifer prodded.

Steph shrugged. "I want to say once a cheater, always a cheater. But I don't know if that's true, and really, I just want you to be happy."

It was true that Evan had been seeing someone else when she'd met him. He'd cheated on that woman with Jennifer and lied to her about it. Jennifer had forgiven him, much to Steph's annoyance. "I need to figure out what I want."

"You need to figure out how to stop being a doormat." Steph paid the check. "Come on. Let's get you some groceries."

The criticism from her old friend hurt Jennifer's feelings. But Steph wasn't wrong. Jennifer bought the basics. Outside, she was getting into Steph's SUV when she spotted the white sedan with the sunflower decal in the back window. She grabbed Steph's arm. "That's the car from cabin three."

The woman with the long red braid came out of the grocery store. "That's her." There was another woman with her, wearing a red coat and white boots.

"Hey." Jennifer called to the woman with the braid. She felt emboldened in the daylight in the middle of town. "Remember me?"

The woman ignored her.

"From Hideaway Lake."

The women looked at each other. "Sorry," the one with the braid said. "You must have me confused with someone else."

"No, I don't. You were there with your husband, or your boyfriend, or whoever." She'd almost spit out the word accomplice. "I saw the two of you kissing last night by the fire."

The woman in the red coat laughed and shook her head as she slipped into the passenger seat. "This is what happens when you legalize weed."

"Lady, I don't have a husband, a boyfriend, or a whatever." The woman with the braid said. "But you have a nice day." She started the car and backed out of her spot.

"She was lying," Jennifer said.

"If that's true, you just confronted a murderer." Steph gaped at her. "Why did you do that? Weren't you scared?"

Jennifer hadn't even thought about it. "I guess I'm just tired of being lied to. And I sure didn't like being called a doormat by my closest friend."

"Believe me." Steph held up her hands. "I won't make that mistake again."

THE SHERIFF OF MOOSEJAW, MAINE, wore jeans and boots and a baseball hat on top of which he propped his sunglasses. He was all of thirty-five, and he was on a first name basis with the locals.

He met Jennifer and Steph back at the lake. They did a more thorough inspection of cabin three than they'd done with Hal, and checked all the other cabins, too. He dug in the snow where Jennifer had seen their fire and found coals, but nothing else.

"You think they'll come back?" Jennifer asked.

"Hard to say." He scratched his chin. "The FBI agent I spoke to after Steph called to fill me in thinks they're on their way to Canada."

"I have video." Jennifer thumbed through her phone and found the video she'd taken of the snow. "Could that help the FBI?" She pointed to the headlights in the frame. And the green hat. "That's them. You can't make out their faces, but at least it shows where they were. Two of them, anyway. I don't see the woman with the red coat. She was in the car today at the grocery store."

Steph nodded her agreement.

"I don't know what they were doing out on the ice," Joe said. "But they're lucky they didn't fall through. You need five or six inches of ice to ride a snowmobile on, and we barely have four, which is what you need for walking. I wouldn't trust it."

That's what Hal had said, too.

"It's usually thicker out there around the island," Steph said. "And they could have accessed it up by Clearwater Point."

"True," the sheriff agreed. "But why?"

STEPH STAYED UNTIL SHE HAD to get back to the hotel, where she and Bill were meeting a business associate. "Are you sure you don't want to come with me? You don't have to stay here at the cabin. The hotel's nice."

"The cabin is nice too, and I'm sure the sheriff was right. If they're on their way to Canada, why would they come back? Especially after they went to the trouble to cover up that they were here in the first place."

"Makes sense. But you're not scared?"

"Who, me? I'm a badass now, remember? I argued with a murderer."

"I remember." Steph hugged her. "I'll see you tomorrow."

The snow started again after Steph left. It mixed with sleet and pinged off the cabin's metal roof. Being snowed in added an extra layer of isolation. Perfect for contemplating life-changing decisions. Was it time for a fresh start? And what would that even look like?

She was sitting in bed, finishing a book, when she heard the crunch of tires on the snow in the parking lot. Her cell chirped with a call at the same time.

"Jennifer." It was Steph. "I'm coming to get you."

"You don't have to," Jennifer said. "I'm fine. Really."

"No, you're not. Joe thinks the bank robbers will come back to the cabin."

"Why?"

"It's that video you posted. The local news showed it in a story about them being spotted in Moosejaw, and it went viral after the FBI offered a reward."

"But you can't identify anyone in the video. Why would they care about it?"

"Joe thinks they may think you saw whatever they were doing out on the ice."

Jennifer heard a car door. "Are you here now?"

"Not yet. Why?"

Her blood ran cold. "Because somebody is." Jennifer hoped it was Hal or Joe, but her gut told her it was neither. There was nowhere to hide in the cabin, and no time to think. She slammed her feet into her boots, grabbed her parka, and bolted out the front door, running toward the trees. Behind her, she heard the ratchet of a shotgun.

Boom!

A full moon illuminated the landscape. Unfortunately, it also revealed her location to the woman with the long red braid, who reloaded and took another shot.

Jennifer ran full out. She slipped and fell and tasted blood. Heard another boom, and the scatter of buckshot raining down on the crusty snow. She scrambled to her feet and ran, not realizing she'd run onto the ice until she heard it cracking underneath her.

The eerie sound echoed across the lake. She considered turning back, but the redhead was closing the gap, and Jennifer didn't know if she had come alone, or if the man and the woman with the red coat were after her too. She sprinted toward the tiny island in the center of the pond. Steph had said the ice might be thicker there.

Someone called to the redhead with a bullhorn. "Put the gun down." Jennifer looked back, saw the redhead whirl and fire toward the red and blue lights lined up along the shore.

But where were the others?

Jennifer kept running, hoping she wasn't heading straight for one of them. Her nose and lungs burned from breathing the icy air. She was near the island, and what she thought was safety. But what she saw beyond it stopped her heart—open water glittering in the moonlight. She had nowhere left to go.

She tripped again and fell. On her hands and knees, Jennifer spotted something under a clear patch of ice. A fluorescent green hat. And a bloated face looking up at her.

A shotgun ratchet sounded right behind her. "End of the line, Miss Buttinski."

"You killed him." Jennifer crab walked backwards away from the redhead. "Why?"

"Because I was done with him." She aimed at Jennifer. "It would have looked like a snowmobile accident if you hadn't gotten involved."

She said it as if what she'd done was Jennifer's fault. The same way Evan had sounded when he'd asked her for the separation.

Rage bubbled up. Jennifer kicked out and caught the redhead in the knees. Because they were on the ice, it was enough to take her feet out from under her. She landed flat on her back with a thud. Jennifer heard a sickening crack before the ice broke, and the lake swallowed the redhead.

The ice undulated beneath Jennifer. The edge of it broke off and her feet plunged into the freezing water. She scooted back, clawing for purchase, but more ice broke. The water covered her calves and knees. She skittered away from the hole with the ice spiderwebbing beneath her.

"Jennifer," the voice on the bullhorn said, "don't move."

Behind her, in the open water, the sheriff approached on a rescue boat. Steph was with him. "Stay put," she called to Jennifer. "Don't move until we throw you a rope."

The ice popped and cracked. Jennifer's lower legs ached and her teeth chattered. It took her three tries to catch the rope Joe told her to tie around her waist. He secured the other end to the boat. "Come on now. You can make it."

He kept the rope taut as Jennifer inched across the splintering ice and hurled herself into the boat. Finally safe, she laid on her back, looking up at the moon. "She fell through."

"We saw," Joe said. "What about the other two?"

"The man is in the water. She killed him last night." Jennifer shuddered. "I didn't see the woman with the red coat."

Joe grimaced. He radioed the information to someone. As he was speaking, another shotgun blast rang out, followed by the report from a rifle. Joe's radio crackled. "The second shooter is down."

The woman in the red coat, no doubt.

Joe looked at Steph. "Is she okay?"

"I figured out what I want," Jennifer announced, violently shivering.

"What's that?" Steph tucked a silver survival blanket around her.

"I want a civilized divorce."

Steph squeezed her hand. "Good for you."

"I don't want to be a doormat anymore. I want to be a badass."

"You are," Steph assured her. "You are."

"I also want a vacation from this vacation. I want a suite at the hotel. With room service. And pizza delivery. And reliable internet. And . . ."

"Yeah." Steph smiled at Joe. "She's okay."

PIER PRESSURE

KATE FELLOWES

OLIVIA PAYTON SET DOWN HER sketch pad with a contented sigh. Before her, the lake was a vision of blue, punctuated by humans at play. Motorboats cruised past, one trailing someone on skis. A young couple in kayaks paddled by, not disturbing two ducks bobbing a few feet away.

This could be paradise, Olivia thought, with a tinge of cynicism, ten years on the job as a police officer having taken their toll on her outlook. But no more. The future spread before her, a blank canvas waiting to be filled. That's what this vacation was about—finding her way forward.

Childish laughter came from a picnic area near the four cabins at Franks' Landing. Shake-shingle affairs, they showed their age, as did the whole resort. Her other neighbors were a family and an elderly couple. The last cabin had held some honeymooners, but they'd left the day before.

The laughter came from one of the family's little girls. Mom and dad had two, four and nine years old, at a guess. A stand-offish teenage boy rounded out the group. The littlest girl, introduced at the bonfire last night as Piper, tossed a bright yellow ball to her sister, Katie. The girls' parents, Jake and Nita, were nowhere in sight, but that was the joy of Franks' Landing: they were all safe here. No urban crime would creep in on paradise.

Olivia drank in the sounds and smells of her surroundings. After the shooting, her therapist had talked an awful lot about mindfulness and being in the moment. This moment—not any of those others that had almost killed her. It wasn't as easy as it sounded, though.

The beach towel beneath her didn't do much to soften the hard earth under the pine trees, but the shade was divine. I'm glad I booked in for a whole month, she thought.

THE DOOR OF THE CABIN closest to the water opened and the old married couple appeared. The Mrs.—that would be Marian—clutched her purse and a scrap of paper. Off to the grocery store, Olivia guessed. Larry settled sunglasses on his generous nose before heading to the car, where Marian waited.

"I don't know why you keep locking the car, Larry," she scolded. "There's nothing to steal and no one to steal it."

Larry made no reply.

Olivia watched them pull up the hill and out of sight.

My world and welcome to it, she thought.

WITH THE FIRST LIGHT OF dawn, Olivia awoke, her heart hammering. She blinked, trying to shake off the nightmare that had plagued her since she'd been shot. Would it ever leave her alone?

At the kitchen sink, she drank a glass of cold water, glancing out the window. Sensing movement, she squinted, making out three figures standing on the pier, talking by the rowboats. Larry and Marian, the old married couple. And with them was. . . yes, Russ Franks, the resort's aging owner. Assessing the situation out of habit, Olivia thought their conversation looked serious, not casual, but a moment later Marian kissed Larry's cheek, and he stepped into a rowboat and pulled the cord to start the outboard. Marian raised a hand in farewell as he puttered off across the calm water.

Yawning, Olivia turned away. She could go back to sleep now. The nightmare never bothered her twice in one night.

Sunlight streamed through the curtains and birds twittered when a shout jolted Olivia awake. Another shout followed, urgent and panicked.

In her pajamas, Olivia rushed from her room. Her bare feet flew over dirt, then sand, to where Jake stood knee deep in the water, bent over, tugging at something. His fishing pole and tackle box lay discarded on the pier, and when he looked up at her, he was pale and wide-eyed.

Face down in the water was Russ Franks, a bloody wound on the back of his bald head. Jumping into the water, Olivia helped Jake drag the old man onto the sand. She struggled to keep her balance when she stumbled over a homemade anchor—a coffee can filled with concrete.

Once on the beach, she pressed her fingers against Russ's neck, already fearing the worst.

"I came down to go fishing and found him," Jake said, words tripping over each other. "Is he dead? Oh my God."

"Call 9-1-1," she said, her voice calm, knowing this was merely a formality.

As Jake gave the basics to the emergency operator, Olivia hopped onto the pier to survey the scene from above. A length of rope stretched from a cleat on the pier to a rowboat bobbing in the water. A smear of blood ran down the bow of the boat into the water.

Jake's wife, Nita, hurried over, Katie on her hip. She moved to Jake's side, gasping at his exchange with the operator. She glanced at the body, then turned away, blocking her daughter's view.

Marian approached, tightening the sash on her robe. She lifted her hand to block the sun's glint reflecting off the water. "What's going on?"

Jake pointed in silence to where Olivia stood beside the dead man, guarding the scene.

"Oh, my word!" Marian said. "Call 9-1-1."

"Already did." The distant sound of a siren pierced the air.

As the EMTs knelt beside Russ, Olivia placed a hand on Jake's arm.

"They'll want to talk to you, so stay here, okay? I've got to get into some other clothes." She tugged at her thin, wet pajamas, adding, "I'll be back in five minutes."

It took less than that for her to change into shorts and a t-shirt. Sliding her feet into sandals, she headed back outside, retreating to the trees to observe. She sank to the ground, arms wrapping around her knees.

What happened seemed obvious. The old man caught his foot in that coil of rope or stumbled over the cleat. Falling, he must have hit the rowboat, sustaining the head wound. Unconscious in the water, he drowned.

Overhead, a bird sang some cheery notes. It was too beautiful a day to die, Olivia agreed. Such a senseless accident, when just hours earlier Russ had seemed fine.

Olivia recalled what she'd seen from her cabin window after waking from her early-morning nightmare.

Russ, Marian, and Larry had been talking on the pier. Larry was leaving in the boat when Olivia lost interest and turned away. But if Russ had fallen as he and Marian walked back to shore, surely Marian would have taken action.

Olivia tried to remember if she'd heard a shout. The water had been running in the kitchen sink, and there'd been a racket from the outboard. She didn't remember hearing anyone call out.

Now, she watched Marian, standing next to Nita. Clutching the neckline of her robe, she looked as shaken as Nita, but neither seemed as unsettled as Jake.

A squad car rolled down the hill. The officer who got out looked middle-aged, nonchalant but focused. This wouldn't be his first time seeing a dead man, Olivia knew.

For the next half hour, Olivia observed the activities—the EMTs assessment of the victim, the officer's examination, his documentation of the scene.

She knew, at some point, he would question her, as he would the others, asking what, if anything, they could tell him about the accident.

After Russ's body had been taken away, Olivia went down to the shore. Approaching the officer, she introduced herself. "I'm Olivia Payton. I'm vacationing at the resort, but I've just retired from the Bradford PD." She named a big city miles away. "If I can be of help, please let me know."

"Thanks, miss, but I think I can handle this." He eyed her with curiosity. "Retired?"

Olivia gave him the short version. "I was injured apprehending a suspect." Her hand moved to the scar at the neck of her t-shirt. "So, I'm out. Life is too short, Officer Schroeder." She read his name badge.

"Tim," he said, nodding. "Did you hear Russ fall into the water?"

She shook her head, recounting what she had seen—Larry, Marian, and Russ on the pier. "But I never heard him call out, or a splash or anything. I wonder if Marian did, since she was right there. But the fall could have come some other time and not when I saw them, after Marian had gone back to her cabin." She shrugged.

"I'll speak with her and the others. Has her husband returned, or is he still out on the water?"

"Still out. There's a boat for every cabin and only three are here now, so one's missing."

"Okay, thanks."

He turned away, and she realized she'd never gotten around to breakfast.

She ate in the picnic area, watching Officer Schroeder speak with her neighbors. Even Dylan, the sullen teenager, took a turn, mumbling single word responses. Once dismissed, he dashed off, vanishing into the woods.

Drinking the last of her coffee, Olivia found the idea of a hike appealing. By the time she'd packed a rucksack and found her hat, the officer was gone. The lake showed no visible trace of the morning's tragedy.

Olivia walked for over an hour, tension releasing with every step. Once, the back of her neck prickled with the feeling that she was being watched. Dylan still taking refuge from parents and family? But when she scanned the woods, she spotted a doe hidden in the foliage, eyeing her with caution. Returning to the cabin, Olivia was ready for a rest.

The patrol car was back, Officer Schroeder emerging as she crossed the parking lot.

"Ms. Payton," he called.

"Yes?"

"Your offer, does it still stand?"

"Of course." She could hear the eagerness in her voice.

"An irregularity has come up. I need to do some additional interviews, check out the scene. It would go faster if you could take notes." Holding up his hand, he went on, "I don't need any assistance with my investigation, you understand, so I'll ask you to keep your participation to notes."

Olivia nodded. She had no doubt he'd checked out her story before making his proposal, but he clarified it now.

"I spoke with your former CO. He had plenty of glowing remarks about you. Sends his regards."

Olivia lowered her gaze, never comfortable with praise. "Thank you. Can I ask what the irregularity was? What information you hope to elicit?"

They walked onto the pier, stopping beside the blood-stained rowboat. Officer Schroeder pointed. "It looks like Russ fell. Tripped maybe, or stumbled. He was frail. It wouldn't take much. So, I speculate he hit his head on the boat and was unconscious when he went under."

Just like my theory, Olivia thought.

"But the doctor tells me there are two head wounds. Not one." Their eyes met. "I don't think he bounced."

"So, this could be murder," Olivia said, and he tipped his head.

"I'd like to take pictures here and in his office. See what jumps out at us. I mean, me." He handed her a notebook and pen.

Taking them, she watched him check out the hours-old scene. The smear of blood on the bow of the boat remained, silent testimony, but other clues seemed elusive.

Pointing with the pen, Olivia said, "When I jumped in to help Jake, I bumped into that anchor." She indicated the submerged coffee can. "He could have hit the boat, then the anchor when he went under."

Officer Schroeder pulled on plastic gloves, then knelt, lifting the can from the water. Any blood on it had long since vanished, but he took its measurements and several photos anyway before bagging it as evidence.

"Or a murderer could have carried a weapon away," she suggested. "But who had it in for the old man?"

"A sick old man. Dr. McIntyre confirmed Russ Franks had cancer. I'd heard the rumors, of course. It's hard to keep a secret in a town like ours."

Olivia made a note. "Is there family?"

"Not in town," Officer Schroeder said.

They walked to the resort office and entered the unlocked space. Sensing her question, Officer Schroeder said, "Only you city folks lock doors around here."

Olivia remembered Marian scolding her husband for bothering to lock the car. Were they locals?

"What are we. . . you . . . looking for here?" Her eyes scanned the dusty office. An old calendar, curled and faded, hung on the knotty pine wall beside framed photos and fishing regulations.

"Don't know." He opened and closed drawers. "An address book listing a relative's name would be a good start."

Olivia examined the photographs. Lots were of vacationers holding up fish. Lots more showed Russ enjoying bonfires with guests through the years.

You can date them by the clothes and hair, she thought.

She checked out the faces, pausing on a distinctive nose. Leaning closer, she rubbed at the dirty glass. It was Larry. The woman beside him, all big glasses and bigger hair, had to be Marian.

"Any luck on the address book?" she asked, scanning other pictures.

"There's a ledger of renters, and I think I also have what I was looking for." He displayed an ancient blue book and flipped the book open. "I'll look for familiar names."

"Found a picture," Olivia began, tapping the photo and reporting its contents. "Has a definite '80's vibe, I'd say. And here," she indicated a small black-and-white picture of two boys, arms around each other's shoulders, "I think this might be Russ and Larry as kids."

Officer Schroeder joined her. "That's them, sixty years ago. Old friends. That's no crime. That's a blessing."

"Old friends, old secrets?" Olivia suggested, as he went back to the book.

"Ah!" He gave a cry of triumph, jabbing an entry. "Jake and Nita Wolter."

"They made Russ's Christmas card list?"

He chuckled. "Look at the heading on this page."

"Franks," she read aloud. "His relatives?" She pointed at the half dozen names filling the paper.

"Let's go ask some questions."

Nita and Jake's cabin door was ajar, and a TV blared as Officer Schroeder rapped on the doorjamb.

"Nita, could I have a word?"

Nita dropped a plate into the sink. "You startled me, Officer. Please, come in."

Officer Schroeder suggested she join them at a picnic table instead.

"Ms. Payton is taking notes today." He showed her the page headed "Franks." "How were you and Russ Franks related?"

Nita blinked. "He was my uncle. Mom's only sibling. Those others are their cousins. But they're all gone now."

"Russ never married? No kids of his own?"

Nita shook her head. "No, there was just me."

"You'll inherit the resort, then?"

Scoffing, Nita said, "Lucky me. A run-down place in the middle of nowhere."

"On ten acres with lake frontage," Olivia said, then grimaced, feeling Officer Schroeder's stern look.

"Worth some money," he said.

"What are you implying? Uncle Russ tripped. Right?"

"You didn't mention your relationship when we talked earlier," the officer said. "How come?"

"It's not a secret. We've been coming here since before the kids were born," Nita said.

"Did you get along?"

Nita's head snapped up. "Why wouldn't we?" Nita asked.

"Honey?" Jake approached. "What's going on?"

"They think I killed Uncle Russ." Tears filled Nita's eyes.

"That's ridiculous." Jake's face turned red, and his hands clenched. "Get out of here. She's done talking."

Olivia scribbled notes as Jake led Nita away. "Seems like an overreaction," she said.

"I'll check their financials. See if there's a motive," Officer Schroeder said.

"She seemed genuinely upset," Olivia said, "but so did Jake when he found the body."

"A shock to see a dead body, especially someone you know," he said.

"Or if it's the first time you killed someone." At his questioning look, she added, "Just saying."

"That's your big city background showing," Officer Schroeder said. "But I'll bear it in mind."

They walked toward the last cabin in the row and found Larry and Marian at the shore, seated on folding chairs, feet in the water.

"May we have a word?" Officer Schroeder dragged another chair across the sand and Olivia followed suit. "I'm following up this morning's events," he explained.

"Anything we can do." Larry shook his head. "Poor Russ."

"You go way back," Officer Schroeder said. "To boyhood, here in town."

"Yes, indeed." Larry's voice cracked. "Lots of adventures."

"They were old friends," Marian said. "May I ask why that matters? His death was obviously an accident." She peered over her sunglasses at them. "Russ was not a well man. He should have retired years ago. So stubborn."

A bittersweet smile crossed Larry's face. "Traveled the world together. In the service, out of it." Retrieving a handkerchief, he blew his nose.

"Which one of you was the troublemaker?" Olivia asked, smiling back. Sometimes with friends, one takes the lead and the other stands in their shadow, she thought, recalling her own relationships.

Officer Schroeder didn't dart her a look this time.

"That was me," Larry said. He looked to Olivia. "Back in the day. Isn't that right, Honey?" He gave Marian's hand a squeeze.

"You were a rascal." Her wistful smile darkened. "Just high spirits, you understand. Nothing criminal."

Olivia drew a question mark on her notepad. Why had Marian insisted on making that distinction?

"We'd have heard, if it were," Officer Schroeder said, his tone conversational. "Knocking over mailboxes and drag racing are our most common violations. And underage drinking." He sobered. "Kills a kid or two every year. It makes me angry, seeing those young lives snuffed out."

Olivia wondered if Officer Schroeder's vehemence derived from his personal experience. His own unending nightmare, perhaps. A movement jarred her from her thoughts.

Across from them, Marian silently struggled to release her hand from Larry's white-knuckled death grip.

"One unguarded moment," the officer went on. "A second's lapse in judgement. Most times it's the reckless driver who gets it, wrapped around a tree or going over the bluff." He paused. "But sometimes there are innocent passengers." Another pause. "Or some poor schmuck in another car, or crossing the road, or riding a bike." He shook his head.

"It was an accident." Larry blurted, his face reddening, sweat on his brow.

"Russ's death is hitting him hard," Marian said.

"She came out of nowhere. Down that hill on her bike. I couldn't stop!"

Olivia realized she'd stopped taking notes and hurried to catch up.

"You were driving, Russ beside you?" Officer Schroeder guessed. Larry nodded.

"He doesn't know what he's saying," Marian said.

"I do," the officer said. "Doc McIntyre mentioned it earlier. Said he hoped Russ would finally have some peace all these years later."

"Those boys didn't mean to kill that girl," Marian spat. "It was an accident."

"Hit-and-run, Doc says, right after he'd come to town. Said there was plenty of talk who did it, but not enough evidence. Franks family goes back a long way here. They protected their own."

"Russ wanted to confess," Larry said.

"As if that could make any difference now." Marian rubbed Larry's arm.

"You tried to talk him out of it?" Olivia asked.

"He wouldn't listen," Larry said. "Told me he needed to tell God and the police before he died. But, he didn't get to." Tears rolled down the old man's cheeks.

For a moment, the only sound was that of Larry mourning his friend. Then, Officer Schroeder spoke.

"Ms. Payton says she saw you head off fishing today. Catch anything?"

Larry shrugged. "Enough for dinner tonight."

"Marian, you were on the pier with Russ after Larry left. Can you tell me what happened?"

"I can tell you he tripped and fell. At least, that's what it sounded like, but I was walking away. I'd had quite enough of him. Too bad I didn't look back." She crossed her arms.

"You heard him?" All color drained from Larry's face. "Why didn't you—"

"Because his talk would ruin our lives. You can still go to prison, you know."

"As can you," Officer Schroeder told her. "Doc says he didn't drown. Hitting the bow of the boat knocked Russ out, but it didn't kill him. That anchor you dropped on him did. And that's called murder."

* * *

THE NEXT DAY, AT HIS invitation, Olivia met Officer Schroeder in town for pizza and beer. He was running late, and she took the time to sketch. As soon as they settled into the booth with their beers, she asked the question that bothered her. "Did you suspect Marian all along?"

He shook his head. "My money was on Jake. Kind of a hothead. Three kids, a mortgage, college to think about. Seemed plausible."

Olivia nodded. "Wouldn't have surprised me. But the truth sure did."

Tim sipped his beer. "The look on Larry's face when I started talking about drunk driving—well, it brought to mind Doc's story. So, I thought I'd push a little. See where it went. And Doc said the second wound was from blunt force trauma. Coffee can of concrete sure fits that bill."

"So, after killing a man to keep a secret, Marian just spilled it out." Olivia shook her head. "Incredible what guilt can do."

The pizza arrived. She grabbed her sketchbook to make room for the platter.

"What's this?" Tim took the pad from her and flipped through the pages. "These are good. You did one of me?" He held up the sketch she had done last night from memory. "Why?"

"It's what I do when I find something—or someone—interesting."

He clinked her glass with his beer. "Well, here's to more sketches, then. Does that mean you'll be staying a while? That all this hasn't scared you away?"

Olivia sipped her drink, then smiled. "Yeah, I think I'll be sticking around."

Salt, Sand, Slay

Cindy Martin

As Steve and I crossed Card Sound Bridge, entering the Florida Keys, the stress of planning this weekend melted away. I soaked in the cloudless sky, painted a vivid cerulean. Along State Road A1A, brilliant green palm fronds swayed above tiki huts and seashell shops. Smiling, Steve tapped his wedding band on the steering wheel to a Jimmy Buffett tune.

"Isn't that a fact? Changes in latitude. Changes in attitude," I said.

"Absolutely, Grace." My husband kept his eyes, covered in aviator shades, on the road.

Even though we were seated with only a small console between us, he seemed miles away—his mind elsewhere.

At fifty-two, Steve had aged gracefully: a full head of chestnut hair with a few stray grays at the temples and an athletic build without a beer gut, unlike his buddies. Despite his insane hours, Steve managed to squeeze in workouts five days a week at the Miami-Dade Police Department's fitness center.

I had overestimated the challenge of convincing Steve to take time off from work and go on this vacation.

After our daughter left for college, I had floated several potential trips by my husband. He found flaws with each and every one. Steve knew the streets of Miami and the layout of the gym better than the interior of our home, especially the bedroom. After twenty-four years of marriage, I had adapted to his adrenaline-charged style of working violent cases—even when he disappeared for three days because he wouldn't quit until he found the guy, gal, suspect, murderer, rapist, fill in the blank. I often joked with my colleagues at the bookshop that I should file a missing person report on my detective husband.

On a rare dinner date a few months ago with our former neighbors, Steve became fired up to go to the Keys. Kaci and Paul bounced between their properties in Miami and the Keys, making a killing on their rentals. They were more like business partners than husband and wife. Paul, the introvert, preferred sunsets and late nights reading. In fact, when he lived next door, Paul and I joked that we were a two-member book club, since we shared crime novels and occasionally met to discuss them over a glass of wine.

On the other hand, Kaci was an early bird with an active social calendar. Coordinating the Seven Mile Bridge Run in Marathon, a small race open to only fifteen hundred runners, was her newest community activity. Steve perked up at the sound of an athletic challenge. Running was one of the things he and I had enjoyed together in our early years—until life got in the way.

Kaci tipped us off on how to register for the race and offered us a free cottage for that April weekend. Steve couldn't say no. It was a win-win decision: a getaway that included running over a causeway with a spectacular view of the Gulf of Mexico's turquoise waters. I was excited about the possibility of drinking fruity cocktails on a white sandy beach and evenings snuggling with the man I loved.

Now, months later, here we were humming along the four-lane highway from Miami to Marathon. After a couple of hours, we arrived at a two-story bungalow owned by Kaci and Paul. The quaint and private beachfront house, painted emerald green with white trim, bore the name, "Key Lime." Dangling over the door was a wind chime made from chunks of a coconut shell.

Kaci emerged from the canary-yellow cottage next door. She wore a short white cotton dress that showed off her sun-drenched skin. Paul followed in khaki shorts and a short-sleeved shirt decorated with flamingoes. After a round of hugs, Kaci and Paul escorted us into our place.

"It's so cute. It reminds me of a gingerbread house," I said.

"Just like Hansel and Gretel." Steve lowered his voice and wiggled his fingers near his face, like he used to do to pretend-scare our daughter and her friends when they were little.

We stepped inside to find a surprise on the narrow kitchen counter: a small white basket containing bananas, granola bars, bottled water, and our rectangular paper bibs for the race.

"See, there's no witch inside," I said, playing off his *Grimm's Fairy Tale* reference.

"But it's like an oven in here," Steve said.

"You guys are too much with your dark humor," Kaci said. We laughed.

Paul tapped a few buttons on the thermostat. "Give it a few minutes to cool down. These things have a mind of their own." Paul gave Steve and me a thumbs up and headed out with Kaci.

I unpacked my suitcase while Steve secured his pistol in the bedroom's safe. His phone buzzed, and he headed for the door.

"Update on the Bradley case," he said. The murder case of a rich Miami doctor who drugged his wife, then fled, was all over the news—and consumed my husband.

Through the years, I'd learned to accept my position as a "detective's widow." Steve was always on the clock.

From the balcony, I watched his familiar form pace the sandy beach. His head was bent with his cell stuck to his ear. I was prepared for this. My bag was stuffed with a few new psychological thrillers.

Twenty minutes and three chapters later, I heard Steve's gruff voice turn sugary sweet. I looked up from my page to find Kaci—in the tiniest pink bikini—posing before my husband. Steve's eyes drifted downward toward her bulging breasts. Suddenly, as if he remembered I was on the balcony, he stepped away from Kaci, patted her on the shoulder, and returned to the cottage with jagged blotches of sweat on his t-shirt.

"Case closed?" I asked.

"I wish," Steve grumbled. He grabbed a beach towel and mopped his brow.

"Hey, Grace, Steve." Paul's voice boomed from below. "We've got some pre-race juice."

"It's margarita time," Kaci said. She held up a full glass pitcher. In her other hand, she carried sliced limes. Paul raised a colorful tray holding four salt-rimmed glasses.

Steve and I waved them up to the balcony.

My husband drained his first cocktail and poured a second. "Geez, how did

I get talked into running a race in April? Don't you know it's the beginning of summer in Florida?"

"The good news is it will be a cool seventy degrees in the morning. Plus, the bridge is only six-point-eight miles and there's free beer at the finish line," Kaci pointed out.

"At least there's one good thing about this race you conned me into running." Steve gave Kaci a fake glare. He got up and entered the bedroom through the sliding glass door. I watched him tinker with the thermostat, then disappear into the bathroom. When he returned to the happy-hour balcony, I noticed he had on a fresh t-shirt.

We clinked our glasses and took in the sunset. The reflection of gold and coral hues streaked the gentle ocean waves as the bright yellow ball in the sky kissed the ocean.

Kaci looked at her smartwatch. "There's pasta salad in the fridge so you can carb up tonight, and those peanut butter granola bars in the basket are fabulous for energy before the race. I'll be up well before y'all open your eyes since I'm part of the set-up crew. See you three at the finish line. Keep your eye on the prize."

"Beer," Steve and Paul said in unison.

"No. The gorgeous medal. I'll be handing them out, so I better see you all there." Kaci waved and headed out. Paul fist-bumped Steve and gave me a hug.

The next morning, I rousted my husband before dawn. "Too many margaritas for you," I said. I pinned the bib to Steve's shirt while he dressed and downed a couple of ibuprofen tablets and a bottle of water.

Paul met us outside the cottage. "I feel your pain, buddy," Paul said. "Margaritas do help you sleep like a rock. I didn't even hear Kaci leave. I swear she's insane, volunteering to be up and out by four in the morning. I'm glad I set my alarm, or I would still be snoozing. Kaci would never let me hear the end of it."

Steve patted the pockets of his shorts. Phone bulge on the right. Police credentials on the left. Steve never went anywhere without his Miami-Dade police credentials—even the bathroom.

Paul teased him. "Geez, are you happy to see me? All that crap is gonna weigh you down."

"This isn't my first rodeo." Steve clearly wasn't in the mood for jokes.

"It's a cop thing, Paul," I shrugged.

We walked the short distance to the bridge where runners had gathered, some in crazy get-ups, including grass skirts over shorts, ball caps with stuffed parrots protruding from the top, and light-up flamingo necklaces. "We are less than seven miles away from enjoying the weekend," Paul said.

After the starter pistol rang out, Paul and I took off at our agreed pace. Steve fell behind. I told Paul I'd see him at the beer tent and dropped back to let Steve set the pace, as slow as it was due to his hangover. I wanted to finish together. Between heavy breaths, he grumbled during the entire sixty-three-minute run while I took in the blue-green waves below. Once I spotted the balloon arch marking the finish line, I grabbed his hand, hoping for a decent photo.

"Smile, Steve." I lifted his arm, and he put on a show for the cameraman.

After we crossed the finish line, volunteers placed ribbons with miniature chunky medals of the Seven Mile Bridge around our necks. My husband stumbled to a grassy area and collapsed.

"Note to self—no margaritas before a race," Steve said.

"Bucket list checked." I let him cool down while I gathered water bottles, bananas, and beers.

Steve livened up at the sight of the plastic cups full of amber liquid. He looked around.

"Where's Kaci? I thought she said she'd be at the finish line," he said.

"Maybe they moved her post." I had to raise my voice for him to hear me over a duo who had launched into a set of Beach Boys tunes. "Paul finished well ahead of us. I don't see him around either." I handed my husband a water bottle and a beer.

"Double-fisted," Steve grinned.

We checked on our race times and headed to our cottage for showers and breakfast. When we arrived, the sandy driveway was jammed with Monroe County Sheriff's patrol cars, an ambulance, and a white truck labeled, "Monroe County Medical Examiner's Office."

"What the hell?" Steve said. We picked up our pace and reached the yellow tape that cordoned off the cottages. He pulled out his badge and ID and showed it to a uniformed officer.

Within minutes, a six-foot-four detective approached. He had a receding hairline of salt and pepper hair, and a goatee even saltier.

"I'm Detective Marc Meade." He shook hands with both of us.

I'd seen it a million times. When my husband meets another officer: instant brotherhood.

The towering detective shared the scenario. He tilted his scruffy chin toward the beach. It looked like a hazmat scene, with men and women dressed in white protective gear milling about under a tent.

"Tourists found a woman's body in a kayak. Next of kin has arrived. Her husband, Paul Sulliman."

"What?" I screamed. "Kaci is dead? How?"

My pulse quickened thinking about Paul having to deal with this alone. Steve wrapped his right arm around my shoulder and pressed his nose into the top of my head. His breath puffed into my hair. A lone tear trickled down my face.

"Oh, man. You know the couple? I'm really sorry. My partner is talking with Paul right now." Detective Meade tapped his blue pen on his miniature notepad. "Since you're friends with Paul and the deceased, I'd like to ask you a few questions."

Steve nodded. "Yes, of course. I just can't believe it. Kaci is so sweet. Who would want to kill her?" He gazed toward the tent.

"That's what we're trying to figure out. Would you mind coming with me?" The detective lifted the crime scene tape and escorted us to the rear of our cottage, where we stood around a circle of faded Adirondack chairs.

"There's no escaping crime." Steve shook his head.

I clutched his hand. "She was so happy yesterday." My mouth filled with the tangy taste of blended sweat and tears. It was hard to form just the right words. Finally, I asked the question I wasn't sure I wanted the answer to. "How did she die?"

"Gunshot." Detective Meade said. "We'll run ballistics on the shell. The squad is in the Sulliman's bungalow with Paul's permission. Would you authorize a search of yours?"

Steve nodded. I turned toward a younger man in khakis and a police-issued polo waddling in our direction.

"Meet my partner, Detective Bowman."

Detective Bowman held an iPhone in his gloved hands. Steve stood stone-faced. I knew the look of my husband's investigative mind.

"This was in the victim's pocket," Detective Bowman said. "Surprisingly, unlocked without a password. It still has juice too."

Detective Meade yanked enormous blue latex gloves onto his hands. Towering over his chubby sidekick, he removed the glowing phone and jammed his index finger onto the glass screen. Cupping his palms around the device to darken the screen under the Florida sun, his eyes scanned up and down. I peered into the investigator's hand as he tapped the settings icon with the gray gears.

"Here it is. Kaci Sulliman." Detective Meade said. "Latest model. Worth some bucks. Since the perpetrator didn't take the phone, I'm assuming robbery wasn't the motive."

"Maybe he didn't know it was there," my husband said.

"What do you know about Kaci and Paul's relationship?" Detective Meade asked.

"We've known them for a long time, like fifteen years, and never saw any issues." Steve said. "Aside from being polar opposites, they seemed happy. We're only here because Kaci and Paul invited us. The race, the cottage on the beach. It sounded like fun to spend a weekend with our old friends."

"That race is a big deal around here. Closing the bridge to traffic for two hours drives the locals nuts." Detective Meade lifted his eyes from the phone to Steve. "Let me ask you something. Paul told us the last he saw Kaci was when he woke up because you called her around one a.m. with an air conditioning maintenance issue."

"No. That's impossible. I was dead to the world after drinking half a pitcher of margaritas." The etched lines on Steve's forehead became more prominent. He swiveled his head in my direction. "Did you call Kaci?"

My eyebrows pinched from my confusion. "No. I zonked out at eleven-ish after texting Carlene, our college daughter in Orlando. Even though she's nineteen, I still like to say good night to her. I slept straight through until the alarm went off at five this morning. Maybe one of their other renters is named Steve."

"Well," Detective Meade said. "Her call log says she received a call at one-thirty-three a.m." He tapped the phone number.

A familiar buzz vibrated, and we all stared at the front pocket of Steve's shorts.

For once, my husband didn't drop what he was doing to answer it.

I resisted the urge to plunge my hands into his shorts and grab the phone. Instead, I crossed my arms over my chest and let out a breath I didn't know I was holding. "Steve? What the hell is going on? Did you call Kaci?"

Detective Meade kept his ear to the cell and let the call go to voicemail. His brows became one and his pupils enlarged, leaving only a small ring of hazel. I heard a male voice. I couldn't be certain it was my husband's.

Without looking at us, the investigator lowered the phone and scrolled through the photos app. He tapped a couple of albums containing photos of properties and landscapes. When he got to one labeled "Miami," Detective Meade paused, and enlarged a photo of a man and woman.

Turning the screen toward Steve and me, Detective Meade's piercing blue eyes zeroed in on my husband. "Can you explain this?"

Steve looked at me and then at the detective. "Like I said, Kaci and I are old friends. Paul too. We met up a couple of times for drinks. No big deal."

On the screen was an image of my smiling husband and Kaci clinking glasses of wine. Detective Meade sideswiped the photo, revealing six images of my husband and friend smooching, selfies with their cheeks pressed together, and one with Steve's hands on Kaci's bikini-clad hips.

"Really, Steve? With one of our best friends?" My heart was pounding so hard I thought I might have a heart attack. "I suspected you were up to something. Late nights at work," I said with two fingers from each hand bent into air quotes. I slapped him, leaving a bright red mark on his cheek. "And then you killed her!"

Detective Bowman snatched my arm, preventing me from slapping Steve again, and marched me away from Steve while his partner hovered over my husband.

"No! I didn't kill her. I, I—."

"What do you carry?" Detective Meade asked in a cool tone.

"Glock twenty-three," Steve said.

"Forty cal?"

"Yes," Steve replied.

The investigators shared a knowing look. Detective Meade bagged Kaci's phone and gave it to his partner, who walked away with the evidence. I stayed put and watched Steve and the detective talk. The only thing I could hear was my heart hammering in my chest, the faint strumming of a guitar and the post-race party crowd singing the song, "Fun, Fun, Fun."

Detective Bowman returned with another clear plastic bag. Inside was a pistol.

I sidled closer to listen.

"With your permission to search the premises," Detective Bowman said, "and with Paul's help to enter your safe, we retrieved your Glock. One round is missing from the magazine."

"No." Steve threw his hands up in the air. "No way. I haven't fired that weapon since I qualified three-four months ago."

Detective Meade Held out his hand. "Can I look at your phone?"

Steve clenched his jaw. He glanced at me, then back at the detectives.

I darted to my husband's side. "You know, you don't have to give it to them. I can call our lawyer."

"Nah. I'm not lawyering up. I've got nothing to hide." Steve placed the phone in Detective Meade's palm.

"Unbelievable. How could you?" I pressed my fist into my hips. and shook my head.

Detective Meade opened up the GPS app on Steve's phone. "Well, Steve, Bad news. The data speaks for itself. You were pretty active between one-thirty and three a.m. walking from your cottage to the beach where you lingered before returning to your place."

The investigator reached for his waist and unsnapped handcuffs from his belt. "Steven Henderson, you are under arrest for the murder of Kaci Sulliman. You have the right to remain silent—"

"I understand my rights. Grace, it wasn't me." Steve took a few steps toward me before Detective Meade's large hand wrapped around my husband's wrist.

"Save it for court." Detective Meade snapped on the cuffs and steered him toward a patrol car.

I yanked my phone from my pocket and shouted back at my husband. "I told you not to hand it over. I'm calling the lawyer now."

I tapped a few numbers then stopped. What would I say to the lawyer? "I think my husband may or may not have murdered our friend?" The evidence was mounting against Steve. I placed my cell on the circular table between the chairs—the place where the four of us had planned to celebrate finishing the race.

Despite the humidity, I stood there shivering. What would happen to my husband, who was ruthless and had spent his career protecting and serving? Inmates aren't very kind to imprisoned cops.

The sound of flip-flops smacking bare heels made me turn. Paul, still in his running shorts and bib, approached. He plopped into the faded blue chair next to me.

For a long time, we sat in silence. At this point, what could we say to one another? His wife was dead and my husband arrested. We watched a pelican land on the small dock next to the rainbow-colored kayaks. The prehistoric bird flapped its wings twice and then settled on a wooden post.

Paul reached for my hand. "We did it, honey."

I squeezed his hand. "All those crime novels paid off."

THE DEFENSELESS COOKBOOK

MARY ADLER

WHILE THE OTHER STUDENTS AT the Villa Rondina Cooking School milled about waiting for the driver to distribute their bags, I wandered away with my satchel. If I stood on my tiptoes, I could just see over the wall encircling the forecourt. Below me, paths and olive trees spiraled up from the plains of Florence.

"Pardon me, Sister, but are nuns not required to travel in pairs?"

The deep voice, one I did not expect to hear in Tuscany, surprised me. I twirled, and the hem of my black habit stirred the dust.

"There are so few of us that we must venture into the secular world unaccompanied and at our peril." I tilted my head down and looked over my glasses at the magnificent man before me. "Perhaps you would like to be my chaperone, quite a burdensome job, as I am not let out often and may be prone to excess."

Carabiniere Inspector Guido Fazio bowed, as our fellow students looked on. "It would be my pleasure, Sister Anne."

We'd met years ago when we'd collided in a Manhattan police station. When he handed me the briefcase I'd dropped, he whispered, "I assume you are an undercover officer."

In near-perfect Italian, I'd answered, "You assume incorrectly. I am a rare book expert and a nun with The Sisters of Perpetual Sorrow."

He was delighted that I spoke his language. One thing led to another, and I invited him out to dinner. At the convent.

"The convent?" He seemed surprised.

"Yes. We eat dinner almost every night," I'd said dryly.

I hadn't seen him since, but we'd kept in touch. I was now thrilled, although a bit confused, to see the Venetian officer, out of uniform, at the cooking school.

As I hugged him, I said, "May I assume you are undercover, Guido?"

He whispered, "Later."

Then, in the European fashion, I kissed him on both cheeks. When in Rome, as they say, although we *were* in Florence. Apparently, we scandalized the bus driver, who glared at us and made the sign of the cross before driving away. An elderly gentleman tipped his Panama hat as his nurse wheeled him to the hotel's accessible entrance, and the French couple smiled as if we were lovers on the Seine. The Americans immortalized the moment on their iPhones.

I visualized the photo—of a nun kissing a handsome man—traveling through the ether to my convent in New York. I hoped the fees I earned restoring books would buy me Mother Superior's indulgence.

I FRESHENED UP AND FOLLOWED mouth-watering aromas to a room with arched windows and faded frescoes.

At dinner, Guido entertained our fellow students with fictional accounts of his adventures as an airline pilot determined to learn to cook risotto.

Bonnie and Helen, the American women, darted glances at us, iPhones ready.

"We are on our honeymoon," Bonnie said.

"Yes, we hope to create a signature dish." Helen lay her hand over Bonnie's.

Mimi shrugged, and Jacques said, "It is, how do you say, a whim?"

Mimi muttered to him, in French, that they would cook Italian food better than the teacher.

"My nurse, Francesca, is the student," Enzo, the elderly man, said. "I will enjoy the fruits of her labors."

"And I think learning a new dish is a splendid way to end my holiday," I said.

After dinner, Guido and I left through twelve-foot-high doors to a walled patio and admired the lights of Florence twinkling below us.

"Alone, at last." I sighed.

"Sister, you are incorrigible. Can you explain how you ended up in a convent?"

"I am more interested in hearing what *you* are doing here."

"The Prefect dotes on his son, whose roommate at the art academy in Venice is Stefano Santilli." He waved his hand to encompass the villa. "Stefano's mother owns this cooking school. When Stefano was home, he intercepted an ominous note addressed to her. Then the brakes on her car failed. Fortunately, she steered into a lavender field."

"And apparently came to a safe, but fragrant stop," I said.

He ignored my interruption. "The mechanic said the brakes weren't tampered with, but the Prefect sent me to look into it anyway. Discretely. Hence no uniform." He raised his shoulders a bare inch in that Italian way that meant, *What could I do?* "I'll investigate and learn to cook risotto. How do you say, *a busman's holiday?*"

"*Si,*" I said.

He looked at his watch. "I have an appointment with Signora Santilli, who knows why I am here. Come with me. Perhaps together we will solve a mystery."

An intriguing invitation I was powerless to resist.

"And why are *you* here?" he asked as we walked toward her house. "At dinner in your convent, you renounced all culinary pursuits—for which your fellow nuns were grateful. I assume a book is involved."

"Well done, Inspector. I happened upon an article about the cooking school—well, I like to think of it as divine intervention. In a photo of the owner's kitchen, a yellow leather-covered cookbook lay near the stove. I believe it to be a rare nineteenth-century tome. The owner doesn't welcome visitors, so I enrolled in the school hoping for a chance to speak to her. God willing, I will rescue the cookbook from the destructive environment of a kitchen."

"Somewhat contradictory, *non?*" He pushed back a lock of dark hair that had fallen over his forehead.

"The book belongs in a museum. At the very least, it should be protected from steam and smells of garlic." I shuddered. "I know it is not my place, but when I saw that photograph—"

Guido caught my arm when I slipped on the catkin-littered stone stairs to Signora Santilli's house. A branch of an ancient chestnut tree arched over the stairs.

"*Madonna!*" he said. "It's a wonder Signora Santilli has not fallen and broken her legs."

"Or her neck." I felt a chill unrelated to the breeze that stirred the leaves above us.

When Signora Santilli opened the door, Guido introduced me. I complimented her on the chestnut tree while wiping my feet on the doormat.

"A nuisance, but it has been here forever." She placed her hands in a prayer position and moved them back and forth. "Thank the Lord there are not any others on the estate."

She was a handsome woman, maybe in her late forties. The Tuscan sun had done her skin no favors, and her features were austere, but she carried herself with a certain grace as she led us inside, where a bottle of Vin Santo sat on an ornate coffee table.

"Please." She invited us to sit. We felt obligated to sip the sweet wine she offered. I ached to see the cookbook.

After Guido talked to her, I would tell her why I was there and convince her to protect the book, perhaps even donate it to one of Florence's majestic libraries.

"I am sorry you came so far for nothing, Inspector," she said. "My son overreacted. No one tampered with my brakes. I am in no danger."

"He said you received a threatening note."

She waved a dismissive hand. "Someone who didn't enjoy their cooking lessons, a disgruntled supplier. The notes mean nothing."

"Then you have received more than one."

She grudgingly admitted there had been several. "But they said only, 'Do the right thing.'"

"Do you know what 'the right thing' referred to?" he asked.

She shook her head and grew increasingly flustered, convincing me that she not only knew who was sending the notes, but why.

When he finished his fruitless interrogation, Guido nodded at me.

I leaned forward. "Signora, I am an expert in rare books and wish—" I faltered when she covered her mouth with her hand. "I'm sorry, Signora. Have I upset you?"

She stood. "Not you, too."

"Signora, I only wish to advise you—"

"Out!"

"But Signora—"

"Come, Sister." Guido's look persuaded me to acquiesce.

As we left, he paused in the doorway. "If you do not tell us the truth, Signora, we cannot help you."

She shut the door in his face.

As we descended the stairs, I said, "She knows what the notes are about and who's sending them."

"Yes. It was obvious, and she seemed frightened when you mentioned books."

I wondered if "doing the right thing" referred to preserving the cookbook. I envisioned vigilante book restorers descending upon the villa armed with archival tape, loupes, and white gloves.

"Sister?"

I did not share my fanciful thought and said only, "We must discover who is threatening her."

"And why. But how, Sister?"

THE NEXT MORNING, I WOKE to bells calling the faithful to Mass. Too many bells. I'd overslept. I said a quick Our Father and promised the Lord more prayers later.

Lidia, our instructor, told us Signora Santilli had gone to town for the day but would see us tomorrow. I blew out an exasperated breath. I needed to speak to her again.

Charitably put, Lidia was not an inspiring teacher. While we rolled out gnocchi dough, Enzo told Francesca to text him when we finished and whirred away in his motorized chair.

Francesca flicked the dough almost as expertly as Guido, who produced near perfect gnocchi. He shrugged apologetically. "My grandmother," he said. Francesca smiled wistfully and said, "Mine too."

Mimi's gnocchi resembled misshapen marbles. She left in high dudgeon when I pointed that out to her—in French. Jacques winked at me as he rerolled the lumps and began again.

Of the Americans, only Bonnie stayed, her iPhone now covered in dough from sharing her progress on social media.

While our gnocchi rested, Lidia demonstrated how to slowly—tediously slowly—incorporate chicken broth into arborio rice.

While stirring, I heard the gate bell and glanced out the window. Signora Santilli had returned. Good. Perhaps she would talk to me during the break.

I'd stirred myself into a dreamlike state when a scream brought spoons clattering against pans. A chill ran down my spine at the thought of Signora Santilli at the bottom of those treacherous stairs, her neck at an awkward angle.

WE RAN OUTSIDE TO WHERE the maid pointed at the house and said Signora Santilli had been attacked. Guido showed his credentials and told Lidia to keep everyone in the forecourt. He took the stairs two at a time, and I followed, careful of my footing.

She lay on the living room floor, moaning.

Guido knelt beside her. "Lie still, Signora. Can you tell me what happened?"

"Someone knocked me down."

"Sister?" He motioned for me to take his place, then phoned for medics and the Carabiniere.

"My purse," she said, and clutched my hand.

I glanced around but didn't see it.

Guido asked, "Did you see who pushed you?"

"*Non*, but I heard him run out the back door."

"Did you smell anything?"

"*Non*." She waved Guido away and tried to stand.

"Please, it is better if you wait for the doctor." He patted her hand.

"But I must check to see—" She pressed her lips together.

"If the book is missing?" I asked. I hoped it hadn't run out the door with the intruder.

Guido asked, "Will you trust a nun to check for you?" His dimple deepened when he smiled. She nodded and told me where to find it.

Not in the kitchen. She'd hidden it inside a corset box at the bottom of her cedar chest. I caressed the raised bands on the spine, now scuffed and dented. Clearly, the book had suffered daily use. Perhaps the tomato stains could be removed, but I despaired at the oil marks on the once-beautiful laid paper. Handwritten notes on many of the pages diminished the book's value considerably, but I carried it reverently as I returned to the living room.

"*Grazie a Dio.*" Signora Santilli reached out for the cookbook, then kissed it.

"Why is this book so important to you?" I asked, for she seemed to have no idea of its value to a collector.

"It belonged to my great-great-grandmother, who passed it to her oldest daughter, then the next, all the way to me. We treasure it and have preserved it through the years."

"Preserved it?" My voice rose to the top of my mezzo-soprano range.

A smile threatened to break through Guido's officerly demeanor.

"Is the book the reason for the threatening notes?" he asked.

She nodded. "I never should have allowed the article about the school." She berated herself until Guido calmed her.

"Why not?" he said.

"It doesn't matter."

"Signora, it matters very much to someone, or you would not have feared the book had been taken."

She closed her eyes. We waited. When she opened them, she looked disappointed that we were still there. She sighed.

"A man named Cesare came here after the article was published. He enrolled in the school, and we became close." She looked at me. "My husband died four years ago, and I thought *maybe*, but . . ." She pursed her lips as if tasting something bitter. "One day, I left Cesare in the kitchen and went to the garden for arugula. When I returned, he held the cookbook. His eyes were shiny with tears."

Her eyes shone like obsidian.

"He jumped, like a thief. And then he said he'd meant to tell me. It belonged to his family. That my great-great-grandmother had stolen it from his great-great-grandfather."

"And then what happened?" I asked.

"I grabbed the book and told him to get out. He kept explaining, but I pushed him out the door and locked it."

"Then what?"

"He came back a few days later. Tried to persuade me he cared about me."

The medics arrived, and while they examined her, Guido smoothed out jurisdictional issues with the Carabinieri lieutenant. After Signora Santilli refused to go to the hospital, the medics left, and the rest of us returned to the forecourt, where everyone had gathered. While the Carabinieri investigated, I paced in the shade of umbrella pines, thinking.

Whoever attacked Signora Santilli was among us. No one had come through the locked gate all morning, except her, and the only people who weren't in class when she returned were Mimi, Helen, and Enzo.

Guido fell into step with me. "I am sure you hope the French woman is the culprit, Sister, but an officer reported that she and the American have alibis."

I squinched my eyes to concentrate better while the swallows, for which the school was named, swooped and darted across the cloudless sky.

"Then Enzo is the only person not accounted for," I said. "Maybe there is another entrance to the property."

"Apparently not," Guido said.

Tires crunched on gravel as Francesca wheeled Enzo to the lieutenant. The elderly man waved his arm toward the wall and said, "A young man ran down the path. He threw something into the bushes."

The lieutenant sent officers to search while another recorded Enzo's description of the robber.

Then an officer held up a purse and yelled, "I found it."

"Enzo's lying," I said. "I had to stand on my tiptoes to see the path below the wall. He couldn't see it from his chair."

"But they *did* find a purse."

I thought for a moment. "*Enzo* could have thrown it over the wall."

"Impossible." Guido pointed to the house. "How could he have climbed the stairs to steal it?"

"An accomplice?"

"Francesca never left class," he reminded me, "and there have been no other visitors."

"If Enzo lied about who threw the purse into the bushes, maybe he's lying about something else."

"Something like . . . ? Ah. Of course," Guido said. "And how will we find out?"

"I have a plan."

We joined Enzo and congratulated him on saving the day. I dropped my hanky beside his chair and glanced at his shoes. Then I stood, smiled triumphantly at Guido, and tilted my head toward the chair's footrest. I caught Francesca watching the exchange. She bit her lip.

Guido bent down. When he stood, he said to Enzo, "The soles of your shoes are worn, and catkins from the chestnut tree are lodged in the heels."

"It means nothing," Enzo blustered. "I can walk a bit. The wind probably blew those things everywhere."

"There is only one chestnut tree on the estate, catkins do not have wings, and it took more than a bit of walking to wear your shoes to that extent."

Enzo protested, but Francesca knelt in front of him and said, "It's over, Grandfather." The voice was loving, concerned. "Tell them."

He stroked her cheek. "I only wanted to borrow the cookbook," he said, as if that excused him. "I waited until everyone had gone and hid my chair behind the garage. Signora Santilli returned too soon."

A young man shouted at the Carabinieri blocking the path to the forecourt, "Let me pass. I am Stefano Santilli. I live here. Where is my mother?"

At Guido's nod, the young man approached us. He broke through the crowd, then stopped short. "Francesca, darling. What are you doing here?"

"Oh, Stefano, I am so sorry." She buried her face in her hands.

Enzo stood and embraced her. "It is not her fault. I begged her to help me. My dying mother wants to hold her family's book one last time."

Stefano looked stricken. "Francesca . . ."

"It's not what you think, Stefano," she said. "When we met, I didn't know your family had the book."

"What book?" the lieutenant asked, and Guido suggested we continue the discussion in the house.

MRS. SANTILLI BEAMED WHEN HER son rushed to the sofa where she lay. Then she asked why he'd come back from Venice early.

Once we were seated, Guido explained what was happening, and said, "We must talk about your cookbook."

"*My* family's cookbook," Enzo said.

"*You* sent the notes," Signora Santilli cried.

Stefano lunged at Enzo, but Guido stepped between them and told Stefano to sit. The boy hesitated, then settled beside Francesca. She took his hand.

Guido said, "Enzo, you came in the house to 'borrow' the cookbook. Why take the purse?"

"When Senora Santilli came home early, I panicked and took the purse to make it look like a robbery. I thought no one would suspect a man in a wheelchair. I didn't mean to push her. I was going to get help, but then I heard someone coming up the stairs, so I ran out the back." Enzo pointed to the sofa. "May I?"

Signora Santilli nodded, and he sat beside her.

Enzo continued. "You are the image of your great-great-grandmother, who broke my great-grandfather's heart and stole the cookery book the Marchesa of Barone gave him for saving her son's life. The one he wrote his creations in."

"As *I* do," she said.

I winced. Neither family deserved the magnificent book they had defaced through the decades.

Guido smiled at me and lifted an eyebrow as if he knew what I was thinking.

"My family lost track of yours, and as the daughters married, their last names changed. Then two wars destroyed our country, and we thought the book was lost." Enzo spread his open hands apart. "But then my son Cesare saw it in a magazine. He came to talk to you, Signora, but fell in love with you and hesitated to speak of the book. Then *you* broke *his* heart and sent him away."

"He said I broke his heart?" Her fingers touched her chest.

"Yes. He cares about you."

Enzo seemed sincere, but Signora Santilli said, "How do I know this is not another lie to steal my family's book?"

The Carabinieri lieutenant interrupted, "Are you pressing charges, Signora?"

Still looking at Enzo, she said, "*Non.*"

"Then we have wasted enough time." The lieutenant bowed. "I will leave you to decide this matter among yourselves."

Guido rested a hand on my forearm. "Perhaps we, too, should leave the family to sort this out."

"But the book." I wailed. "They might divvy it up, like a pizza."

"Come." He guided me to a bench under an olive tree. "Seriously, Sister. Even I can see the book is severely damaged. How much value does it have now?"

I thought about the stains, the handwritten notes, the broken spine, the burn mark on the cover—the evidence of several generation's use—and of the two families who cherished it.

"Perhaps more than it did in its flawless state, Guido. To the families, it is priceless. And perhaps it will bring them together."

"*Sì,*" Guido said. "Enzo's mother will die in peace, holding her grandfather's book. Signora Santilli may forgive Enzo's son and find love. It appears Stefano has already forgiven Enzo's granddaughter—" he paused "—and they will continue the family tradition of preserving the book."

He hit "preserving" with just the right amount of irony to make me smile.

"Oh, my, Guido. That poor defenseless book."

THE BLUE-FOOTED BOOBY

CYNTHIA RICE

SAMMIE ALCIVAR'S CHUBBY, CALLOUSED HANDS trembled as he sorted nine pairs of still-damp swimming fins by size into their storage bins on the lower deck of the Emerald. He shook the droplets of salt water off his own navy-blue fins and leaned them against the bin to dry next to Marco's bright-blue pair. It was easy to tell them from the tourists' supply, which were all black. Sammie had missed a near-perfect opportunity—or had it been something else entirely, a fiasco, which would cost him his job, if not his freedom? He wasn't sure. He had come so close, and now time was running out.

It was already the fifth day of the nine-day sightseeing cruise through the Galapagos Islands. At each island stop, after the 145-foot yacht the Emerald anchored offshore, Sammie and the other naturalist, Marco, would split the sixteen tourists between their two Zodiacs and head to an island for a guided hike.

As had been the case on every trip Sammie and Marco worked together, the tourists preferred to board Marco's raft each morning, with the late risers reluctantly climbing into Sammie's. The men took turns providing the naturalist lectures each evening after dinner, and Sammie knew his talks fell short of Marco's, the tourists checking their watches and even ducking out midway to head to the bar on the upper deck. Marco's, by contrast, were full of amusing anecdotes and facts about the various islands and animals that had never been covered in Sammie's four-week naturalist certification course. It didn't hurt that Marco was ten years younger, thirty pounds lighter, and an engaging speaker.

A few nights before, Marco had entertained the group with a slide presentation on their next stop, which would include sightings of the blue-footed booby, one of the most popular and recognizable birds in the islands. The name, Marco claimed, derived from their blue feet combined with their clumsy behavior on land. He described their unusual courting habits, how the females were attracted to the males with the brightest blue feet. Sammie's cheeks burned with embarrassment when Marco reminded the tourists of the vivid blue swim fins he wore, compared to Sammie's darker blue pair. Marco used the same tired joke every tour, and it never failed to elicit an appreciative laugh. Sammie hated him for it. This time was worse than most. One passenger, an eleven-year-old brat named Theo Regler, had taken to calling Sammie "blue-footed booby," after Sammie had tripped climbing from the Zodiac and face-planted on the rocky shore.

That morning, the group had enjoyed an uneventful hike on North Seymour Island, where they saw hundreds of frigate birds and blue-footed boobies, then returned by the Zodiacs for the short ride back to the Emerald for lunch. The ship then motored a short distance to the northeast corner of the island for a few hours of snorkeling. That's where Sammie missed his opportunity.

Marian Stuckey was an overweight, shrill woman from Chicago in her mid-fifties, and her husband had paid good money to have her die on this vacation. The Tres Banderas Cartel, one of the strongest in Ecuador, was happy to oblige for the right price. Marian and Lillian, Marian's traveling companion, had been inseparable since they boarded the Emerald. This time, however, Lillian, along with a half-dozen of the other tourists, stayed on the ship rather than snorkel, citing the choppy conditions that afternoon. Sammie knew his odds were good when only Marian and the elderly couple from Miami joined him in his Zodiac.

The Zodiacs anchored fifty feet offshore, where they were likely to find schools of colorful fishes and an occasional sea turtle. Sammie frightened the elderly couple into staying in the Zodiac by claiming he'd seen a jellyfish.

He guided Marian away from the Zodiac, and further away from Marco's group, claiming there was an abundance of sea turtles in the area. She paddled after him, and to Sammie's surprise, they did see the largest sea turtle he had ever seen swimming just a few yards away. Marian followed it toward the Zodiac and witnesses. It took considerable urging on Sammie's part to get Marian turned and again swimming away from the Zodiac.

Just a little farther, he thought. When she had managed another ten meters, he closed the distance, preparing to make his move.

His plan wasn't foolproof, but it should work. He would swim up behind the woman, yank the snorkel out of her mouth, and use his considerable body weight to hold her submerged until she drowned. It didn't hurt that she had three glasses of wine with lunch. The deed done, he would shout for help and make a terrific show of trying to save Marian. By the time Marco and the others responded, it would be, sadly, too late for Marian. Sammie would feign guilt and despair over her death. He'd lose his job with Emerald Tours. A small price to achieve the fifty-thousand-dollar payday, which would nearly cover his past-due gambling debts to the Tres Banderas Cartel.

Sammie took one last glance back at the Zodiac, where the couple from Miami huddled with their backs to him. He steeled himself, took two strokes to position himself behind Marian—and she lifted her head from the water, yanked her snorkel from her mouth, and screamed, "SHARK!"

She pointed at a four-foot blacktip reef shark swimming fifteen feet below them. Before he could reassure her it was nothing to worry about, she shrieked "SHARK" again, even louder. She attempted to paddle, flailing her arms, frantically trying to reach the Zodiac. Forty feet away in the Zodiac, the elderly couple was now standing, yelling, and pointing in his direction. He saw Marco swimming his way, and he knew he had waited too long. Marian Stuckey would not drown that afternoon, ironically saved by the very creature she feared, a harmless blacktip reef shark.

It was two days later before Sammie had another chance. Marian and Lillian climbed up to the top deck bar that night, like they did every night. By closing time, two empty and one half-full bottles of cabernet decorated their table. Sammie was friends with the bartender and most nights helped him gather empty glasses in exchange for an occasional six-pack of beer, which he would take to the cramped quarters adjacent to the engine room he shared with Marco.

The other tourists trickled back to their cabins, with just Marian and Lillian remaining.

"Ladies, mind if I remove the empty bottles?" Sammie asked.

"Sure, thanks." Marian slurred the words, then reached out protectively and pulled the half-full bottle closer. "Not this one." She hiccupped loudly, which sent Lillian into a fit of loud laughter.

"Have a drink with us, Sammie," Marian said.

Sammie suspected the women knew it was against the rules for the staff to drink in the bar. Was there some way that by accepting he could get Lilian to leave him alone with Marian? He couldn't think of how that would work, and besides, even if he got Marian alone, Lillian would know he was with her. That wouldn't work. "Not for me. I want to be bright-eyed in the morning."

It was now day seven of the cruise, and Sammie knew what would happen if he returned to Quito without the money.

He couldn't imagine getting Marian alone on Isabela Island, their next stop. The Emerald would anchor offshore, and Marco and Sammie would accompany the tourists on a hike to take photos of the sea iguanas and birds. There wasn't another snorkeling session tomorrow. The final day, they would visit the tortoise breeding center before returning to San Cristobal Island. There, Marian and the rest of the passengers would disembark and head for the airport, eliminating Sammie's only option to pay back his gambling debt.

He supposed there was a slight chance he could waylay Marian on the walk back from the tortoise center. But Lillian would be with her like a barnacle. He *had* to kill Marian.

Sammie considered using the bar knife his friend used to slice lemons. He could cut both of the women's throats. He picked it up and stared at the blade, then placed it back on the counter. Despite his need to do *something soon*, this wouldn't work. After he'd killed one, the other would scream and wake the crew before he had time to throw their bodies overboard and clean up the blood. Sammie was running out of time.

The Emerald had crossed the equator a few hours earlier, complete with the cheesy ceremony the tourists loved, which included a champagne toast. The ship would motor all night as it headed south towards Isabela. The noise and vibrations from the engines would make it hard to sleep. Sammie planned to down a few beers in his room before retiring.

He returned to his quarters to discover Marco had finished off Sammie's beer stash and was snoring loudly from the top bunk. Sammie stripped down to his boxers and climbed into bed. He stuck in ear plugs, which muted the engine noise and Marco's snoring, but did nothing to lessen the vibration from the grinding of the large engine just feet from his bed.

After tossing and turning for two hours, Sammie climbed out of bed and slipped on a pair of shorts. He grabbed a pack of cigarettes and lighter from his locker and headed for the main deck.

The engine noise was barely audible on the deck. He stood at the railing and stared at the dark water churning from the ship's motion. The night sky was clear with a small crescent moon above, adding little to the dim night-running lights of the Emerald reflecting on the rough water. The ship's speed and cool air caused goose bumps to pop on Sammie's arms. He should have grabbed another layer, but he wouldn't be long. He lit a cigarette, inhaled, and tried to concentrate on the beauty of the Milky Way, the myriad stars forming a broad band of light stretching across the sky. It was different in Quito, where the city lights obscured the splendor of the night.

Instead, his mind returned to the dangers awaiting him back in the city if he returned without a way to pay his way out of trouble. Sammie had his passport with him, but was there anywhere he could go that the cartel wouldn't find him?

Footsteps on the port side distracted him. A woman staggered to the railing, leaned over, and vomited. Retching complete, she turned away from the railing and Sammie recognized Marian's pink sweatshirt from earlier that evening. He couldn't believe his luck. The deck was empty except for the two of them, and she was too inebriated to put up a struggle.

Sammie glanced around one last time, then rushed at the woman. He grabbed her ankles and flipped her over the railing into the dark water below. She made a soft cry as she tumbled down. Sammie's heart pounded in his chest as he watched. She resurfaced, flailing her arms, but by then, the ship was a considerable distance away. If she had cried out for help, Sammie didn't hear her.

He lit a cigarette and slumped on a deck chair. He had done it! With any luck, her roommate was sound asleep and wouldn't discover Marian was missing for hours. By then, the ship would be miles away, and no one would suspect Sammie's involvement.

Sammie drew hard on the cigarette and felt a surge of nausea. He fought down the urge to vomit, flicked the cigarette into the water, followed it with the butt of his first smoke. He needed to get back to his room in case anyone else wandered onto the deck and could place him there.

After changing into a sweatshirt and pants, he climbed under his blanket, but he couldn't shake the chill. At some point, he must have fallen asleep, because when his alarm woke him, he was gasping for breath, memories of a bad dream in which he was in the water next to Marian. As she sank, she gripped his ankle and pulled him down with her.

He was surprised he hadn't heard Marco leave. He sat on the edge of his bunk and settled his breathing. Pull it together, Sammie. You need to prepare for someone to discover Marian is missing. After ten minutes, he felt calmer, and he dressed as if he expected to hike on Isabela Island that day. Sammie started up the ladder towards the dining room.

He froze on the top rung. The ship's captain, Marco, and two men in National Park Patrol uniforms stood outside the entrance to the dining room. The Park Patrol policed the waters around the islands, alongside the Ecuadorian Navy and U.S. Coast Guard. He forced himself to finish the climb and walk towards the group.

"We're heading back to San Cristobal this morning," Marco said.

"What's going on?" Sammie asked.

"One of the passengers is missing," the ship captain said. "I suspect she went overboard during the night. We've searched the entire ship. I can't believe it. The Emerald has a spotless safety record."

After one more search of the entire ship, the National Park Patrol officers returned to their vessel, and the ship captain went in to comfort the passengers, who huddled around the tables with coffee but no food. Sammie followed Marco into the dining room, where he heard an ear-splitting nasal wail from the corner of the room.

It couldn't be, he thought.

But it was.

"Lillian! My poor Lillian," Marian Stuckey howled, while the other passengers sat in stunned silence. The elderly woman from Miami sat next to Marian and ineffectually patted her arm. "How could Lillian be gone?"

"Do they know what happened?" Sammie whispered to Marco.

"Not really. Both women were drinking till the bar closed, like they do every night. You've seen them put it away. Marian said Lillian had felt nauseated and wanted to go up on deck for fresh air. She'd grabbed Marian's sweatshirt because the temperature had dropped. When Marian woke up this morning, she realized Lillian had never returned." Marco poured himself a black cup of coffee. "We assumed we'd find Lillian sleeping it off on one of the deck chairs, but no such luck."

"That's terrible," Sammie said, realizing he meant it.

"Yes, of course. And we're ending the trip a day early. Most of the passengers will have to find a room in San Cristobal for the night, which may not be easy. What a mess, and worse, I won't get to give my gratuity pitch at dinner tonight. These people are going to be depressed or angry when they get off the ship a day early." Marco glanced around to be sure no one was close by and lowered his voice. "Tips are going to suck."

Marian started in on a fresh round of wailing. Sammie grimaced, filled his coffee cup, and carried it to the relative quiet of the deck. He, like Lillian, was nauseated and in need of fresh sea air. What a failure he was. Not only had he botched the murder of Marian Stuckey, but he had also drowned Lillian, her nice roommate. Without the fifty thousand dollars he needed, and as Marco had said, he'd earn little in tips for the nine days, especially considering the tourists always stuffed the larger bills in Marco's envelope, and the fives and tens in his, it was *his* death to return to Quito and face the wrath of the cartel to whom he owed money.

On the captain's order for departing passengers and crew to pack their belongings, Sammie loaded his swimming mask and blue fins into a gear bag and put the rest of his clothes into a small duffel bag. Marco and Sammie usually flew back to Quito, having a full week off between their cruise assignments. Sammie didn't know what he would do, but flying to Quito was not a choice. He had to disappear.

He carried his bags to the main deck and set them next to Marco's suitcase. Most of the ship staff would stay with the ship on the next cruise, with two days of shore leave in San Cristóbal.

Later that day, Sammie and Marco stood on the dock to pose for final pictures, bid goodbye to the passengers, and collect their gratuities. Marian, her eyes swollen and red from crying, walked past them without even a nod. As Marco had predicted, few envelopes of cash were handed to either man by the departing guests. The last family off the ship were the Regler parents and their obnoxious son, Theo. Mr. Regler handed a thick envelope to Marco and a much thinner one to Sammie.

Theo posed for one last picture with the naturalists. As his mother snapped the photo, the boy looked down at Sammie's shoes and laughed. "Sammie, you'll always be the blue-footed booby."

Sammie trudged up the gangplank to retrieve his luggage, realizing that the boy was right.

Dunes, Dogs, and Du Mauriers

Allison Baxter

As a Chicago teacher, the summer is long, and the money is short. The last two summers, I've had a "workcation" as a dog walker to the elderly residents of the Dunes, trading bathroom passes for poop bags. I relocate from my South Loop studio to a spacious attic apartment facing Lake Michigan in the breathtaking Indiana Dunes, where the aging NIPSCO—the Indiana power and gas plant to the east—casts cool shadows over the beach.

Each morning, depending on which clients are in residence, I walk the dogs in my charge to the beach. I start with my landlady Gertrude's Chihuahua, Chester. Then I pick up one or two others from nearby owners and exercise them together. Sun and breeze follow me as I run the dogs around the neighborhood before reconnecting them with Gertrude and her clan of retirees to spend the morning at the beach. Before lunchtime, I reverse the process. Late afternoon walks are shorter and just around the neighborhood.

But yesterday the routine had a few hitches and my world fell apart.

Gertrude didn't answer my morning knock. No note on her door, so, as agreed, I entered and secured the pooch to his lead. I would meet Gertrude at the beach after the walk. My usual second client was away with her grandkids and my third had gone to the city, so it was only Chester.

We arrived at the beach about 7:15. A clutch of senior citizens in an array of visors, orthopedic shoes, and folding chairs had gathered next to the lake in front of an imposing sand dune—but no Gertrude.

I shouted hello to Renfro, Gertrude's friend who walks his own dog. He waved me over.

While his cocker spaniel, Federico, smelled Chester's butt, Ren whispered into my ear, "You seen Gertrude today?"

"You neither? I collected Chester and expected to find her waiting with my morning brew."

Gertrude was not great about taking her heart meds. I exhaled, not realizing I'd been holding my breath. "I'll head back and check the house."

"I'll come with," Renfro said, handing Federico to a friend.

We hoofed back to the two-story clapboard, Chester catching a ride in my arms. Gertrude's adult tricycle was parked as usual outside the back door, a light wind blowing the handlebar streamers.

Inside, I shouted, "Gertrude, you here?" Nothing. I put Chester down and trotted frantically from bedrooms to bathrooms while Ren took the basement and storage room. In her usually tidy bedroom, her bed was unmade and her pillow on the floor. The rest of the room was as it usually was. *Golden Girls* video cassettes, seasons six and seven, stood in order under her antennaed TV. I practically ran to the bathroom, but everything from her Donald Duck toothbrush to the orange floral shower cap was in its place.

Renfro and I met in the living room. My mind was racing with worry. The unmade bed and the parked tricycle suggested a quick and unplanned exit on foot. What if she'd fallen or had a stroke? "I'll call the police."

Ren ran a hairy hand over his hairless head. He sighed loudly. "You know, I can head back to the beach and ask if anyone has seen her."

Because of her age and health history, the police put a BOLO—Be On the Look Out. I wasn't going to wait for our tiny police force when seconds might count. And, I'd recently overheard information—through the floor—that worried me.

The thing about living above Gertrude's place is that you couldn't help but know her. Even if you didn't spend time with her, you *spent time* with her. First, you'd hear the Golden Girls theme song play as her cell phone ringtone. Then after the lovely: "Thank you for being a friend," she'd answer with a gruff, "Whaddya want?" She's a loud talker, an exuberant critic, a relentless gossip, and insists on using the speakerphone. Even when talking to her ex-husband, who likes to shout and still resents that she took his mother's Fiesta Ware. She's embroiled in a $500,000 lawsuit with the neighbors, the Tristans. And I've heard her argue with Frank, another neighbor, about the property line.

What worried me was a one o'clock in the morning call the day before. She took it off the speakerphone . . . and lowered her voice. Did she know I was listening? Or was she being thoughtful given the hour? Either way, after the call, she left with a loud door slam.

When I collected Chester the next morning for his walk, Gertrude was sitting on the patio drinking coffee and smoking. Her swollen eyes and pale skin added ten years to her eighty.

I sat in the rattan chair across from her. "Are you OK?"

She took a deep draw on her cigarette and scratched her bright orange hair absently. "I've got a lot on my mind."

"Want to talk?"

She inhaled deeply, the cigarette dangled from her lips, so precarious I worried it would fall into her coffee. "Naw. Divorce. Ex-husband."

But Gertrude has no poker face, and her darting eyes told a different story. And working with teens has made me a lie detector. It wasn't her ex-husband that was ruffling her feathered hair. Someone was pressuring her. I wondered who and why, but I wouldn't add to her worries by pestering her to talk.

"Meet you at the beach?"

She nodded and rose to go inside without saying a word.

THE FIRST TIME I MET Gertrude was when I came to look at her rental. She opened the door dressed in orange polyester pants and a poet's blouse in coordinating colors.

Over a glass of sherry, I explained that I needed a vacation, time out of Chicago. "This place is magical. Give me a few days. I'll find a roommate," I said.

She frowned. "No roommates."

At my look of disappointment, she said, "Do you like dogs? You could cover your rent as a dog walker. There's nobody young to exercise these athletic dogs we all keep buying. Our clan in this neighborhood are Bengay and mobility devices. There's a demand. You could be the supply." Then Chester nuzzled my hand in agreement.

Two summers later, Chester still nuzzles, Gertrude still shares sherry with me, and I still love my summer place.

WHILE REN LOOKED FOR GERTRUDE at the beach, I knocked on doors, starting with Frank, Gertrude's neighbor on the right. He must have noticed the panicked look on my face because he used his captain's hat to wave me in to sit at his glossy mahogany table. I was slapped by a salmagundi of smells. There was a distinct smell of . . . ketchup that danced with smoky cigarettes and a lavender air freshener.

"I'm worried because Gertrude is missing. Did you see her walking around early this morning?"

"Nope. But, she doesn't," he chuckled softly, "check in with me. She doesn't even keep her fence on her own property." He smoothed his comb-over with a well-manicured hand. "Check with the Tristans. Their reputation precedes them as lawyer-loving and accident-prone, and they're always spying on Gertrude. I sure hope you find her." His face saddened. He must have realized how serious her absence was, too.

I was haunted by the tomato and corn syrup smell. But more haunted by the idea that I'd have to visit . . . the litigious neighbors.

Mrs. Tristan answered my knock with a glare and adjusted the cervical collar she still wore two years after she "slipped" on Gertrude's steps. "Come on in, dearie." Her mouth said dearie, but her eyes said something else. "I've seen you around Gertrude's."

While Mrs. Tristan was telling me in one run-on sentence that she had recently risen and had no idea where Gertrude was and she couldn't imagine why I would think she'd know what Gertrude was up to, I examined the living room for pentagrams or sacrificial goats. Instead, a Canadian flag almost as big as the country itself had pride of place. Next to it, a photo of the family on a large boat. Mr. Tristan looked young and spry with thick dark eyebrows, dark hair, and a black captain's hat.

"Who's from Canada?"

"Dearie, we all are. We sure were younger then. Lacey," she tapped a young girl in the picture, "my eldest is about your age."

Would this family have motivation for making Gertrude disappear? If anything, they'd want her alive so they could have their payday.

I returned to Gertrude's and sat on the patio to think. I was troubled by the ketchup. Then, it hit me. Who eats ketchup potato chips? Canadians. Frank also was Canadian.

I went into Gertrude's place to do a deeper dig. Maybe I expected to see a plane or bus ticket. A ransom note? But there was only yesterday's newspaper on the dusty glass coffee table next to a pack of her cigarettes, a Canadian brand she'd picked up from her ex-husband, she told me, du Maurier. There was a full ashtray of butts with orange lipstick, smoked all the way down. Under the table, on the peach rug was a stack of unopened mail. I sorted through utility bills, diner ads, junk mail, and an oversized envelope, unpostmarked, with the letters Z.S. on its front.

I took out my handy Swiss Army knife, kept Chester away with one hand, and sliced open the Z.S. envelope to reveal an enlarged photo of the back of a convertible with the license plate KNUX N LUV. Canucks in love? The slang term for Canadians. In the car were two people, both with long ponytails, one blonde and one dark. The car was parked in front of a sign that promised the best Hoosier Cream Pie in Indy.

Everyone knew my mom had the best Hoosier Cream Pie. She and I had spent hours engaged in Hoosier Cream Pie lessons. I never mastered fluffiness. I slapped my head. The only room I hadn't rechecked at Gertrude's was the kitchen.

There I found next to the humming refrigerator a blinking answer machine dating from the 1980s. I pressed the play button. The disembodied alarmed voice spoke. *We've been trying to contact you about your automobile warranty.*

Ren buzzed my cell phone. He spoke quickly, an edge of panic in his voice. "I found Gertrude's orange slip-on Sketchers, size five. Just one. I called the police, but they say I can't prove it's her shoe." Panic changed to anger. "But they *might* be willing to send it in for DNA if she doesn't show up. A little late."

"I'll be there in a minute." I jumped on the tricycle and soon the spokey dokeys were clicking, the patriotic red, white, and blue streamers stretched horizontal in the wind, and the orange flag warned everyone I was coming. A few minutes later, I found Ren.

"When the police realize their error, we need to have the evidence," Ren explained, lying on the sand to get a close-up photo of the shoe. Then he picked it up with his sleeve covering his hand and put it in his Indy Indies tote bag. "I'm keeping this. Now, help me up, please. My knee replacements aren't so good. I have something else to show you."

I extended my hand and leaned backwards until he was unsteadily standing.

While we walked down the beach, I told him about the photo. He hadn't seen the license plate but knew that sign was at the local yacht club.

"There." Ren pointed in the shadow of the towering dune at a smoked du Maurier cigarette. With orange lipstick on it. Nearby was a pile of du Mauriers without lipstick and not smoked to the filter . . . and a piece of green plastic rope next to it, a knot tied in the end. Had she drowned alone in the water? Was she abducted from the beach?

Mr. Tristan and the smarmy Frank were both Canadians, smokers, and boaters. So was Gertrude's ex, who owned a boat, lived right over the border in Michigan, and wanted his mother's Fiesta Ware. But would an elderly Lothario (a serial cheater from what Gertrude said) kill over plates? Maybe.

Ren pointed down the beach to a man walking with a metal detector. "I almost didn't recognize him with his hair all tucked under his hat. It's Mr. Tristan looking for treasure. That family is something."

With Mrs. Tristan at home and Mr. Tristan occupied, now was an excellent time to poke around the boats at the yacht club. Maybe see the convertible. I hoped Frank was still at home, since he was not off my list of suspects. Property lines can be serious, especially with a permanent fence being contested. But like the dishes, would someone kill over chain-link, even if it was ugly?

I left Ren to collect his dog and rode the Cruiser Trike as fast as I could, my stomach sinking. What kind of danger was Gertrude in?

Twenty minutes later, I hid the tricycle behind the club dumpster. The dock master was talking to one of the club members. I tiptoed into the office. I'd been here a few times, and I knew there was a list on the wall of boat slip assignments. The ex had a boat named, what else, The Gertrude. The list said it was out for repairs the rest of the year. So, the ex was off the hook for this, anyway.

I found the Tristans' Sérendipité moored in Slip 5 with a green rope. Green rope on Frank's Chris Craft Catalina in Slip 7, right next door. Actually, Slip 3 and Slip 1 also had green rope.

The dock master shouted, "Young lady, can I ask what you are doing? This is private property. You have to be a member of the," he cleared his throat, "yacht club."

I put my shaky hands in my pockets, thinking cool thoughts. "Ummm, I'm a friend of the Tristan Family. We went out on Sunday, drank too much, and I forgot my . . ." What could I produce from the trip down to the cabin if I needed? Surely they had a miscellaneous sweater or sweatshirt laying around for the chill of the lake. "My sweater. Shirt. Sweatshirt. You know, I borrowed it from my aunt and need to return it. She's livid. I don't want her to know that I was out with my boyfriend and not at church. Help me out?" I offered him my most helpless look.

"I'll give them a ring and check. What's your name?"

I put my finger on my lips and winked. "To be honest, it was just me and their daughter, Lacey, and our boyfriends. Her mom didn't know. Can't we just keep this on the DL? I'll run down really fast, grab it."

"Okay. We've been doing some maintenance on it. The cabin's unlocked."

Nothing interesting on deck, I hustled below and yanked open doors and drawers, whirling like a waterspout around the small sleeping quarters. Only a few dirty glasses and junk. I tried the bathroom door, but it was locked.

"Hurry up!" The dock master yelled down into the cabin, making me jump out of my body. What was I expecting, that they would have a box of evidence on the table ready for me to take to the police station? On the way out, I grabbed a sweater off a hook by the door and took the stairs two at a time to the deck.

As I climbed back onto the pier, I spotted a cigarette near Slip 6. About half-smoked. No lipstick.

"Sir," I shouted as he turned to go. "Whose cigarette is this? It's du Maurier."

"Oh, any number of Canucks smoke that brand."

I walked away, dragging my feet, listening to the dock master and dock hand chatting. The words "oil change" and "long trip north" floated through the air. Were they talking about the Sérendipité, the Tristans' boat?

I took a table at the outdoor café, ordered a slice of Hoosier Sugar Cream Pie, and ate it at a glacial pace while I surveilled the harbor like a regular detective. My mom's was definitely better. I called Ren. No news from the beach. He was plumb tuckered out. Would I consider adding his dog, Federico, to my client list? Chester would love the company, and I would love more cash for my teacherly habit—an espresso and two chocolatines, small chocolate croissants, from the Quebecois bakery across from my school every morning. And Ren was such a homebody; he wouldn't be gallivanting all over like my other clients and leaving me unemployed.

The dock hand carried a toolbox and a five-gallon container of oil to Frank's Catalina, not the Tristans'. Was Frank the one taking a long trip? Had he been gaslighting me?

Fifteen minutes later, the worker hauled his toolbox off Frank's boat and disappeared inside the office. The dock master wasn't around. Now was my opportunity to take a look inside Frank's Catalina.

I paid the bill at the cashiers and exited the restaurant to discover a black convertible had backed into the restaurant lot. KNUX N LUV. I'd never seen the driver's face. She was my age, had a long blond ponytail, and wore a red sundress that was shorter than I would wear. Should I follow her or investigate Frank's boat? The woman made no move to get out, and the car was still running. Waiting. For whom? The person with the dark-haired ponytail from the photo?

The dock hand stuck his head out the door, scanned the area, like he was looking for me, and went back inside. That did it. The woman could wait. I had to check Frank's boat. I scooted to Slip 7 and hid in the shadows of Frank's mast. Over the sound of my pounding heart, I caught a familiar ring tone. The theme from *The Golden Girls*, "Thank You for Being a Friend." But from where? Frank's boat? Or elsewhere?

In most crime fiction, the villain comes back and catches the nosy neighbor/amateur detective who isn't smart enough to get in and out. I peeked down the stairs and scanned the cabin. There was a pack of du Maurier smokes and Frank's captain's hat. I felt warm breath on my neck. I turned quickly.

"What are you doing, young lady?" Frank shouted, his face red, a cigarette dangling from his lips.

My heart was in my throat, but I managed to squeak, "I was looking for . . ."

I took a chance and held up a finger, signaling Frank to wait while I used my cell phone and dialed. A feeble Golden Girls ringtone came from the Sérendipité. "That's Gertrude's phone. We need to check the boat."

Frank nodded. "Old Zacharie Satan."

"What?"

"Oh, we all call Tristan that. And Mrs. is the W.O.S. Wife of Satan."

Z.S.

We jumped onto the Tristan's boat. I rang Gertrude again and found her phone in the glove box and a lipstick tube pushed between the cushions. Persimmon. Gertrude's color. I couldn't imagine an alive Gertrude would abandon it or her phone. My stomach clenched, and I choked down the bile. I prayed silently that we'd find her alive. And in good health.

We descended the stairs, both of us shouting Gertrude's name. A light rattle came from the bathroom. I took out my pocketknife and jimmied the door open. From the shower floor, a crumpled, taped up, single-shoed, gagged Gertrude looked up at me, her leg poised to kick the door. If only I'd shouted her name and listened before, I might have found her.

I took all the tape off and hugged her tightly.

At that moment Mr. Tristan came running down the stairs, his captain's hat in his hand. "Gertrude tried to make herself look like a kidnap victim. I'm gonna sue." He grabbed an attaché and ran back off the boat, his dark ponytail bouncing on his back.

Gertrude shouted out, "Were you going to dump me in the lake with concrete boots? Sell my kidneys?"

Now I saw it. Tristan—Z.S.—was the dark ponytail in the car. He was having an affair! I released Gertrude from her tape manacles while Frank called 911. "Were you blackmailing him to stop the settlement?"

She sat up, wiggling her fingers and shaking her wrists. "He told me to meet him, and we'd do an exchange of papers for photos. Of course, I made two sets of photos, thank goodness. When I arrived . . . wham-o. Into the boat."

I ran off the boat and down the pier just in time to see Z.S. jump into the waiting convertible. Cars with vanity plates make poor getaway cars, Mr. Tristan. Within minutes, we heard sirens and saw lights. Frank and Gertrude, on deck now, lit up their twin du Mauriers to celebrate.

Frank took a deep draw and, flicking his ashes, said "Lots of good things come from Canada, like me. But that old Zacharie Satan will rot in an American prison. Oui?" He snickered at his rhyme. "And Gertrude, you can keep your fence as long as you grab some more ketchup chips next time you visit your mother-in-law in Canada."

"Ex," she said with a snort. "I'll buy you a whole case. And we can eat them together on my Fiesta Ware. I'm giving the damned dishes back and getting rid of that old bag of bones."

Happiness comes in sand mountains and cold Lake Michigan waves. All in one afternoon I found Gertrude alive, saw Zacharie Satan hauled off, got an offer of a boat weekend on the lake with Frank, and gained Ren's dog, Federico, as a client. My heart was singing. The whole summer lay ahead of me, full of Chester nuzzles, Golden Girls reruns, and coffee under the shadows of the NIPSCO. And no one will ask me for a hall pass.

LESSON LEARNED

SALLY MILLIKEN

ANDREA HADN'T SLEPT WELL, STRESSING over her plans for the day, the second of their three-day reunion. For months, she'd been looking forward to sharing her home with her friends. The house had been built along the Ventura River located in a narrow Southern California valley. Although the river was home to an endangered Steelhead Trout, birds were more her passion. Vanna, Carla, Bob, and she had stayed up late, laughed over old photos, and updated each other on their lives. The first day was easy. Today . . . not so much.

As she plugged in the teakettle and cracked eggs, she marveled that thirty-five years had passed since they'd spent three months together studying wildlife conservation in Kenya.

Bob, now a Yellowstone Park Ranger, had risen before her. Through the window of her 1930s stone house, she saw the bearded giant walk the nearly dry riverbed, likely looking for the tarantula they'd seen the day before.

A door slam reminded her that others were up too. She surveyed the eight teapots collected while leading birdwatching tours throughout the world and chose the one from Africa—for old time's sake.

Vanna and Carla entered the kitchen with wide smiles. Vanna, her short dark hair tucked under a baseball cap, was tan and muscular from years of tracking wildlife as a Montana biologist, and Carla, a life coach with a big heart, was a half-foot taller with long blonde and curly hair.

"Tea?" Andrea asked.

Vanna chuckled. "Still not drinking coffee, Andrea? I'll make it."

Andrea pushed a bag of coffee toward her. "Thanks. Bob's outside. Carla, would you mind telling him breakfast is almost ready?"

Vanna ground the beans. "What's on the agenda today, Andrea? Bird watching?"

She caught Vanna's grin. "Always." Andrea had her priorities—and a pair of binoculars at the ready. "I have something else in mind first."

"I'm up for anything," Carla said. "It's just so good to be together."

When the door closed behind Carla, Vanna sobered. "Any word from John or Ray?"

"John's due in an hour." Andrea checked her phone and her smile fell. "Nothing from Ray. He promised, but that was two weeks ago. You know how he is . . ." Andrea let out a long sigh. Even though he'd committed to arriving that morning, Andrea figured it was fifty-fifty that Ray would show up. And what would they do if he didn't appear?

A LOUD KNOCK INTERRUPTED THEIR breakfast.

Andrea dropped her fork. "John must have made good time."

She opened the front door. "Ray? You're here. Come in, come in." She didn't see any new vehicles. "How did you get here?"

Ray dumped his faded backpack on the tiled floor and gave them each a hug. "My car has a flat tire, so I got a ride. I'm hoping one of you can drop me off in town later."

Bob slapped him on the back. "No worries. We'll make sure you get where you need to be. We're just relieved you made it."

Andrea closed the door. "I texted, but you never answered."

"Oh, I dropped my phone in water last week." Ray shrugged. "I told you I was coming, didn't I?"

Andrea cleared her throat. "It's perfect timing. We were just finishing breakfast and about to pack lunches. I've planned a hike for today." She glanced at his dusty boots. "And you're already dressed for it. Have you eaten?"

Andrea had helped everyone prepare lunches and was finishing her own when a car horn sounded three short beeps.

Bob stood to meet the newcomer. "Right on time."

Ray's brow furrowed. "Expecting someone else?"

Andrea slid a plastic bag of snacks across the counter. "Here, Ray, can you put this trail mix in your pack? Let's greet our newest addition."

Everyone followed Andrea outside to find John arriving in a black MINI convertible. This should be interesting, Andrea thought and checked Ray's reaction.

He had frozen in place with his arms crossed. Not even his mustache twitched. "Why is John here?"

John exited the car and pushed up his wire-rimmed glasses. "Uh, Bob invited me."

"I ran into him at Yellowstone," Bob explained. "And the others said it was okay. I tried to get ahold of you to ask, but . . ."

Ray pulled at his ear. "Oh, well . . . Great to see you, John. It's been a while."

John's shoulders relaxed. "Thirty-five years, almost to the day."

Andrea waved them all back inside. "We can get reacquainted while we hike."

THEY PILED INTO TWO CARS and drove above Ojai toward the Topatopa Mountains. Andrea led them across a dry riverbed and onto red sandy trails in the rugged foothills still recovering from a wildfire. The trail reminded her of those they had climbed together in Kenya.

They hiked for hours, stopping to look at wildlife tracks and watch birds flicking within oak and coniferous woodlands. They crossed grasslands dotted with scrub before returning along a streambed lined with chaparral.

After a swim in the pool, dinner cooked on the grill, and a few after-dinner drinks, they all turned in for the night. Andrea snuggled into bed that night as the crisp night breeze flowed through the open window. The day had gone better than she'd hoped. But not well enough.

A SCREAM OUTSIDE HER BEDROOM window woke Andrea. She bolted from her bed and tore open the sliding door to the back deck, stopping only to flick on the outside lights. Carla was screaming and pointing toward something in the pool. At first, all Andrea could see was the large inflatable llama. Bob and Vanna pushed past her and jumped into the water, shoving aside the toy animal.

A man floated face down.

Andrea's heart pounded against her ribs. Ray appeared and she and Ray watched as Bob and Vanna dragged him to the edge of the pool. Working together, they pulled him out.

Carla checked his wrist. Then his neck. "There's no pulse. Andrea, call 911," she shouted. "We need an ambulance."

Bob leaned close over the man's face. "He's not breathing."

Carla hovered nearby, wringing her hands. Vanna began chest compressions as Carla and Ray stepped forward.

"Stay clear," shouted Bob. "We've got this."

Andrea shook herself into action. "I'll get my phone—be right back."

Andrea grabbed the phone next to her bed, pressed the numbers, and returned outside in time to hear Bob say, "He's dead. Vanna, you can stop. I think . . . he's been dead for a while."

When Vanna stood, it provided her first clear view of the dead man.

Carla hugged herself and rubbed her arms. "Poor John."

"John?" Ray scanned the grounds as if looking for a living John.

Bob gestured toward John's chest, where Andrea now saw a dark stain. "I think he has a gunshot wound." Bob peered into the pool, dove to the bottom, and got out with something clasped in his hand.

John's wire glasses.

Andrea told herself to stay calm. "I've got the 911 operator on the line." Her voice shook as she reported the conversation. "A truck fire damaged the bridge across the river and the ambulance can't get through. Not until they make sure it's safe."

With tears leaking down her cheeks, Vanna shuddered. "It's too late for an ambulance, but we need the police."

"Okay. I'll tell them." When Andrea hung up, she swallowed to stop herself from crying. "They said we shouldn't touch anything."

"So, what do we do?" asked Ray. "We just leave the body there?"

"Yes. It's a crime scene," Bob said. "They won't want us to contaminate . . . him."

Andrea exhaled to calm herself. "Everybody come inside until the police arrive."

ANDREA BROUGHT CARLA AND RAY into the kitchen as Bob and Vanna changed into dry clothes. Andrea's legs felt like lead, and she sat hard on a stool, while a headache throbbed behind her eyes.

"I hope the police get here soon." Carla's eyes darted toward the still-dark windows and whispered, "What if someone is out there?"

Andrea's voice cracked. "I locked the doors."

"But what if it was one of us?" Carla whispered. Her hands shook so badly that most of the grounds missed the coffee maker. "Vanna carries a gun for work. She and Bob both hunt."

"There's no way," Andrea said. "We've known each other almost our whole lives. Not one of us would . . ." She fluttered a hand, unable to finish the sentence.

Ray followed Carla to the window and peered outside. "What if she's hiding the gun as we speak? How well does one know anyone, really?"

Carla turned and pointed her finger at him. "Was it you? Did you kill John?"

"Of course not. I can't believe you—"

"Maybe walking the trails today brought it back, and you wanted revenge for what he did to you."

Ray's face flushed and his nose flared. "You were the one who found him. Maybe it was you."

Andrea wondered how things had gotten heated so quickly. She pushed herself between them. "I'll search the bedrooms for a gun."

Carla took a long, calming breath and stepped back from Ray. "Good idea. You can easily make up an excuse if you get caught."

"We'll need to get everyone out of the house," Andrea said. "The courtyard by the firepit would work. It's nowhere near the pool."

"Okay," Carla said. "When they get here, you suggest it. Ray and I will make sure they don't go inside. Right, Ray? And Ray, I'm sorry for what I said."

Ray nodded. "Yeah. Me too."

* * *

A LEAFY PASSIONFRUIT VINE GREW along one edge of the courtyard and continued up and across a set of string lights, giving the space an intimate feel. The sky wouldn't brighten the horizon for several hours. Not soon enough, thought Andrea, as she lit the fire.

Other than the crackling wood and the occasional creak of an Adirondack-style chair, they were quiet around the firepit. Andrea wasn't the only one mesmerized by the flickering flame. The smell of smoke reminded her of their semester, so long ago. How many times had they sat around a campfire together? Too many times to count.

"Carla, why were you outside?" Vanna asked.

Carla pulled a blanket around her shoulders. "Today's hike with John got me thinking about Kenya and what happened. I couldn't sleep and thought the hot tub would help. If only . . . I might have . . ."

"Don't think like that," Bob said gently. "You might have been killed too."

"How could this have happened?" Carla covered her face with her hands.

Andrea exhaled deeply. "I don't know."

Ray roused himself. "It wasn't one of us . . . but who else could it be? This place is isolated." Ray tugged at his shirt collar. "John told us he's a college professor, but we have no idea who or what he could be mixed up with."

"I suppose," murmured Vanna.

Andrea threw another log on the fire and grabbed her empty mug. "I'm heading inside for more tea and to call the police again. Anyone want anything?"

Carla said she'd make a plate of snacks. Ray stretched his legs toward the heat. "How about a beer?"

CARLA AND RAY WERE WAITING for her in the kitchen after she had searched the entire house. "I found no sign of a gun anywhere. Not that I needed that as proof, but I feel better all the same."

Ray's voice was low. "Unless he or she dumped it outside."

"It's possible," Carla said. "But wouldn't we have seen them?" She rinsed her mug in the sink. "What do we do now?"

Ray stood. "I'm going."

"No," Andrea shouted, louder than she meant to. Ray flinched and Carla cringed.

That was not productive, Andrea thought and rushed to add. "The police said no one can leave until they talk to us. Besides, with the bridge closed, there's nowhere you *can* go."

ANDREA, CARLA, AND RAY RETURNED to the firepit, interrupting a heated conversation.

Vanna asked, "What about it, Ray? You must have mixed feelings about John's death. We were just talking about what happened that night he pushed you over that cliff. I've always wondered what made him do that. You could have died."

"John didn't seem the type to hurt anyone," Bob said.

Carla nodded. "He wasn't in Kenya very long before . . ."

After an uncomfortable pause, Ray finished the sentence. "Before what he did to me. Is that what you were going to say? It's too bad, but it all worked out."

Bob's head snapped up. "What do you mean?"

Ray straightened in his chair. "He's had a good life. He must have turned himself around because he had a successful career, a family, a home . . ."

Bob's eyes went wide. "Had you been keeping track of him? You've never mentioned that before."

"I Googled him." Ray opened a beer. "Are you all wondering if I killed him? Because I didn't."

"No, of course not." Carla's tone was neutral, professional. "But do you feel guilty because of what happened, that he got sent home?"

"And that he dropped out of college," added Vanna. "Then his parents kicked him out."

"No, that was on him." Ray scoffed. "He shouldn't have done it. How can I feel guilty for something he did? Besides, he eventually graduated. I'd forgiven him a long time ago."

"Did you ever tell him that?" Carla asked.

Ray gave her a quizzical look. "No, why would I?"

"You're amazing, Ray. Many would feel guilty." Carla patted his hand. "Many of my clients would benefit from your confidence."

Andrea's cell phone rang, and she looked at the screen. "It's the police." Into the phone she said, "We're okay. Yes. When are you . . . ? Okay." After a pause, she repeated, "Okay. Thank you." She disconnected and threw up a hand in despair.

Bob squeezed the bridge of his nose. "I take it they still can't get through."

Andrea let silence be her answer. Ray slumped in his seat.

"Ray, you look exhausted," Vanna said. "Why don't you head back to bed? We'll wake you when the police arrive."

"Okay." He yawned. "If you're sure."

After Ray was in the house with the door shut, Carla asked, "What if he takes off?"

"I just set the alarm," Andrea said as her phone vibrated. "It'll send a text to my phone if any of the outside windows or doors are opened."

Carla sighed. "Will this night ever end?"

"It'll be over soon," said Bob. "Did anyone else notice how Ray responded when Andrea mentioned the police? He seemed to fidget and look for an excuse to leave. Does Ray have a reason to be concerned about the police finding him here?"

Vanna chuffed. "Knowing him, probably."

Silence settled around them. Andrea noticed that the sky above began to lighten but couldn't keep her eyes open.

The sound of a loud bang woke her. She blinked to focus. Bob, Vanna, and Carla were standing, staring at the house. The sun was low in the sky. The fire had long died out, but the smell of smoke lingered in the air.

Ray flung the nearest door open and ran toward them, panic in his eyes, his face pale as an egret.

Andrea's phone buzzed with a text from the alarm service. "What—"

"Someone tried to shoot me." Ray patted his body, from chest to legs, as if to check if he had all his limbs.

"Are you sure?" Bob asked. "Sounded like it might be a truck backfire."

He paced. "No. Someone opened the window and tried to kill me."

"I wish I had my rifle," Vanna said. "Or at least bear spray. Let's look for clues, scuff marks, footprints, something. Outside first. Then inside. Stick together."

They followed Vanna around the house to Ray's window.

"See." Ray pointed as he knelt on the ground. "Footprints."

Andrea cursed. There they were: two footprints pressed into the red soil in front of the open window.

Even Vanna, an experienced tracker, could not find any other prints as they worked their way around the house toward the pool.

When Vanna stopped suddenly, Ray ran into her. She pointed to the spot where John's body had been. He was gone.

The only thing that stirred was the blow-up llama—which floated across the water—and the leaves of a lemon tree.

Andrea's heart was pounding. "Back inside everyone. I don't know what's going on, but we should stay in the house until the police arrive."

WHILE ANDREA CLOSED AND LOCKED the window in Ray's room, Carla shut the shades, and Bob and Vanna inspected the room.

Vanna dragged her fingers down the wall. "You were right, Ray. There's a hole here. Looks like a bullet to me."

"Double-check the locks," Bob said.

They huddled in the large living room. Andrea passed around a bottle of wine to settle their nerves. When that ran out, and everyone was still tense, she switched to tequila.

After an hour, a glass empty in his lap, Ray muttered, "I think John's after me."

"Why would he be after you?" Andrea added the obvious. "He's dead."

"I was drunk," Ray whispered.

"What?" Carla asked.

"John didn't push me." Ray's voice grew stronger as he explained. "When we were in Kenya. He didn't push me off the cliff. I fell. All on my own."

When no one spoke, Ray continued. "I didn't want to admit that I'd been drinking. No one liked John anyway. I figured it wouldn't matter."

Andrea was glad when Bob spoke. She was speechless.

"You mean to tell us you've been lying all these years—" he said. "That John didn't do it?"

Ray nodded. He picked up a wine bottle, shook it, and tilted it into his glass. Only drops came out and he growled as he dropped it on the sofa next to him.

Andrea drew Ray's attention to her with an audible swallow. "Why? Why didn't you say something sooner?"

Ray scratched his chin. "I would have gotten in trouble. And sent home—well, I'd already gotten kicked out of one program. That was my last chance. My parents were going to make me pay for college and then cut me off. How was I supposed to deal with that? It was just a little lie." He lifted a shoulder. "No one got hurt. Besides, I was so drunk that I wasn't thinking straight. So I blamed it on him. Well, him and Andrea."

"Andrea?" they all repeated, except for Andrea, who said, "Me?"

Carla leaned forward in her seat, her elbows resting on her knees. "That wasn't it at all. You were in love with her, weren't you? You thought she had a crush on John. You wanted her for yourself."

"Oh, *that* makes sense." Vanna shook her head in disgust. "You set him up. You wanted him out of the way. You planned it all."

"Were you even drunk?" Andrea asked.

Ray's face flushed. "Why are we rehashing this? It was thirty-whatever years ago. It doesn't matter now anyway."

Vanna crossed her arms. "Because John's family deserves to know the truth. And so do we."

"Alright. Fine." Ray stood. "I set him up." He glared at them one by one.

Until that moment, Andrea had never considered the expression about hearing a pin drop.

Bob broke the silence. "Finally."

Vanna added, "We've been waiting a very long time for you to admit that."

After a moment, Andrea quietly said, "I believed you, Ray. I thought John had deliberately hurt you, and I didn't speak to him again after that. None of us did. Not for a very long time."

Vanna shouted, "John, you can come out now. It's over."

Ray looked around, his eyes wider than the bottom of the glass, as John—very much alive John—appeared.

"We've been trying to get you to admit what you did for a decade," Vanna said. "Ever since John told us what really happened." She moved over to make room for John and patted the sofa. She handed him his glasses. "I just wish we'd found out the truth sooner."

Ray's face turned red—as brilliant as the cap of a woodpecker—and he collapsed back onto the sofa. He gritted his teeth so hard a vein streaked across his forehead. "Ten years?"

"You've had many opportunities, but you refused to come clean," Bob said. "And when you didn't attend the reunion five years ago, despite saying you would, we—" He waved to include the others. "—realized we needed a different approach. With John's agreement, we decided to stage this little drama."

"All we had to do was get you here," said Vanna, "and give you a strong enough reason to tell us. So we ratcheted up the pressure again and again, until . . ." She waved her hand.

"You broke," Andrea finished.

Bob explained further. "We just had to keep you from getting too close. Vanna released the fake blood. When that didn't work, John fired blanks and added the footprints to make it seem like you were being shot at. I even knocked a hole in your wall."

"You hurt one of us, you hurt all of us." Carla nodded toward John. "And we're trying to make up for not believing John when it happened."

Resembling the trout in the river, Ray opened and closed his mouth several times before he choked out, "What about the police?"

Andrea gave a half shrug. "I never called them. When my phone rang, that was John."

Beads of sweat glistened on Ray's forehead. He licked his lips, and his eyes darted from Andrea to each of them, stopping at John's. "All this to get me to admit that I lied?"

John nodded. "Yes."

"Why?" Ray asked.

Vanna pressed a hand to her heart. "Because actions have consequences. You never learned that. We decided it was long past time that you did."

With those words hanging in the air, a flash of blue lights appeared through the windows.

Ray peered outside. "I thought you said you didn't call the police."

"Andrea didn't, but *I* did." John used the tail of his shirt to clean his glasses. "I think they'll love hearing where you were the night before last."

Ray shifted in his seat. "You followed me?"

"Yes." John put his glasses back on and then looked at Ray. "Selling fentanyl, Ray. Really? That's what you're doing with your life? Hurting more people?"

"What?" Ray shrieked and sprang up. "I never . . ."

"Oh, no?" John tsked. "That'll be hard to argue when they find a plastic bag—covered with your fingerprints—filled with the stuff. It's just a little lie. No harm done."

A River in Egypt

Mary Dutta

UNTIL SHE MET LYNN, THE self-styled influencer, Joanne had not thought there was anyone she would hate spending a vacation with more than William, her hopefully soon-to-be ex-husband. Lynn was yet again gesturing at her to move out of her "perfect shot." Joanne was glad she had begged off the first leg of the Egypt tour. She probably would have pushed the other woman off a pyramid by now.

When she had agreed to join her spouse for the Nile cruise portion of the trip, Joanne had envisioned a glamorous, Agatha Christie-style excursion. But William, without consulting her of course, had instead booked them on a traditional dahabiya, a small wooden sailing ship with a handful of cabins, wonky Wi-Fi, and no bar. The only thing Christie about it was Joanne's desire to murder someone.

She dawdled her way out of Lynn's frame and joined her fellow passengers at the table on the deck, where the guests shared all their meals and suffered through William's endless, unasked-for seminars. No one got a bite of basbousa or kushari without a side serving of Egyptology or astronomy or some other topic on which he considered himself an expert. At least everyone else would be free once the cruise ended in Aswan. Joanne would be stuck until her divorce lawyer got things sorted. She prayed to Horus, Isis, and all the other Egyptian gods that the paperwork would be ready by the time she got off this boat. She fully intended to sail up the Nile and out of her marriage, even if that meant checking her phone for legal updates as often as Lynn checked hers for likes and mentions.

The honeymoon couple at the far end of the table seemed too lost in connubial bliss to pay William's speechifying any mind. They had introduced themselves, but Joanne thought of them as Honey One and

Honey Two, since that's all they ever called each other. She had never called her husband by anything but his name, at least not to his face.

The only one in their group even feigning interest in William's latest lecture was Rose, who made up for her lack of personality with an excess of politeness. Joanne had tried talking to her, hoping that a woman her own age would be better company than the honeymooners, who had eyes only for each other, and the influencer, who had eyes only for herself. But Rose had about as much to say as the flower whose name she shared. No wonder she was traveling solo.

The arrival of their guide, Ahmed, put an end to her musings. "My friends," he said, "today we will visit a very special temple."

"Great," Lynn said. "More hieroglyphics. Thank God I packed so many outfits, otherwise my followers wouldn't know I was going to different places."

"I'm sure you will look very nice," Ahmed said, seemingly unfazed by her rudeness. It probably made a nice change from William's constant interruptions to chime in on his professional guidance.

"Oh, I will," Lynn said. "Today's vibe is pure Cleopatra."

William sat up straighter in his chair. "You know, of course, that Cleopatra was Macedonian. The last of the Ptolemaic dynasty."

"Yeah, well, I'm going for a snake armband and some chandelier earrings." Lynn grimaced and put a hand on her stomach.

"Aren't you feeling well?" Rose asked.

"Ah, the famously lethal snake," William powered on. "An asp, from the Greek aspis."

Ahmed was more sympathetic. "If you are ill, you can stay here on the dahabiya. The crew members can bring you anything you need."

"It's just this weird Egyptian food," Lynn shook her head. The only thing weird about the food, Joanne thought, was how long they all had to wait to serve themselves while the influencer styled the platters to her exacting standards. "Besides," Lynn said, "I have to go and get some new content. If I don't post at least twice a day, I could lose followers."

William raised his hand to regain everyone's attention. "Cleopatra actually tried out various poisons on her handmaidens before choosing the venomous snake for her suicide. It was—"

The honeymoon couple pushed back their chairs, making a great fuss about whether they had all their belongings. "I think I left my sunscreen downstairs," Honey Two said. Her husband scuttled after her toward their cabin. Joanne seized the opportunity to escape William as well. Only Rose remained, smiling blandly as he blathered on.

Joanne avoided her husband until later that morning when the group clustered around Ahmed in a patch of shade as he pointed out highlights of the ancient site before them.

"Fascinating," William said. "You know, of course, I have a special interest in ancient temple construction."

"I'm going to walk around and do some filming," Lynn announced. If she weren't quite so unbearable, Joanne might have fled with her.

"We'll see you back at the van," Ahmed said, "in one hour, please."

But an hour later Lynn was not back. Rose wondered out loud if Lynn was all right. Joanne didn't particularly care, but Ahmed asked them to wait and went off to consult with nearby security guards.

Two hours later, he returned with a limping Lynn, who had lost one earring and whose white linen ensemble was brown with dust. "My friends," he said through a strained smile. "I must remind you not to go past any barriers you encounter. They are for your safety. And the safety of our priceless cultural heritage."

"Well, I can't just take pictures from the same angles every other influencer uses," Lynn snatched her bag from the temple attendant who had escorted her back. As she boarded the van, Ahmed murmured something to the man and slipped a folded bill into his hand.

Back on the boat, Lynn lowered herself onto a chaise longue. Rose handed her a pillow to elevate her foot.

"What happened?" she asked.

"I had found a perfect spot, just past some stupid barricade, when I lost my balance."

Rose murmured sympathetically.

"I must have been dehydrated," Lynn said. "I felt a little dizzy."

Or wasted, Joanne thought, given the size of the influencer's pupils. She hoped that the next time Lynn decided to get high, she would think about how the rest of them were stuck sweating and fending off souvenir hawkers while the search for her had dragged on.

"You can go back to your husband," Lynn said to Rose, arranging the cushion under her foot for a perfect photo op.

After an awkward silence, Rose said, "William is married to Joanne."

Lynn looked back and forth between the two women. "I thought . . ." she said, then shrugged. "Whatever, I'm fine now."

Rose wandered off, but Joanne stood fuming at the classic invisible middle-aged woman syndrome. To Lynn, she and Rose were valueless to the point of being indistinguishable. She bet the younger woman would be surprised to learn that Joanne not only had a husband, she had a lover as well. William would be shocked too, but no way was he finding out before the divorce settlement. She pulled out her phone and sent another message to her lawyer, one with extra exclamation points.

Lynn remained blissfully unaware of Joanne's outrage and unchastened by her temple experience. She gloated over the responses to her string of postings on her injury, and judging from her slurred speech as she recorded herself watching sunsets, exploring tombs, and gazing at the banks of the Nile, was toasting her success a little too frequently.

Joanne spent more and more time with the Honeys, leaving Rose to dodge Lynn's camera angles and absorb the brunt of William's instruction. The woman should make some friends if she wanted a better time.

"Too bad you missed Cairo," Honey One said. "The museum was amazing."

"That's right," his wife said, clinging to his arm, "you weren't there with William."

Joanne wondered if their closeness was new love or if they would achieve the happily-ever-after state she and William had never achieved. Maybe the Honeys could achieve it with others after they went their separate ways. That was her plan. After an equitable distribution of assets, of course.

"And the shopping!" Honey Two continued. "I loved the Khan El-Khalili market. And Rose raved about the antique shops."

Joanne struggled to picture dull Rose being passionate about anything.

"William told us a lot about the Antiquities Protection Law," Honey One said, "and tomb raiders, and the illegal transportation of artifacts, and . . . a lot."

Joanne suppressed her usual impulse to apologize for her husband. Very soon he would no longer be her problem.

Luckily, the next day's desert camel ride involved plodding along single file, which thwarted William's attempts to capture everyone's attention. Lynn brought up the rear, the better to avoid people intruding on her video. Rose kept turning around to check on her as she fell further and further behind the group. "Something's wrong," she called out. "Lynn dropped her phone."

Ahmed halted the procession. He had the camel driver guide Lynn's mount into a kneeling position, at which point she slid off onto the sand.

"I got so hot," Lynn fanned herself with her oversized sun hat while their guide plied her with water, and she groped around for her phone. "I don't get it. The sun doesn't usually bother me."

Joanne suspected Lynn was faking the whole incident, given the social media success of her first injury. She was even more convinced it was a production once they returned to the boat. Lynn seemed none the worse for wear, brushed off Rose's questions and immediately started recording.

"It's real, y'all." The influencer brought the camera close to her face and lowered her voice. "The mummy's curse." She regaled her followers with a dramatic retelling of the camel calamity until William interrupted.

"You know, of course," he said, "the mummy's curse is a modern idea, built up by Hollywood and a misunderstanding of the aspergillus fungi found in newly opened tombs."

Lynn hit pause and heaved an exaggerated sigh. "I am *filming*, can you not? And what is it with you and your wife? This is exactly how you messed me up in Cairo."

"I wasn't *in* Cairo," Joanne said, "and I don't appreciate—"

"Jeez, whatever," Lynn said. "Could you all just stay out of my way and let me work?"

Joanne managed to do just that until the last night of the cruise, when the crew came up after dinner to perform some traditional Egyptian music and encouraged everyone to dance. Lynn joined in with unbridled enthusiasm, staggering as she held her phone up to capture her increasingly frenetic moves.

She stopped suddenly, causing William to crash into her. "Cleopatra." Lynn pointed into the night. "She's right there!" She looked around at the group. "Can't you see her? She's wearing my missing earring." She let her phone fall and started climbing over the ship's railing. The crew abandoned their instruments and rushed to stop her.

The Honeys stared wide-eyed as Ahmed ushered Lynn down to her cabin. "I think this evening's entertainment is over," he said.

"What the hell was that?" Honey One said. No one answered. Joanne looked around the group. Instead of her usual expression of solicitous concern, Rose wore a tiny smile. *And what the hell is that*, thought Joanne.

The next morning, the dahabiya docked in Aswan. Lynn filmed a farewell for her followers without a hint of embarrassment. She didn't bother saying goodbye to her shipmates. The honeymooners disembarked hand-in-hand with promises to stay in touch. Joanne watched the crew load luggage into the car that would take her and William to the airport. She had left the packing to him rather than endure a lecture on the proper way to fill a suitcase.

She was abandoning her baggage, anyway. Her lawyer had finally come through with good news on the divorce filing and Joanne would soon be free. Maybe she would become an influencer like Lynn, traveling the world on a permanent, William-less vacation. She headed to the car, leaving him to finish a final glass of hibiscus tea, and presumably one final monologue, with Rose.

"I KEPT A CLOSE EYE on Lynn," Rose said to William in a flirtatious tone that would have astonished Joanne.

"And?"

"Dizziness, dilated pupils, heat sensitivity, hallucinations. The belladonna I've been dosing her with works exactly as promised."

"You know, of course, Cleopatra used it on her handmaidens," William said. "We had it on good authority."

"So, if Lynn ever says she saw us in a compromising situation in Cairo—"

"She would be a totally unreliable witness." William winked. "Although she did think you were my wife. Which you soon will be."

Rose looked around to make sure they were alone, then smiled and ran a finger down his arm. "And an unreliable witness means that your hopefully soon-to-be ex-wife will have no evidence to contest a divorce."

"True, and I'll have plenty. Adultery for one. Plus, she'll have trouble contesting anything from a jail cell, which is where she's headed after Customs gets a tip about the illicit antiquities I packed in her luggage. You know, of course, about the Antiquities Protection Law."

"I had a wonderful teacher," said Rose. "That's why I only shopped at the sketchiest stores in Cairo for him."

"Joanne will deny everything."

Rose clinked his glass with hers. "Denial is just a river in Egypt."

The Centerpiece

Beth Irish

Détective Pierre Tremblanc of the Service de police de la Ville de Montréal leaned over the lifeless body of Farrah Rocher. She was sprawled in the hors d'oeuvres. One hand rested on the jumbo shrimp wrapped in lean bacon, the other was immersed in sturgeon caviar, the kind harvested by gentle massage. Her neck was twisted, with the right side of her head resting on the Brie and Prosciutto tray. Her eyes blankly stared at the ornate fountain surrounded by ice sculptured roses. But one thing to be said for Madame Jacques Rocher, the blood matting at the base of her head could not be mistaken for anything as bourgeois as ketchup.

While Farrah Rocher nee McAlistar was a central figure in the campus Greek Life community forty years ago, the sisters of Chi Psi Omega Sorority's Centennial Ball Planning Committee most assuredly did not have her in mind as the centerpiece of the appetizer station.

"Inspector Chatham, is that a stick of ice laying beside Madame Rocher?"

The recently retired Inspector Chatham of the Royal Canadian Mounted Police, also known as my writing partner, Victoria, shook her head. Despite not looking the part in her full-length royal navy ball gown, pearls, and high heels, she immediately assumed her professional persona.

"To be more precise, Pierre, it's part of a rose ice sculpture. The stem I believe. The red rose is our sorority's official flower. Although unlike a real stem, this one is rather sturdy."

I'm only guessing, but I don't think there's a Canadian law enforcement officer that Victoria hadn't met in her thirty-five years on the force. She and Pierre first met when he was a patrolman, and she was a constable attached to the RCMP's C Division. He moved up in the ranks, choosing to make his mark on the Montréal force. Victoria, never Vicky, also climbed the ranks, but transferred to Toronto. To say they go way back is a masterpiece of understatement.

Détective Tremblanc sighed. "Victoria, let's take it from the top. Exactly what happened?"

Although Victoria had already flipped from sorority sister to RCMP investigator the moment the screaming began, I could hear her brain's gears pick up speed.

"At 6:00 PM, the 250 sorority sisters and their guests attending the Centennial Ball made their way to the Vieux Montréal Ballroom. Formal attire required. At 7:42 PM there was a loud boom, then the lights went out. There were multiple screams, not from one person or location in particular. The lights were back on in less than five minutes. During that brief time, someone killed Farrah. Cory, didn't you see her talking to someone just before the lights went out?"

The détective turned his attention to me. "Are you one of the alumni too? Do you know the deceased?"

"Oh, Pierre. This is Dr. Cory Shore. When my husband Nigel suddenly had to fly to Vancouver on business, I twisted Cory's arm to replace him as my plus one." Anticipating his next question, she continued, "It may seem silly, but coming back to Montréal for my sorority reunion was important to me. The sisters are honoring the memory of one of our sorority sisters, Shea O'Rourke, who was a dear friend of mine. As Shea and Cory were also close friends, I thought she might like to drive up from Albany for the weekend to attend. She's never been to Montréal before.

"It didn't take much twisting. She also promised third row center seats for the Montréal Symphony Orchestra at Place des Arts tomorrow night. I love symphony orchestras, but never had the chance to make it to one of the MSO performances. Détective Tremblanc, it's nice to meet you. I wish it were under better circumstances." What I didn't add was that solving Shea's sudden death had brought Victoria and me together. We, unfortunately, are becoming crime-solving partners as well as writing ones. I extended my hand to the skeptical détective.

Détective Tremblanc hesitated for a moment before reluctantly shaking my hand. "Nice to meet you, Dr. Shore."

Turning to Victoria with a meaningful look, he added, "Victoria, you know we don't accept lay help. You are an exception, given my knowledge of your exemplary career. I'll interview Dr. Shore along with everyone else—"

"Pierre, don't be such a stick in the mud. Cory is not just Dr. Shore. She's C.M. Shore, author of the Abby Duncan series. I've found she's second only to me in her observation skills. Besides, we need to solve this quickly, as many of the alumni have plane tickets to return home tomorrow."

Really? Second? I would have to talk to her about that later. For now, I'd let it slide. The détective's attitude took an immediate 180 turn.

"C.M. Shore? I've read *all* of your books. As a matter of fact, I read them in English and then read the French translations to be sure I didn't miss any important details. You are—" He stopped mid-gush. "Anyway, Dr. Shore, if Victoria trusts your observational skills, I will also. Did you see anything unusual immediately before or after the lights went out? You told Victoria you saw the deceased talking with someone? Anyone else? Was there anything you noticed about Madame Rocher that struck you as unusual?"

Victoria made a poor attempt to hide a grin. When she entered law enforcement, it was still a man's world. I think she still takes pleasure when she can surprise her male colleagues.

"Please, Détective, call me Cory. I'm not sure I can be of much help. I only met Farrah an hour before she died. She seemed to enjoy being the center of attention, despite not being savvy to social cues."

"How so?"

"When we arrived, she flew across the floor shouting Victoria's name. Gave Victoria a big hug. After she loosened her grip, Farrah showed off the new necklace and earrings her *thoughtful* husband bought her for the evening. She made a big to-do of the fact he remembered the sorority's stone is a deep-red ruby. Victoria's face was a study. Anyone who knows her realizes she prefers to blend into the scenery."

The détective grinned. "She's been shy ever since I've known her."

"Ahem, I'm not shy. I choose to remain in the shadows. I can learn more about a situation when people forget I'm there. Besides, I'm not the topic here. Unless I'm a suspect?"

"The members who Madame Rocher knew well would be the most logical suspects," he teased, "but no. Not unless there's a reason for you to be one?"

Victoria shook her head. "Farrah and I were in the same pledge class, but we didn't run in the same circles. She always had illusions of grandeur. Her goal in university was to graduate with an MRS. She had to be the center of attention, good or bad."

The détective looked puzzled. "MRS?"

"She wanted to be a Madame." The détective's eyebrows rose. "Not that kind of madam. Madame, as in Madame Rocher," Victoria explained the nuanced joke to her francophone colleague.

"Ah, of course," Détective Tremblanc nodded. As bilingual a city as Montréal is, not all jokes translate well.

"You know, almost immediately after she let you out of her bear hug, I noticed her having a heated discussion with a man." I tilted my head in the direction of a gray-haired gentleman hugging a woman. "But just before the lights went out, that same man was arguing in the corner with that man." I pointed to a table in the corner of the elaborate ballroom where one of the sisters was comforting a visibly distraught man.

Victoria provided the identifications. "The first man is Edward Franklin. He's comforting his wife, Vanessa. She pledged with Farrah and me. The second man is, excuse me, *was* Farrah's husband, Jacques Rocher. Jacques is a criminal lawyer. Ginny Bloomberg, also one of our pledge sisters, is with him. He and Ed were arguing? Interesting. Farrah dated Ed in our senior year when he and Vanessa broke-up for a few weeks, but it's hardly a motive to kill someone forty years later."

"Are the Franklins happily married?" Détective Tremblanc asked.

"For years, as far as I know. At least, their Christmas card pictures imply they have been," Victoria commented.

"Did Ginny Bloomberg stay close with the Rochers?" Détective Tremblanc looked pensive, and I didn't blame him. Maybe it's me, but she looked a little bit too cozy with a man who had been widowed less than an hour.

"I don't know. Ginny, Vanessa, Farrah, Shea, and I were initially very close. Our first year in the sorority, we were inseparable. But as time went on, I became close friends with Shea. We found we had little in common with Ginny, Vanessa, and Farrah. Although I understand the three of them remained friendly over the years. You know how every group has one person who keeps everyone caught up? That was Ginny. She even continued to co-edit the sorority newsletter after graduation while she was training to be an RN. Last I heard, she was a trauma nurse at the Montréal General until she retired four years ago. Never married."

"Did she ever date Farrah's husband?" Détective Tremblanc asked.

"Not that I remember, but she could have. It was the first time we were away from home. We all tested our freedom to some extent."

Détective Tremblanc shifted uncomfortably, "Victoria, did you ever date Jacques—"

Victoria's icy stare froze Détective Tremblanc mid-sentence. "Never. Except for Shea, once I became immersed in my criminal justice program, I rarely associated with the other sisters."

As Détective Tremblanc regained his composure from asking his friend such a personal question, I wondered if he had a thing for Victoria back in the day.

I casually shifted my attention back to the table to give him a moment to regroup. As I returned Farrah's blank stare, something about her didn't look quite right—aside from not breathing, I mean. Then it hit me.

"Victoria, would Farrah be caught dead in anything other than a designer original at a society function?"

"She wouldn't be caught dead even gardening in anything other than a designer original. Why?"

"Look at the label of her evening gown. *Joseph Rib.* I'm sure it's a Joseph Ribkoff design, but there appears to be another label sewn under it."

We all leaned in for a better look at the classic floor length evening gown. Détective Tremblanc carefully revealed both labels. I was right about the first. The second label read *Propriété de la Maison Hebert.*

Victoria answered Pierre's unspoken question. "It's a real Joseph Ribkoff alright, but it's a rental from a high-end boutique. I can't see Farrah renting a gown. But it would be less expensive than purchasing an original. Perhaps a slight concession to Jacques if they were arguing over finances?"

"There's something else." I pointed to the ruby in her necklace. "See that slight chip? I don't remember it being that way when she ran over to hug you. It must have broken when Farrah hit the table. Rubies are like diamonds. They don't damage easily."

"Yes," Détective Tremblanc enthused. "Exactly the reasoning Abby used to solve the murder in *Blood Red Ruby*. The real rubies were switched with fake ones by the victim's husband to help pay his gambling debts."

"I doubt Farrah knew the rubies were fake," Victoria said. "Not the way she was showing them off as a gift from Jacques to commemorate the evening."

Détective Tremblanc nodded and made a call. Whoever was on the other end got quite an earful. Unfortunately, my high school French was useless when faced with his rapid-fire colloquialisms.

Noticing my puzzled expression, Victoria whispered, "He's checking the Rocher's finances."

The moment he hung up, Victoria began to postulate her theories. "Pierre, if I were you, I'd begin by focusing on Jacques Rocher, Edward Franklin, Vanessa Franklin, and Ginny Bloomberg. It may be financial, but there could be another motive. As hard as it is for me to believe, there may have been multiple love triangles going on. Jealousy can be as deadly as greed."

"*C'est vrai.* I couldn't agree more."

As Détective Tremblanc rounded up his main suspects, Victoria discreetly pulled me into the conference room the hotel management had made available for questioning.

I asked, "Should we be here?"

"Absolutely not. But Pierre will either thank me or kick us out."

Why did I think it was going to be the latter?

Fortunately, I was wrong. Sure, he gave us a wonky look when he saw us there, but his nod to Victoria meant that our fly-on-the-wall routine wasn't going to be disrupted.

One by one, characters from Victoria's past sat in front of Détective Tremblanc, answering questions about their relationship with Farrah. Each seemed to be genuinely in shock.

Although I still had the uneasy feeling that one of them was a murderer.

But who? Victoria kept complimenting my observation skills, so what else had I observed beyond the dress and the ruby?

While not yet confirmed, I'm positive Jacques Rocher was having financial difficulties. Did he have a hefty insurance policy on his wife? Ginny Bloomberg clearly has feelings for him, but are they strong enough to kill over? If Jacques reciprocated those feelings, that could be more reason for him to want his wife dead. And where do the Franklins fit in the picture? It wouldn't make sense for either of them to kill over a forty-year-old fling, without some darker secret. What could that be?

"Mr. Franklin," Détective Tremblanc's voice brought me back to the interrogation, "why were you and Monsieur Rocher arguing? For that matter, why were you and Madame Rocher also seen arguing?"

Edward Franklin looked uncomfortable. He shifted in his seat so often I was beginning to get seasick watching him.

"Mr. Franklin, I asked you a question."

"It isn't what you think. I love my wife."

"I'm sure you do. That's not my question. Does this have to do with the Rocher's financial situation?"

Edward Franklin looked stunned. "How did you know? I promised I wouldn't tell, but they've been pressuring me to back them on a new investment that would help them get back on their feet. Farrah had been pestering Vanessa to get me on board. I refused."

"Why?"

"Because it's a bad investment. Jacques and I go way back. As a criminal lawyer, he's top in his field. He earns top dollar, but he's nearly bankrupt from his investment decisions. Farrah has really suffered."

"Were you having an affair with Madame Rocher?"

"NO. After we dated those two weeks in university, I broke it off with Farrah to get back with Vanessa. Vanessa and I have been together, and faithful to one another, might I add, ever since. Farrah was always materialistic and self-centered. I don't know what Jacques saw in her. He wanted to be a civil rights lawyer or legal aid lawyer. He only went into criminal law to keep Farrah in the lifestyle to which she wished to become accustomed. That's why he made those disastrous investments."

That's it. I had it. I knew who killed Farrah and why. Now, I had to prove it. At the moment, I just had a theory and circumstantial evidence. As Détective Tremblanc consulted with the other officers, I pulled Victoria aside and shared my suspicions.

"And this is why I trust your instincts." She grinned. "We're going to get you to that concert at Place des Arts tomorrow night, no problem."

"But how do we prove it?"

"Leave it to me." Victoria walked over to Détective Tremblanc and whispered in his ear. A slow smile spread across his face as he nodded.

"Done. Pierre is bringing the four of them back into the room."

Victoria's pledge sisters somberly entered the room, followed by Edward and Jacques. Détective Tremblanc positioned officers at each of the two exits. That done, he eased into the room's far corner, like a watchful cat. Realizing he had cleared the stage for Victoria to take the lead, I slid beside him, waiting for the plan to unfold.

Once everyone settled, Victoria joined her old friends around the wooden conference table. Jacques rested his head in hands as Ginny sat on one side of him, and his fraternity brother on the other. Victoria took a deep breath, and began, "I can't believe Shea and Farrah are gone. Both so unexpectedly. What is the likelihood of that happening?"

Ginny's focus changed from Victoria to the ceiling, and I could see her mental wheels turning. So, apparently did Victoria, who said, "That's rhetorical, Ginny."

Vanessa, her face stained with tears, sniffed. "I can't say Farrah and I always saw eye to eye, but what a terrible way to die."

"Oh, I don't know about that. I've seen worse. I wonder though, why didn't the killer use a knife? Far more effective than hitting someone with a piece of an ice sculpture. You'd have to be sure the blow landed just right to get the job done. You'd have to know what you were doing."

"Maybe because there wasn't a knife available?" Ginny suggested.

"No, the roast beef carving station was just a few feet away. It would have been easy to squirrel away a knife for later. Maybe the killer, in a fit of anger, grabbed whatever was close."

"What do you mean?" Jacques cried out, "Who would want to kill my Farrah?"

Boy, is he clueless I couldn't help thinking, but it was the spark that triggered the response we needed.

"Who would kill her? Who would kill her?" Ginny jumped out of her seat. "She ruined your life," she shouted. "*You* wanted to be a legal aid lawyer. *You* wanted to help others. She always had to be the center of attention. Even tonight, flouncing all over the room, making a spectacle of herself. I was the one who kept us all together. I was the one who supported everyone. Did that matter? No! She was the one who got all the attention. Always. Farrah McAlister. Farrah Rocher. It made no difference."

The rest of the table sat in stunned silence, having never heard Ginny so passionate about anything except the annual Sorority initiation ceremony.

Everyone except Victoria, of course.

"Ginny." Victoria's tone softened to that of sorority sisters sharing a confidence. "What was the final straw?"

"Tonight," Ginny whimpered, "I heard her and Jacques begging Edward and Vanessa to invest in their new company. Farrah didn't love Jacques. She loved his earning potential. I loved Jacques. He wouldn't be in any financial hardship if he was with me."

"And then Farrah was in front of the hors d'oeuvres when the lights went out." Victoria's empathetic tone encouraged her to continue.

"She always wanted to be the center of attention. So, let her be a centerpiece. I grabbed one of the ice roses. I knew I just had to hit her hard enough at the base of her skull. Everyone was screaming in the dark, and I just kept hitting her. For the first time in her life, no one heard her."

Ginny's tone was pure hatred, but then she surprised us by starting to sob.

"It was perfect. Even my fingerprints on the ice would melt and just disappear. Just disappear," she added bitterly between tears, "just like I had my entire life around her."

The room was silent except for the sound of Ginny's sobs.

I'd like to say I felt a sense of satisfaction solving the mystery, but all I felt was sadness over a life lost. Both Farrah's literally and Ginny's figuratively.

As the police led Ginny out of the hotel to a life without the sorority or the illusion of one with Jacques, Victoria walked over to me.

"I'm starved. Come on, let's get changed, then head to Sir Winston Pub for a Molson, and we can split a *pizza toute garnie*—all the toppings and maybe some poutine on the side."

I looked at her and wondered how she could think of food after tonight.

She wasn't close to these women anymore, but they were still a part of her past.

She must have read my mind, because the next words out of her mouth were, "I'm fine. It was a lifetime ago. We've all grown over the years—well, most of us anyway. I barely knew Farrah and I've already grieved Shea. For now, I have the rest of the weekend in town with my bestie, who I want to show some of the hotspots where Shea and I wasted our youth."

"Fine, but no way am I eating poutine."

"Okay, no poutine." Victoria put on a fake pouty face. The pout disintegrated and became a devious smile. "But yes to nightlife." She grabbed my arm and steered me outside. "How do you feel about escargot?"

VOICES IN THE CAVES

MARGARET S. HAMILTON

Dordogne, France

SAVORING HER FIRST SIP OF café au lait, Kate Carmody beckoned to her husband, Jack, who put his plate filled with eggs, sausages, and cheeses on their breakfast table. The hotel terrace overlooked the medieval town and the *Monument aux Morts*, honoring residents—civilian and military—who had lost their lives during World War II.

A middle-aged man and woman stood in front of the monument having a heated argument in loud, rapid French, the woman shaking her fist, the man pointing to Gaston, Kate and Jack's friend from their university days and their local guide. After a final verbal fusillade, the woman turned her back on the man and approached Gaston. The man stormed away.

"I wonder what their fight was about." Kate cut a forkful of omelet. "If they're meeting Gaston to go to the cave with us, we might be in for some drama."

Kate and Jack had been delighted to accept Gaston's offer of a week-long tour of the Périgord region. Each day had brought new adventures—a boat ride on the Dordogne River and visits to castles, churches, ruins, and caves. Lots of caves, dry, sweet-smelling but chilly, each with prehistoric paintings of horses, bulls, and bears painted with black charcoal, red iron ferrite, and red ochre.

In one of the caves, momentarily transported to the Neolithic age, Kate extended her arms, holding a squealing child to dab paint marks with her fingers on the cave ceiling. Still immersed in her reverie, Kate had followed the children's laughter down a side passage in the cave.

After Jack had guided her back, Gaston had given her a knowing look. "You hear the children, *n'est-ce pas?*"

"Yes. In some ethereal form, they're still in the cave."

Gaston had smoothed his luxuriant mustache. "You have a gift. Use it wisely."

GASTON APPROACHED THEIR TABLE. "*BONJOUR,* mes amis. My friends, Sylvie Moreau will be part of the group today."

They introduced themselves to Sylvie while Gaston went inside for coffee.

"Sylvie, are you interested in prehistoric caves?" Kate asked. "Gaston has taken us to several in the area. I'm looking forward to seeing the cave on his cousin's farm."

"As a young child, my mother was hidden with a family on the farm now owned by Gaston's cousin."

"Intriguing." Katie slathered a croissant with strawberry jam and took a luscious bite before she continued. "Does you mother have memories of the farm?"

"Only the cave, where she hid while the Germans killed the French family. According to the local archives, members of the *Maquis*—the Resistance—were relatives. I don't know if the Germans realized that the family also sheltered a refugee child."

Kate shuddered, imagining the young girl's devastation after she found the carnage of her French foster family members.

Gaston handed Sylvie her coffee and sat with them. "Sylvie is seeking confirmation of her mother's original name and birthplace. We had many refugees in Dordogne during the war, including those from Strasbourg. Kate, perhaps you'll be able to assist her."

"I'm on vacation, but happy to help." Kate savored her last bite of *cabécou noix*, the local goat cheese encrusted with chopped walnuts. Which version of Sylvie's story was true, the German massacre, or the search for her mother's birth certificate? Or did Sylvie have an entirely different agenda?

After Kate finished her breakfast, she pulled a spiral-bound pad and pen from her crossbody bag. "Sylvie, I'm a research librarian, specializing in genealogy. Perhaps I can assist you in your search. Where do you think your mother is from? Perhaps Alsace?"

Sylvie furrowed her brow. "Ninety thousand refugees fled from Alsace to Dordogne in 1939. My mother would have been a baby."

"Have you asked the Red Cross and other refugee organizations for assistance?" Kate made a note.

Sylvie stirred sugar into her coffee. "The only information I have is that my mother hid with the Rousseau family in this area from 1942 to 1944."

"What name did your mother use?" Kate continued to make notes.

"The name on her falsified French identity papers, Marianne Rousseau."

"After the Allied invasion and death of the French family, what happened to Marianne?"

"My mother grew up in a succession of orphanages and refugee camps. After she married my father, Claude, they lived in Lyon."

"Does Marianne still live there?"

Sylvie nodded and continued to sip her coffee.

Kate turned to a fresh page in her notebook. "After the slaughter of the Rousseau family in 1944, someone must have cared for Marianne until the Germans left the area. Any idea who that would have been?"

"No." Sylvie dabbed her lips with a napkin. "My mother was only six. I suspect she suppressed her memories of the horrific event and the two years she spent on the farm."

"Gaston, when did your uncle acquire the farm?" Kate asked.

"After the war. Relatives of the Rousseau family sold it to him. My cousin now owns it."

"And does your cousin live there?" Kate asked.

"He built a one-room house to use during hunting season."

"When was the last time you visited the cave on his property?"

"Not long ago. We cleared the trail to the cave."

Kate tapped her pen on her notebook. "Sylvie, I understand why you want to visit the cave and perhaps take some photos to show your mother. But I doubt you'll find evidence of Marianne's stay there." She paused, trying to phrase her next question. "Is it possible your mother was a biological member of the Rousseau family? Perhaps a niece or granddaughter?"

Sylvie shook her head. "She's not a relative. The Rousseau family had a young daughter, Christine, who was Marianne's age. I found Christine's birth and baptismal certificates."

Kate dabbed flakes of croissant with her finger. "What about DNA testing?"

Sylvie's face flushed. "Nothing of interest."

Kate pushed her chair under the table. Sylvie's focus seemed to be on the cave, and hiring Gaston as a guide was her only option to explore it.

TEN MINUTES LATER, KATE AND Jack stood at the hotel entrance wearing daypacks and carrying their jackets. Sylvie emerged from the hotel lobby, a chic silk scarf artfully draped around her neck, fresh gloss on her pursed lips. She ignored them.

"I don't trust Sylvie." Kate murmured to Jack.

"Besides your recent experience in the cave, you have an uncanny knack for ferreting out the motives of people researching their ancestors." Jack brushed a tendril of hair off Kate's face. "What do your finely tuned instincts tell you?"

"Sylvie's lying about her mother, Marianne. She's after more than her refugee mother's birth certificate, which, with some archival research, would be available to her." Kate watched for Gaston's four-wheel-drive vehicle. "Keep an eye out for the man Sylvie had the fight with. He's somehow connected with our cave visit."

Sylvie sat next to Gaston in the front seat of the rugged vehicle, silent, clutching the door handle during their hour-long drive on winding country roads.

Kate immersed herself in the hilly terrain, imagining Resistance fighters hiding behind trees, and trucks filled with German soldiers making the rounds of local farms, searching for French operatives.

Kate and Jack had seen many graves describing German atrocities in retaliation for the actions of the Resistance, which had sabotaged German operations and pulled off a huge robbery from a *Banque de France* rail shipment.

Who had reported the Rousseau family to the Germans? The family massacre would be listed in the town records, their graves in the local cemetery. Local diaries or letters might identify the informant.

After eighty years, what could Sylvie hope to find in the cave? Valuables or perhaps information about the informant?

GASTON SHIFTED INTO FOUR-WHEEL DRIVE and crawled up a pot-holed dirt track through the dense woods. He pulled into a clearing ringed with walnut trees and turned off the engine. "We will see the original stone farm buildings, which are in ruins, before we hike up to the cave above the tree line. Bring your jackets and water bottles." Gaston distributed head lamps and hard hats and filled his rucksack with flashlights. He presented Kate with a wooden hiking staff. "For you, *Madame*. You may need it today."

Gaston knew her fear of snakes. Kate hefted the heavy stick. Her eyes glued to the ground, she walked toward the ruins of the Rousseau farm. Remnants of a large vegetable garden and trellises of climbing roses lay under a brilliant autumn blue sky. Flocks of cawing hooded crows populated the tall trees. A serene and safe place for children as they gathered walnuts and waded in the nearby stream.

Kate offered to take some photos of Sylvie in front of the farm buildings. Sylvie initially declined, then posed with her back to Kate. Didn't she want to share photos of the Rousseau farm with her mother? Without Sylvie noticing, Kate grabbed a quick shot of the woman's face. Imposter or genuine?

Gaston motioned them toward a rugged trail, which quickly turned steep. A rough climb for anyone, especially children. Kate wondered if members of the Resistance had sheltered in the cave. Sylvie hadn't mentioned if other *maquisards*, Resistance fighters, had been killed at the farmhouse.

After a thirty-minute climb, Gaston led them along the path bordering a limestone cliff above the tree line. Below, fields and woods stretched for miles, Gaston's cousin's house the only dwelling in sight. Swifts and swallows chittered and swooped around the cliff faces.

Gaston stopped at a large crevice, the entrance to the cave blocked with heavy chains secured by eyebolts drilled into the rock. He used a key to open the padlock before he loosened the chains enough to allow them to step into the cave. After they pulled on their jackets, Gaston distributed flashlights. They clicked on their headlamps.

Kate took a deep breath and held Jack's hand. Their visits to the famous caves in the region, including taking an electric train two kilometers into the earth, had been child's play compared to exploring this remote cavity. Gaston hadn't mentioned interior rockslides or underground lakes. Or bears. Kate suspected the chains at the entrance would allow air flow, but prevent large animals from entering the cave. But not snakes. She thumped the ground with her walking stick.

Gaston tucked the padlock and key in a jacket pocket and shouldered his rucksack. "Now we will walk approximately one kilometer on level ground. I will show you the cave paintings. Sylvie will be able to experience the same cave her mother did as a young one."

Sylvie compressed her mouth in a tight line and followed Gaston into the cave. Gaston shined his flashlight on the ground and warned them not to trip on rocks and rubble. The air in the cave was chilly and dry, the ceiling height less than six feet. The walls of the cave might reveal inscriptions or drawings—or bear claw marks. Kate still found it curious that the cave paintings didn't portray humans, flowers, or trees.

Jack brought up the rear, one hand on Kate's shoulder.

After Gaston told them to turn off their headlamps, total darkness enveloped them. Kate gasped for air, as if suffocating under a blanket of black silence. She slowly breathed in and out, her feet steady on the cave floor, and ran her hands across the granular limestone walls. Up, sideways, and down. The prehistoric cave dwellers would have used flaming torches to find their way.

"Not too much farther," Gaston called.

They clicked on their headlamps. Kate shuffled forward, tapping her walking stick on the cave floor.

At the end of the cave, Gaston shined his light on the ceiling. "Here we have prehistoric animals and child-sized fingerprints." Kate scanned the paintings. The animals were not for worship. They were prey, a source of sustenance for the cave dwellers. Raising her hands and extending her fingers, she matched her adult-sized digits to the smaller ceiling prints.

Squeals of laughter emerged from a large fissure in the limestone wall. Where were the children? Inside a special hiding place?

"Kate, again, you encounter the children?" Gaston said. "Just as before."

Sylvie pointed her flashlight at Kate's eyes. "Ghosts? Where?"

Kate averted her face. "It's nothing. Please put down your flashlight."

Sylvie stood face to face with Kate. "You heard the children. You know they were here. She gestured toward the fissure. "Through the opening? Show me."

Not a chance. Kate's torso under several layers of clothing was too thick to fit through the opening. And what lay beyond the fissure? "No, I'm leaving."

Sylvie stripped off her jacket and sweater to reveal her petite frame. "Show me!" She yanked Kate's arm.

A man's voice echoed behind them. "Gaston, *où es-tu?*" Where are you?

"*Ici*, Henri." Here. Gaston edged past the two women, and Kate followed, clutching her walking stick. Jack stayed behind her. They met Henri, the man they had seen fighting with Sylvie earlier that morning.

Who was Henri, what was his relationship with Gaston, and why was Sylvie involved? And had Gaston and Henri planned a confrontation in the cave?

"Where is Sylvie?" Henri shined his flashlight toward the rear of the cave.

"She's small enough to have slipped through the crevice." Kate hefted her walking stick. "We'll return to the entrance."

"*Non!*" Sylvie shrieked and popped out of the fissure in the cave. "I found nothing behind the wall."

What had Sylvie hoped to find? Sacks of French francs, jewelry, or perhaps a child's toy?

Henri crossed his arms. "You demanded to see the cave. You found nothing. Now, we leave."

Sylvie shivered in her thin cotton shirt, her jacket and sweater still on the cave floor. "The cave has prehistoric paintings. You didn't register it with the authorities. Unless you pay, I will report you."

Henri laughed. "All you care about is money. Time to leave."

Kate and Jack started walking to the front of the cave, Gaston behind them.

When they reached the cave entrance, Gaston separated the chains to allow Kate and Jack to climb through. Gaston followed, hooking the open padlock on an eyebolt. "It's safe. We will walk back to my car."

Gaston thumbed his cell phone. He left a brief message and terminated the call.

"Gaston, why are Sylvie and Henri still in the cave?" Kate pulled off her jacket.

"Henri is my cousin. Sylvie is convinced there is treasure in the cave and demanded access. She made other threats against Henri and his family. Henri asked me to include her on our excursion." Gaston adjusted his rucksack. "We are finished with Sylvie. Henri will deal with her. We have one more visit today. I hope it gives you pleasure."

"Gaston, Sylvie lied, didn't she?" Kate asked. "You knew Marianne wasn't her mother. I'm sure you've checked the cave many times. There's nothing hidden inside. With your suspicions, why didn't you record the conversation on your cell phone?"

"Ah, Kate, so quick, so intuitive. In France, we have strict privacy laws about phone recordings. I could not tell you the truth until now. Come, let's visit Marianne—the real Marianne, from Alsace. To ensure her safety, her parents hid Marianne with the Rousseau family."

"What really happened to the Rousseau family?" Kate asked.

"They received word the German soldiers were on their way, and the whole family, including Marianne, hid in the cave. The soldiers threw grenades through the farmhouse windows and barn and destroyed the buildings. The Rousseau family stayed in the area until after the war, then hired a relative who was a lawyer to sell their farm to my uncle. Marianne rejoined her parents in Sarlat later in 1944."

"Did the Rousseau family, including Christine, leave France?" Kate asked.

"Yes, for the United States."

"And they had the funds to do it?" Kate asked. "Perhaps from a Resistance train robbery?"

Gaston smiled. "Perhaps."

* * *

GASTON DROVE THE SHORT DISTANCE to Marianne's home at the end of another rutted dirt track. "Kate, I promised you a visit to a local farm."

"How lovely!" The red-roofed stucco house was surrounded by beds of lavender, roses, purple asters, and pink anemones, the floral-scented air abuzz with bees. A stooped woman with white hair stood on the front steps, leaning on her cane. "*Bienvenue, mes amis.*" Welcome, my friends.

Marianne's daughter Louise introduced herself. "I'll serve tea on the terrace. *Maman* has some photos to share with you."

Kate sat next to Marianne, with Gaston nearby serving as an interpreter.

Marianne opened an album and showed Kate photos of her mother and father. Gaston explained that Marianne's parents were Communists. In 1942, suspecting they were to be deported to work camps in Germany, they went into hiding and joined the Resistance. The Rousseau family volunteered to care for Marianne, who was the same age as their daughter, Christine.

Kate asked, "Gaston, can Marianne tell us what happened in 1944, or is it too painful?"

Louise spoke. "I'll tell you. An informant told the Germans that the Rousseau family harbored members of the Resistance who had taken part in the train robbery."

Kate thought for a minute. "Was Sylvie after the money from the robbery?"

"*Oui,*" Louise said. "She threatened *Maman* with prison. Though the money from the train robbery was never found, Sylvie believed it was hidden in the cave. Sylvie threatened me, too." Louise's eyes flashed with anger. "I told her only Gaston and his cousin had keys to the padlock on the cave entrance. Sylvie was determined to visit the cave, so Henri asked Gaston to take her."

Gaston said, "Today, Sylvie threatened to tell the authorities about the cave if Henri didn't pay for her silence."

Gaston's cell phone chimed. He read and translated a text message from Henri. "The gendarmes met Henri and Sylvie at the cave. The woman who calls herself Sylvie is wanted for fraud and extortion, threatening the survivors of the war years." He clicked off his phone and smiled. "We no longer have to worry about Sylvie. And the cave is of no interest to the government. Henri never shows it to tourists. Kate and Jack are friends."

"Gaston, you knew Sylvie lied to us." Kate clenched her fists.

"Henri and I needed to be sure of her intentions before we called the gendarmes," Gaston said. "I'm sorry I misled you." He paused. "Because of your genealogy expertise, Marianne asked to meet you."

Kate slowly exhaled. "I understand." She turned a page in the photo album. "Marianne, did your parents survive the war?"

Louise replied, "Yes, instead of returning to Alsace, they stayed in Sarlat."

Marianne tapped a photo of two girls wearing cotton dresses and aprons, each holding a doll. "*C'est moi et Christine.*" Me and Christine. She gently caressed Christine's face in the photo.

Kate squinted at the three-and-a-half by two-and-a-half black-and-white image. "Very pretty. Would you like me to search for Christine and her family in the United States?"

After Gaston translated, Marianne nodded her assent.

Louise removed two dolls from a cabinet. "One doll for Marianne and one for Christine." Louise displayed a neat row of hand stitching on a doll's cloth body. "When my grandparents left Alsace, they converted their savings into diamonds and sewed them in the dolls. The diamonds in one doll were payment for Marianne's care with the Rousseau family. The other doll hid Marianne's diamonds—the diamonds that paid for this farm."

Kate knitted her brow and looked at Gaston. "Not loot from the train robbery, but diamonds. And what I heard wasn't squeals of childish glee from prehistoric children, but laughter from Marianne and Christine."

Gaston gave her a smile. "Perhaps both, Kate. You have the gift of hearing those who lived before us."

As she squeezed Marianne's hand, children's laughter momentarily enveloped Kate. "I will search for Christine and her family in the States and let you know if I find them." Louise translated for her mother.

Marianne smiled her thanks, clutching the baby dolls, her eyes brimming with tears.

DOWNWARD DOG

VINNIE HANSEN

"BOW YOUR HEAD. CLOSE YOUR eyes. It's time for gratitude." The yoga teacher, Robin, who had turned out to be a man, commanded the class. Nash Barnett did not like taking orders.

Beneath the rustling fronds of a *palapa*, he dipped his tanned face without closing his eyes. He was grateful, yadda yadda, for the chalet in St. Moritz and the new Hacker-Craft 33.5-foot mahogany tender for his yacht, for his daughter being nearly as hot as the girl in front of him. He would have left the class before it started if she hadn't unfurled her mat when she did. Instead, he'd stuck it out. Only a few minutes ago, she had been doing downward dog, her perky ass outlined by apricot-colored yoga pants, ripe enough to . . .

"Inhale."

Nash sucked in a big breath, covertly eyeing the braid of strawberry-blonde hair snaking down the girl's slender back. He'd learned years ago that yoga retreats at posh resorts provided fertile hunting grounds for rich, trusting souls and tasty morsels to bag.

"Ommmmmmmmmmmmmmm," the others chanted while Nash admired smooth shoulders curving from straps of teal.

"Namaste." The instructor bowed.

Finally.

Nash made a mental note not to take this teacher again. The hottie in apricot pants joined her friend on the other side of the concrete slab. They chatted as other students left. Nash stayed put, rubbing his calf as though he had a cramp. He timed rolling up his mat to correspond with their approach.

Standing, he asked, "What did you think of the class?"

The friend glanced up at him, masses of black curls spilling from a hair band. "That instructor sucked."

Nash barked a laugh, then quirked a brow at the hottie.

"Easier to imagine him as a WWE wrestler," she said.

At the edge of the open-air shelter roofed by palm leaves, the three slipped their feet into beach sandals.

"In what way?" Nash asked. If you wanted to tap some ass, best to slot in a few questions.

The friend cut in, "Too brusque."

The hottie smiled mischievously and said, as though continuing her thought about the teacher, "Wrestler or maybe Drax the Destroyer."

Nash had no idea what she was talking about, one of the downsides of chasing the silky flesh of youth. Conversing with someone his age who didn't worship Taylor Swift was the only thing he missed about his marriage.

The trio started down a steep path, cliff and ocean on their left, luxury resort nestled at sea level on the right. "I'd think they wouldn't want that vibe here," Nash said. "They wouldn't even allow me to bring security." It never hurt to work in that he was a man of enough wealth and importance to warrant bodyguards.

"Guns and Yoga." The friend smiled. "Yeah, I don't see that working. I'm Thena, by the way." Her grip was crushing. She may have been a chatty-receptionist type, but she had the strength of a weight lifter. Early in class, while surveying the field, Nash had noted her arm muscles as she held the plank position.

"Nash Barnett." Neither face flickered with recognition. Well, they were young. And when you made money with money, you didn't create a brand like a TikTok boy band with merch.

Nash seriously wanted to get rid of Thena but couldn't think of a way short of pushing her off the cliff. It wouldn't be hard. There was no fence. Gotta love the lax regulations of developing countries, the whole reason he chose them for his bases of operation. The resort didn't even supply a flimsy rail. Just an unguarded, 100-foot rocky drop to churning surf. A rush of vertigo caused him to step back. He landed on Thena's toe.

She laughed and Nash really wanted to give her a swift shove, but pitching Thena into the ocean wouldn't accomplish his objective, and Nash Barnett was a mission-oriented guy. "Would you ladies care for a drink?"

Thena grabbed her friend's arm. "Let's go, Daniela. The hotel cantina has the best *horchata.* I'm dying of thirst."

The hotel's walkways meandered through lush green hillocks interrupted by benches, fountains, and metal sculptures of sea creatures. The open-air cantina perched on a mound at the far end of the development and provided an unobstructed ocean view. Nash waited until both girls chose their bar stools and then positioned himself next to Daniela.

Thena stood and moved to the stool on his other side. Annoyed, Nash waved over the barkeep, wondering how the two girls had come to be at the resort. Neither exuded the subtle touches of money.

Daniela ordered fresh-squeezed orange juice. "Without a straw."

Nash would have preferred a vodka tonic but ordered juice. If you wanted to dance, best to watch your partner's moves.

When Thena's *horchata* arrived, she stretched across his body to accept her drink. "Daniela didn't have to forego her security."

Nash turned to Daniela. Flawless skin and blue-green eyes. Dazzling without a trace of make-up. "Are you some famous actress?" he asked.

She looked away to her arriving orange juice and shook her head.

"She drove a forklift," Thena said. "At Home Depot."

How did a forklift driver make the dough to come to a place like this? he wondered. "I haven't seen any security." Could Thena be punking him?

"Yes, you have." Thena flexed a bicep.

"You?"

She smiled and took a sip of her drink. It smelled like cinnamon and left a milky mustache. Thena licked it away.

Maybe she meant *security* in a generic way, not as a bodyguard. Thena did seem to watch out for Daniela. "You said *drove* a forklift." Nash addressed the comment to Thena, the better source of information, even if he couldn't get a bead on her.

"Before she won the lottery."

Again, Nash couldn't tell if she was serious or playing him, but a lottery win would explain a lot. It also meant that plopped down beside him in paradise was a perfect customer—loaded and naive. Not that he needed to find clients. He had underlings for that. But landing a fish still provided a thrill—better than cocaine, not quite as good as hang gliding.

Damn, he wished he had a business card to hand her and wasn't wearing shorts and a tee. It was hard to make a powerful pitch without the trappings of Burberry suit and subservient muscle. He angled himself toward Daniela. "If you need advice on what to do with your newly acquired capital, I'm your man."

Daniela took a sip of orange juice and regarded him from under thick eyelashes. "Is that right?"

"I'm the CEO of Worldwide Investment Strategies."

She gazed away from him at a parakeet in a palm tree.

"As a matter of fact," he lowered his voice as another woman strolled behind them, wafting expensive perfume and alerting Nash's sensors, "we're launching a brand-new fund—Global Markets Initiative."

The new woman leaned over the bar to order a lemon drop martini. Without breaking its focus on Daniela, Nash's radar absorbed the woman's manicured hands adorned with expensive jewelry, but no wedding ring. He raised his voice. "It's a great opportunity to get in on the ground floor." Completely true, because as with all of his funds, *ground floor* was the only floor that could provide the promised profit.

"We know," Thena said.

He spun toward her. "You know? How could you know?"

"Part of my job." She sipped her drink.

Nash twirled back to Daniela. The middle-aged woman hovered, waiting for her martini. Her wrap was expertly tied off one tanned shoulder, the blue of her hat and tall wedge sandals a perfect match for the print. Large sunglasses with white frames protected her face. Her presence was distracting, but Nash said to Daniela, "We could use your fortune to make you another one."

"Why would I want another one?" Daniela finished her orange juice and placed her glass on the bar counter. "It's hard enough to manage this one." She slid from her stool. "Thank you for the drink."

Thena took a final gulp of *horchata* and hopped down after Daniela.

Nash watched them leave. *Unbelievable.* Had he lost his touch?

The bartender came over with the woman's martini.

Nash used the opportunity to order a vodka tonic. "With a goddamn straw."

"Mind if I join you?" the woman asked.

Now we're talking. Hoop earrings and necklace with . . . he squinted . . . opals. She reeked of money and was alone.

"I'd be delighted," he said. "Let's move to a private table."

She set her cell phone and drink on the table and introduced herself as Krista. "I couldn't help but overhear your conversation."

Holy shit. Could it get easier than this? He was the one who'd won the lottery. "About the Global Markets Initiative?" he asked.

"Yes. *The ground floor?*" A sandy eyebrow arched above the white frames of her sunglasses. "I especially liked the bit about taking a fortune and making another one." She slipped the glasses from her slender nose.

"You look familiar," Nash said. "Have we met?" Unless people looked like Daniela, he didn't pay much attention. That was security's job. Although, in fact, this woman did look a bit like Daniela, aged by thirty years.

"Now *that*," she said in a teasing tone, "has to be the oldest line in the book." She leaned close.

She smelled great and was flirting with him. Not a yoga hottie, but fuckable. She did seem familiar, though, and that distracted Nash. He stared at a little mole on her earlobe. You could change a lot on a face but not so much the ears.

"Admiring my earrings?" she asked.

"They're nice." Nash cleared his throat. "So, let me tell you how to turn your money into a real workhorse."

"Back to money, are we?" She ran fingertips along his forearm.

Nash hoped she was not just after a quick tumble. If that were the case, he'd seize the opportunity, but in the meantime, he'd try to reel in this catch. "Could I take you to dinner tonight?"

"I'd be delighted."

Nash's forehead creased slightly at the mimicry of his earlier words. "How about another drink?"

With older women, nothing opened pocketbooks like romantic flourishes. And alcohol.

At the bar, he ordered another vodka tonic and lemon-drop martini, the combo jabbing at a nagging sense of déjà vu. *Another place but the same drinks and the same situation of bringing in a client.* From the distance, he studied Krista. It might help if he could see her hair, but her floppy sunhat covered every wisp.

When he returned with the drinks, he asked, "Have you been taking any of the yoga classes?" That might explain her familiarity.

"Contorting myself into a pretzel?" She laughed. "No, I'm here for a completely different reason."

"To find investments?" he suggested.

She sipped her fresh drink. "More like looking for the right returns."

Wow, talk about feeding him his line. "Global Markets Initiative delivered an unbelievable nineteen percent return this first quarter."

"Unbelievable, for sure," she murmured.

Nash started his spiel, conspiratorially close so she could feel his body heat. "Global Markets focuses primarily on developing nations with untapped resources . . ." He stayed alert to waning interest, but Krista listened intently.

After he'd drained another drink, Krista checked the time on her phone and suggested a stroll along the cliffside path. He rose from his seat and extended an arm.

Even though balanced on sandals that added at least two inches to her height, she didn't wobble. She hooked her arm on his.

A short walkway led to the bottom of the path. As they promenaded up the hill, Nash ventured, "So what do you think?"

She extracted her arm and looked up to the palapa. "Fool me once, shame on you. Fool me twice, shame on me."

Nash frowned and followed her gaze. A figure was approaching. Male. It could be that yoga teacher Robin, but why would he only now be leaving? Had he taught another yoga class?

Nash peered. No yoga mat. The man strode with purpose. Obviously not wearing sandals.

Nash scooted to the landward side of the path.

It *was* the yoga teacher, walking toward them like a heat-seeking missile. But then, hadn't everything about him been . . . what was the word Thena used . . . *brusque?*

Easier to imagine him as a WWE wrestler Daniela had said.

Nash's instincts flashed code red. An impulse to turn and run to the nearest path into the resort surged through him, but 1) he was quite aware of the difficulty of sprinting in beach sandals 2) if the situation were nothing, he'd look like an idiot in front of Krista and 3) Nash Barnett was *not* a coward.

He repeated *not a coward* like a mantra as the distance between them shrank. He checked Krista to see her reaction, but she contemplated the ocean. "Dolphins," she said, motioning him to join her at the cliff's edge.

Nash didn't move.

When the yoga teacher was six feet in front of him, Nash said, "Namaste."

Robin smiled thinly. He veered toward the ocean side of the path near Krista as if there might be dolphins to view.

A breeze gusted up the cliff, carrying the yoga teacher's words. It sounded like he said that in yoga, karma was not about revenge.

"What's it about?" Nash tried to back away without appearing to move.

"Investment." Robin's word hung, vibrating, in the air.

Nash's stomach turned.

Robin continued, "In yoga, karma is a recognition that actions are transformative, and our fortunes are made . . ."

Had the yoga teacher emphasized *fortune?* He stepped toward Nash, ". . . and remade."

Nash's sandal slipped off the edge of the walk. His toes pulled loose from the thong. He stumbled backward. *Damn third-world construction.* By the time he'd regained his balance and dignity, Robin was toe-to-toe with him, dark eyes drilling into his. Nash swallowed. "You're not a yoga teacher, are you?"

The man shrugged. "You don't believe it? Let me show you a new downward dog." His voice was even. Calm. Nash had a glimmer of hope. For one second.

The next second, a hand grabbed the waistband of his shorts, yanking them into a painful wedgie, while Robin's other hand twisted the neckline of his tee into a garrote. Nash shot a beseeching look to Krista.

"Still don't recognize me?" she asked sweetly, whipping off her hat and shaking out strawberry blonde hair, transforming into an older version of Daniela. "Playa Bonita Investment? I did not get in on the ground floor."

"You seem to have done okay," Nash stammered.

"Daniela's lottery money." Krista wagged a finger at him. "And shame on you for hitting on my daughter."

The man—probably not named Robin—frog marched him to the other side of the walk.

Nash struggled as the serrated cliff, the surf churning below, zoomed into sharp focus. His body lifted onto tiptoes.

"Downward," the man said as he pitched Nash into the air, "dog."

"Namaste," Krista trilled into the whoosh.

DRIVE

ANN MICHELLE HARRIS

"ARE YOU SURE YOU STILL want to do this?"

Henry's voice buzzes beside Audrey as the car rumbles along the mountain road. This weekend getaway was his idea. Three days of relaxation and a chance to see her younger brother perform at the fall music festival. A perfect, easy vacation. Until her brother stopped answering his phone. Until the police used the word *missing*.

Henry probably expects her to scream, to break down in tears. Instead, Audrey focuses on the scenery, watching the gray stone cliffs slide past her as Henry drives. The tops of the cliffs are covered in trees blazing in shades of red, orange, and yellow, overpowering the last bits of summer. Back home, everything is still robustly green, like winter will never come. Henry wants her to prepare for the worst. To the left is the runaway truck ramp, an upward, dead-end slope that leads nowhere. You just slide up, out of control, until you run out of speed. She's done this drive many times. Today is different.

Henry keeps his eyes on the road. The sharp, elevated curves of this mountain require him to pay attention. But the phone buzzes through the SUV's dashboard, startling them both. Audrey silently reads the text.

Joshua missed the audition. The machine voice living inside the SUV reads the message aloud, so Henry hears it too. That audition was everything to Joshua. Nothing would have kept him from it. The text from her brother's friend has effectively announced that her brother is, in all likelihood, dead. She thinks of the runaway truck ramp again as they finally pull into the city.

* * *

AT THE HOTEL, THE POLICE detective gives her his business card. Joshua was last seen leaving this spot, the Leland Hotel. It's a historic space, popular with the tourists—high ceilings, marble, dark wood paneling. Joshua loves it here. He is old fashioned too.

The police don't have much more to tell her, but the lead detective is sympathetic. Josh is a local university student who has always been in the spotlight. He grew from a young piano prodigy to a budding virtuoso, a genius of classical music and jazz. The tourists enjoy having a celebrity at the music festival. It adds depth to the small city culture. Audrey knows it's why his disappearance is being given this much attention. And, their parents were both professors at the university. They were part of the local elite in academia, politics, and society. It's another reason Joshua's disappearance is being given priority. It's a token of appreciation for the two well-dressed corpses buried in the city cemetery. They were killed by a hit-and-run driver on their way from a televised awards ceremony, but no one was willing to come forward and provide any useful evidence, so their killer escaped.

Audrey stares at the phone in her hand, reading the text message again while Henry talks to the staff at the hotel. They remember Joshua. He played the lobby piano and the guests loved it. Many were moved to tears. He has that effect on people. It's not just the music—it's him. He becomes one with the notes, inhabiting them rather than just playing them. And Josh is beautiful in a way that mystifies Audrey, who considers herself average and acceptable. Checking the boxes of what the world needs from her, but nothing more. Her life is her law practice and Henry. Her hobbies are wine and books. She's not chasing glamour or even self-actualization. Glamour leads to danger, and then those adoring fans disappear and abandon you. Ordinary is enough. She wishes her parents and her brother could have known that. How satisfying ordinary can be. Maybe they would still be alive.

"It's like the police said . . ." Henry leans close to her. "He was here. He played the lobby piano for a while. Then he met up with two friends and went up to the friends' hotel room. Afterwards, they all three left together. They were a little drunk apparently, but they said they were walking to their next destination, the riverwalk, so no one tried to stop them."

"His phone is dead." The word 'dead' sticks in Audrey's throat. "I mean, it's gone silent. I can't track it."

"The manager at the front desk showed me the security camera footage from yesterday." Henry holds up his phone. He's videotaped the hotel's security screen. Henry's a visual person. He'd rather snap a picture than take notes or just listen. On the screen, Audrey sees her brother arrive alone carrying his music folder. He's wearing the baseball cap she got him for his birthday last year. It says "Music Nerd" on it. She hears the piano sonata. It's mesmerizing. As with everything he plays, it's difficult to listen to it without crying. His playing feels personal to each listener. Then the video skips and she sees him leaving, laughing, wearing the baseball cap again, carrying his music folder. His face is partly obscured by the cap. He's with two of the people she'd seen watching him in the audience. She doesn't recognize them. But Joshua seems to know them. He's laughing and nodding with them. He doesn't look afraid. Something isn't right. Of course, nothing is right today, but something about the video is off. She's missing something.

"Any word from his girlfriend?" Henry speaks in a lowered voice.

"When I called, she said Joshua told her he needed his space before the audition." Joshua's girlfriend Renee is a violinist. "She was crying. She sounded devastated."

Henry nods and heads back to the lobby desk to book a room for the night while Audrey searches for caffeine. Her boots click on the marble floor as she follows a sign that leads to the rich smell of sweet, buttery pastries and fresh-roasted Columbian coffee. She texts Henry, asking him to send the video to her phone. Henry expects her to move on at some point. Not today, or this week, but eventually. Everyone will expect her to accept that Joshua is no longer her physical, breathing brother, but a 'missing person,' two-dimensional on the police posters that live online or printed on eight by ten copy paper tacked on bulletin boards for the next five years until they find his corpse decayed and floating in the river.

It's him, they'll say. They'll recognize his water-logged college sweatshirt, and what's left of his designer wallet with his photo identification in the skeleton's pocket. The vision makes Audrey search her phone for the forwarded security video from Henry. It's still downloading. Audrey pulls her attention back to her surroundings. In the mostly empty café, a young woman with light brown skin and loose, curly brown hair sips a cup of espresso. She holds a quiet preschooler on her lap. The child's hair and coloring match the woman's. They are clearly mother and daughter. The woman looks up at Audrey.

"Did you know him?" the woman asks. "The piano player who disappeared yesterday." The question surprises Audrey, but she accepts this small, strange mercy from the universe.

"He's my brother. What made you ask?"

The woman stares at her. "You look alike."

She and Josh do not look alike. The statement indicates a different kind of insight. More than the physical.

Audrey sits at the table with the woman and the child. She's drawn to them for some reason. The child waits quietly, staring at nothing, and for a moment Audrey worries about the little girl. Something in her quiet black eyes. But then the little girl leans abruptly against the woman and blinks silently. Audrey relaxes.

"I'm Audrey." Audrey glances at the child. "She looks just like you."

The woman smiles. "Everyone says so. So, it must be true." She watches Audrey. "We're up from Atlanta for the music festival. My husband is helping manage the hotel while his uncle recovers from surgery." She sips her espresso. "It's a family business."

Audrey leans towards her. "Have you seen him? My brother, Joshua. The pianist?" Audrey suddenly realizes how out of her depth she is. Hunting for one young man in a city overrun by tourists. She's not even sure he's still in the state. The woman stares back at her, noncommittal. She wants something more from Audrey.

"I'm from Atlanta too," Audrey says. The woman's expression remains neutral. "I do banking law. It's super boring." Audrey inhales softly, trying to connect. "So, what do you do?"

The woman gives her a quiet smile. "A little bit of everything." She pulls a piece of pastry towards the child, who accepts it and chews quietly. "But mostly, I watch out for my family." She stares at Audrey. Her eyes are accusatory. "Their safety is everything to me."

Audrey breathes softly, understanding. No one ever wants to get involved.

"I won't tell anyone." Audrey breathes in again to keep her desperation from overtaking her. Inside, she is screaming. "Please."

The woman toys with her small espresso cup.

"He came in and played the piano. It was astonishing." She pauses at the memory. "Then he went upstairs with two men. He was drugged. People thought he looked drunk. But I know the difference."

Audrey feels herself breaking to pieces. She wants to hear that he booked a flight to California or eloped with his overbearing girlfriend Renee. Drugged. The woman seems confident.

"I was told that he left with the two men a few hours later," Audrey says. "With his music folder. There's a video of them. Do you know where he went?" *Please.*

The woman strokes the child's hair. "That wasn't him. He didn't leave." Audrey stiffens. The woman feeds more pastry to the child. It looks like an almond croissant, a food that would have killed her brother. He is allergic to almost everything. "My daughter and I are very observant. We can read people."

"That means he's still here?" She knew something wasn't right about that security footage. Audrey grabs her phone and plays the newly downloaded video. She watches Josh exit the hotel. The height, build, and skin color are right, the shirt is the same, the hair is right—a neat nondescript afro. But the baseball cap fits differently. She thought she was imagining it in her smothered hysteria, in her grief.

The woman hands Audrey a hotel key, the override kind the staff uses.

"Room 502. I don't think you'll like what you find."

AUDREY ENTERS THE ROOM. JOSHUA'S lifeless body is lying on the bed, on his back. His shirt is gone. The pillow beneath his head is dotted with small splatters of blood, the same blood that flecks his mouth. Audrey's mind skips past grief or revenge and lands on the blandness of difficult phone calls and funeral arrangements. These are the mundane tasks her spinning thoughts can accept. She wants to scream, but she stands there frozen. Henry pushes past her to the body. He's got his medical bag with him.

Joshua's girlfriend Renee huddles on the floor sobbing, indifferent to their arrival. Audrey wonders how long she's been sitting there.

"I'm sorry, I'm sorry." The words leak from Renee in an unending loop.

Henry injects the body with something and begins pumping his hands into Joshua's chest. He probably thinks she won't forgive him if he doesn't at least try. There's nothing for her to do as she hovers in this in-between moment. The ambulance and police are on their way. So she turns her growing fury to Renee, who sits weeping and mumbling on the floor.

"I'm sorry," she sobs, "it was an accident."

Audrey squats down and grabs the young violin player's shoulders. She and Joshua had met in music school. "What did you do, Renee?"

"He was going to leave me after the audition. Everyone knew he'd get the spot. The others had no chance. Three other music students heard us arguing. The one guy, Jared, was desperate and asked me to help get Joshua here. Jared and his two friends were just going to drug him so he'd oversleep and miss the audition. There'd be a scandal. The conservatory would turn Joshua down and Jared would get the spot instead. But something went wrong. Josh started choking."

"He's allergic," Audrey stares at the girl, not quite comprehending her brother's murder, "to so many things."

"No." Henry's voice floats over from beside Joshua's body. "It's not an allergic reaction. They poisoned him."

Behind her, the hotel door opens, and the paramedics enter along with the police. Henry keeps pumping Joshua's chest. The only movement from Joshua is the pressure of the body under Henry's fists. She wants to tell him to stop. Finally, he does stop, and she hears someone . . . choking. Tears leak from Audrey's eyes as she processes the sound. Henry yells for oxygen and soon her brother is on the stretcher, gasping into the plastic mask. There's more blood. Tiny flecks of it splattering the clear covering over his face. Audrey struggles to keep from passing out as the paramedics pull him to the elevator, shouting instructions at each other, and whispering encouragements to her brother, urging him to live.

Henry glances at her and then leaves with the paramedics. Audrey is not ready to cry, not yet. She has one more thing to take care of. The police are handcuffing Renee, who sobs her confession freely. So much for her budding violin career. Audrey steps in front of the girl. Audrey is not a cop, she doesn't have to worry about Miranda rights. She keeps her voice calm, free from the murderous venom she feels, as she stares at Renee.

"Where are those music students?"

The lobby of the hotel is busy with more police, startled hotel guests, and reporters from at least two news stations. She overhears the three boys' names announced as suspects. Audrey imagines their startled faces as they watch the news in their apartments or at a local bar. And she imagines them all in prison, using their talents for the other inmates. Audrey scans the hallway for the woman from the cafe to thank her and return the passkey, but she is gone. The hotel manager walks towards her from the front desk. He keeps his voice low to avoid attracting the reporters to her. She appreciates that kindness.

"Is he okay?" the young manager asks.

"He will be. My husband is with him. He's keeping me updated." She shakes her head and looks over at the car valet stand. "I have to go see him."

"How did you know he was still here? We all saw him leave."

Audrey searches for something to say.

"It was just instinct," she says. Then she walks away. She'll tell the police she had Renee's location on her phone and that's what tipped her off. Hopefully, it's enough to make them move on. And they have a confession. Renee genuinely loves Josh. But it's the grasping, cruel kind of love that drives people away. Instead of a stellar violin career, she'll go to prison too, as she deserves. As far as Audrey is concerned, life in the shadows has its advantages. So she will keep her promise to the woman in the café because all that matters now, as she gets into her car, is that her brother Joshua is alive.

Travels for the Traditional Man

Lisbeth Mizula

I COULDN'T STOP MYSELF. "OH boy, we're going on a car trip!" I clapped my hands as Greg jammed his key into the ignition. The baby, Jonathon, the orange and white kitty I inherited when my mother died, was in his cat carrier belted onto the backseat of the car. Our clothes, the diary mother left me, and Jonathon's kibble and scratching post were all packed neatly into suitcases in the trunk.

"Mee-oow-ow, meow, meow, meow, meow." Jonathon sang from the backseat.

"Do you hear that, Greg? Jonathon's singing "Keep on the Sunny Side." The little angel knows how much I *love* being positive. He's happy we're going on an adventure, and me too. We're doing what we've needed to do for months. And now we are, because of you, Greg."

Greg gave me a sweet grunt and kept his hands at ten and two on the steering wheel, his head faced directly toward the road ahead. I'd never seen a safer driver!

"Oh, this is nice. Nice, nice, nice. The views through each and every window of the car are spectacular. The *trees*. Ohhhh. And the *weather*. Mmm. There's never been a more perfect day. Except maybe for the day we met at that dating website, *Men Lead Women Follow*. For the traditional man. That's you."

Greg leaned closer to the wheel, concentrating even more on his driving. And Jonathon sang from his carrier in the back seat. And I rolled down my window and waved my arm out the window, the air bouncing playfully against my hand and arm as the car zipped along.

"I'm just so darn happy. Happy. Happy. Happy." I inhaled a lungful of happy air. "Oh, look, Greg. We're in downtown Houston. This *is* a surprise. I never dreamed our trip today would be into the heart of our great city."

Greg grumbled, and it was such a masculine grumble—I felt proud to be in the same car with him. And then, though it seemed like we'd barely gotten on the road, Greg said, "We're here," and he parked the car perfectly within the lines of a parking space.

"Thank you for getting us here safely." Unbuckling my seatbelt, excitement made me bounce in place. Greg unfastened his seatbelt slowly and controlled, guiding the strap off his shoulder.

"You parked with the precision of a cake decorator. There's so much *room* between us and the other car. I couldn't hit their car with my door if I tried. Not that I would, or *could*, ever even think of causing damage to another person's property." Once out, I swung the door back and forth, marveling at all the available space, then turned to make sure Greg could see all the room he'd allowed for my side of the car. But Greg was already through the lot and about to cross the street.

Hurrying, I unbelted Jonathon's carrier and had to run with our baby to catch up.

"Oh, my Heavens. This building's *amazing*." When we reached Greg, I pointed back at the cornerstone. "Built 1967. We're going to be walking into a piece of Texas history. You didn't tell me we were taking an historical vacation."

"What's that, Jonathon? You think there's a bed-and-breakfast coming up somewhere? Me too, me too, me too."

Smiling, I held up our orange-striped baby so Greg could see how happy little Jonathon was, but the dear man kept his eyes looking straight ahead. That's my Greg, putting safety first when walking into a large building near a busy street.

Greg pushed through the doors, and I scurried in to join him at the line to the metal detector.

"Thank you for bringing us here today, Greg."

"You never give up, do you?" Greg said.

"You got me. You know me inside and out. You understand that I make my residence on the sunny side of life."

"I *know.*" He shouted that last word, and I must say, his voice was quite manly. People were staring at us, and it was easy to guess their thoughts. The women wished they were me. The men wished they were more like my Greg. And all of them wished they had a little Jonathon to carry around in a stylish carrier.

"Look. Where. We. Are." Greg raised his arms over his head and slashed the air to punctuate each word.

"Yes, my love. We're here in this beautiful building. Standing with all these nice people."

"Meow," Jonathon said.

Greg closed his eyes, his jaw working back and forth, like he was praying. I never interrupt his praying. Neither does Jonathon.

When Greg opened his eyes and spoke, his voice was perfectly controlled. Perfectly modulated, if I'm using that word right?

"I got fired from my job. I've been out of work two *years.* No one will hire me. We sold our furniture last week for groceries. And today, we were evicted from the crappiest apartment complex in Houston. But still. After all that," he took a ragged breath, "every *damned* day, you keep singing that song. Over and over again. That *idi-otic* song. Until I want to rip the ears off my head." His face had turned a nice, cheerful red color. And he was pulling at his hair until it all stood out from his head in a beautiful halo.

Greg began to sing, which was quite unlike him. In fact, I'd never heard my husband singing. It's possible he was imitating me, and, if so, he made me sound good.

"*Keep on the sunny side. Always on the sunny-side. Keep on the sunny side of life—*"

"Gee, if only I *could* sing that well, Greg. You always do everything better than I could ever hope to—"

"Damnit, Carol Lynn. We are standing in the Family Law Center. I have brought you to divorce court. It's *over.* I'm not even getting back in the car with you because I can't take one more minute of—" He shook his fists in the air over that beautiful halo. I've never seen such passion! "—your *inane,* happy GARBAGE." His face had turned a much darker red now. Probably from shouting. Greg has taught me so much about men, like how much they need to be heard.

Even unshaven, his hair dirty, and his face almost black from his passion, he was still the handsomest man I had ever seen.

"I'm just so glad we're husband and wife. And that we have Jonathon to love. Darling, you know . . ." Shaking my head, I continued. "I could never, never, never divorce you. We've only been together four years. Give me one more year. I promise." I placed the hand not holding the carrier over my heart. "It will be the *best* year of your life. Jonathon promises too. No, we don't just promise, we *guarantee* it."

I winked. Blew him a kiss and held Jonathon up in his carrier. Greg's eyes got a funny look in them. Everyone was staring at the striking figure he made. This may have been when the police officers came out of a nearby office, wanting to help. Greg reached under his fishing vest and pulled out a *gun*!

Everyone around us seemed to be pushing or shoving someone else—so impolite and uncalled for. I was quick to act myself. With prayer. "Heavenly Father-Mother God. Hallowed be thy name—"

Whose gun went off first? There were so many bangs. It was eardrum-shocking. Greg twirled closer to me, like he was dancing, before slumping onto the marble floor at my feet.

"Greg," I knelt beside him with our Jonathon. "Stay with us, darling."

"Life insurance—canceled because no . . . money." Greg's voice was a hoarse whisper as blood leaked from his body. The floor around him would be very slippery. People would have to watch their step.

"Oh my, oh my, oh my. If only you'd said something about running out of money sooner. Mother left me plenty of money so I'd always be able to take care of Jonathon. You just needed to ask Jonathon, and I know he would have been happy to share his money with you. But he never would have offered because he wouldn't want to hurt your male pride. Because as we all know, you're a traditional man. And you married me because you knew that, as a traditional woman, I'd always put you first."

Greg screwed up his face, and I'm pretty sure with his dying breath he was trying to say, "Thank you, Jonathon," it just didn't come out right.

I hugged the cat carrier close as I was helped to my feet by police officers who crowded around us. That's when I first laid my eyes on Teddy Sherrell. He was a manly man: The sleeves of his orange jumpsuit rolled up, revealed colorful tattoos on his muscular arms. They showed off his knowledge of how every woman wants to be seen, completely naked on someone's forearm with her legs in an impossible position. He had very good posture, and as he walked by in a line of men dressed in orange and paired with police officers, Teddy leaned away from his officer as he passed near me.

"I'd never be too proud to ask your kitty-cat for some cash. And I'm outta here in three days." He partly lifted one arm, which also raised the arm of his officer.

The man's type couldn't have been more obvious if he'd had a neon sign flashing on his forehead. Traditional Man. Traditional Man. Traditional Man.

Peeking back at my beloved, the way the officers stood around him, I knew Greg was no more. "My name's Carol Lynn. That's two separate words, Carol as in sing me a carol. Then Lynn."

I held up Jonathon in his carrier for Teddy to see. "And this is my baby."

"Teddy Bovine Sherrell. Inmate 555683," he called as he was led away. "Send me your address."

Mr. Sherrell made it quite clear that I was in the company of another traditional man. And one who knew how to make use of a woman's assets.

Jonathon and I said our final goodbyes to Greg, then allowed the police to escort us to an office for, frankly, some overzealous questioning.

When we finally made it back to the car, I got the leash and took Jonathon on a little walk so he could do his duty, then secured him once again in his carrier in the back seat. I got out mother's diary and read Mimi Sinclair's recommendations, her very last words to me, then made my notes for the day.

Not much of a writer, I wrote one short line. There would be an adjustment period, life without Greg, but when Jonathon started singing, I added my voice and knew we were on the right track. The jail guards made a big to-do out of my calling Teddy Bovine Sherrell, inmate 555683. When Teddy got on the line, I told him my plan—withdraw cash from the bank in San Antonio where mother set up Jonathon's account, then drive to Massachusetts, to the beach bungalow she willed to Jonathon and me. He said he'd be de-lighted to meet me.

From Houston to San Antonio, Jonathon and I belted out one golden oldie after the next, starting with "Raindrops Keep Falling on My Head," moving right along to "Put on a Happy Face," and my favorite childhood gems like, "Ninety-Nine Bottles of Beer on the Wall," and "There's a Hole in the Bucket."

By nightfall, we made San Antonio, where Jonathon's litter was from and where mother left funds for Jonathon's benefit and to carry out her wishes. The bank being closed that late in the evening, we bunked overnight with Jonathon's cousin, Jonathon V, and his human, San Antonio Sandra. A little too much catnip was had at the Jonathons' reunion. Both kitties had to run off their energy in the backyard, but eventually all settled in for a good night's sleep.

The next morning, we said our goodbyes. After a quick stop at the bank, we were back on the road to Massachusetts and my dear mother's last home; a tiny, beachfront cottage, currently unoccupied.

Also in Massachusetts, Jonathon could visit the grave of his great-great-Grandma, Mildred Kitty.

"GET THAT FUR BAG OF yours to stop that racket or I'll skin him alive."

"But Teddy, Jonathon loves singing Christmas carols. Just like his mommy." Holding a cluster of mistletoe over Teddy's head, I went in for a kiss.

"What've you got in your hand?" Teddy grabbed my arm and pulled it down to see what I held. His eyes grew wide, looking at the harmless little sprig. "Arrggghhh. More Christmas crap." He ripped the bit of plant from my hand and threw it into the fire—the one I'd kept burning in the fireplace since Teddy arrived, because it's another way to say, "Merry Christmas," every day.

And everything in our little Cape Cod bungalow screamed Merry Christmas. I made sure of that. Of course, we couldn't keep the front yard decorated. We wouldn't want trouble with the Home Owners Association. But I made up for that on the inside of the house. Every room had a giant wreath and a fully decorated Christmas tree. There were three trees in the living room. And a tree in each of the two bathrooms. I used some of mother's money to install house-wide surround sound speakers that pumped out Christmas carols every hour of the day.

With Nat King Cole singing all my Christmas favorites in the background, Jonathon and I danced around the tree in the living room until I had to hurry back to the kitchen to get ready to serve dinner.

When I had all the food on the table, I started the Santa Meal Alarm—a six-foot plastic Santa Claus who merrily announces, "Ho-ho-ho. Time to eat. Ho-ho-ho. Time to eat." His arm pumps up and down, ringing a brass bell until you shut him off. Teddy never forgets to turn off the meal alarm.

Today he forgot.

I found Teddy in the living room. Santa was "Ho-ho-ing," and you could see immediately Teddy had that look on his face. That same expression that was on Greg's face on our last day together. Maybe not exactly the same? Yet. Time for a little more celebration and he'd be ready.

"Oh, there's no place like home for the holidays," I sang to Teddy as I watched him staring at the big screen TV. It only got the one station; the Christmas channel. In a marathon of lesser-known Christmas movies, "Rudolph and Frosty's Christmas in July" was playing. A sequel to "Rudolph the Red-Nosed Reindeer," in this version Rudolph's nose stops glowing, and he's accused of theft.

Teddy looked at me and suddenly began tearing his clothes off.

"What's for *dinner*, Carol Lynn? Huh? What the *hell* have you *made* us for dinner *tonight*?"

"Why the same thing I serve for every meal. Every day. You silly. All the traditional Christmas dishes." Turning, I pointed at each individual dish. "Dressing. Sweet potatoes with tiny marshmallows. Cranberries. Green beans with pearl onions. Fresh rolls. And of course, hot cocoa and mulled cider to make our Christmas toasts."

Teddy bolted from the room. He grabbed the keys to the car and ran butt-naked out the front door, knocking over our life-sized Santa on his way out.

"We've got plum pudding for dessert," I called after him from the front door.

Teddy looked back at me and I could tell he was done. At that exact same moment, the bell in the kitchen rang and, in a cute coincidence, the Christmas turkey in the oven was done too.

Teddy jumped into the car, started up the engine, and backed out into the street. He didn't have far to go. We lived right by Pier nine-oh-nine, a real sturdy number just as strong as any bridge. Where it ends, it's a twenty foot drop to the old rock jetty.

Teddy got up enough speed so when he drove off the end of the pier, the car seemed to hang in the air for a fraction of an instant, before it nosedived with Teddy and crashed on the boulders below.

For the first time since Teddy moved in, Jonathon looked relaxed. He always pretended Teddy's bad manners didn't bother him, but animals know when someone can't be trusted.

Right now, I'm outdoors on the deck, the wind in my hair and the sun on my face. I'm taking pictures of the sea and of Jonathon digging in the sand. And of our Christmas trees. Our absolute favorite pictures will be made into postcards for Jonathon V and Sandra back in Texas.

After dinner tonight, I promised Jonathon I'd take him to a Christmas carol meet up that matches people and their furry friends with others who really do love Christmas all year long. We're looking forward to singing the carols everyone loves, starting with Jonathon's favorite, "We Wish You a Merry Christmas." For myself, I don't care if we sing, "Here Comes Santa Claus," or, "What Child is This?" My favorite is anything Christmas.

I've got a meeting lined up tomorrow for another man I met online at MenLeadWomenFollow.com. Of course, I'll only go out with him if he truly is the type of traditional man father would have approved of. Right now, this second, I'm recording my notes below mother's last words to me.

The Diary of Mimi Sinclair

Dearest Carol Lynn,

If you're reading this, your father has murdered me. It will look like an accident. Your mother married a greedy bastard, not an idiot. Because of his connections, we both know he'll get away with it.

Should you feel compelled to get justice for your old Mom—never be afraid to use a method that makes sense to your way of thinking. You are my unique, my original, my dearest Carol Lynn. I'll love you forever—
Mom

Carol Lynn – Progress Notes:
    Dinner for Daddy
    Joy for Greg
    Christmas for Teddy

The Ned I'm meeting tomorrow deserves something uniquely his own—I don't think anything says *Kill Me* quite like the eighties disco scene.

CASANOVA TAKES A HOLIDAY

NINA WACHSMAN

"WELCOME TO THE CONTINENTAL," SAID the footman, opening the carriage door.

Casanova exited first, ready to help the ladies descend, while the uniformed footman lent a hand to the older gentleman.

Giacomo Casanova looked away as the well-endowed woman leaned over, giving him a full view of her charms. For the third time. He did not like women who made such an effort to capture his attention. Unlike the other lady, whose lovely, white-gloved fingers intertwined with those of the young man beside her. Casanova imagined they were running away to elope and wished them luck; young love should always be indulged.

Inside, a lively looking older man, a Monsieur Bonnard, welcomed them again, and interviewed each in turn, writing their names in the hotel's ledger.

The mature lady introduced herself as the Contessa Maria di Antonini, a widow from Umbria. Monsieur Bonnaire gave her a deferential nod, but Casanova could tell the proprietor was as skeptical of the lady's title as he was.

Next was the elderly gentleman. "Reverend Isaiah Blackstone, originally from Bristol, staying two nights before continuing to Vienna."

Monsieur Bonnaire beamed at the young couple. "Madame and Monsieur Niccolo Foscarini. Such a lovely room I will have prepared for you. Your first time in Trieste?" As he entered their names, he gave them a good look. Noticing the clasped hands, he asked, "Newlyweds?"

The young man blushed more deeply than his bride, who answered for him, "Yes, only last week. We are so excited to visit Trieste. First our honeymoon, and then a bit of business, since we are to meet Niccolo's future employer here."

"You are quite young to already be married and beginning a new position. What type of work is it that you do?" asked the proprietor, looking at Niccolo over the rims of his glasses.

Niccolo's voice came out unnaturally high, but then he cleared his throat, and in a lower pitch he said, "I am to become the personal secretary of a famous man who is to visit here. I am to help him with his memoirs."

"Really? A famous man?" repeated the Contessa, batting her eyes coquettishly, "Oh, perhaps you can give us a little thrill and tell us his name?"

The young couple exchanged looks as if they were making a silent pact, and then said, "Casanova."

The older woman's laughter rang out like the clanging of a bell. "Why are you laughing?" asked the young lady. "Do you know him? Is he awful?"

The Contessa controlled her laughter and said, "May I introduce you then to your new employer? For he is Giacomo Casanova."

Knowing full well he had not hired a personal secretary, Casanova played along. "How extraordinary. We have been companions on this entire journey without recognizing each other."

The young man and his wife looked as if they had been struck by lightning. Casanova doffed his hat, and bowing, said, "It is a pleasure to meet you at last, Niccolo."

The Contessa gave him a cat-like smile, knowing they were all lying.

The proprietor became very tiresome, bowing and apologizing for not having recognized such a famous personage as Casanova. He asked if Casanova would like the chamber adjacent to the contessa's and gave a little wink as he pushed the key towards him, but Casanova shook his head, and politely requested another.

Monsieur Bonnaire promised to have hot water and fresh towels brought to their rooms immediately, and pointed out the dining room where their dinner would be served.

It was a lovely evening, and upon opening the shutters in his room, Casanova appreciated his view of the main square. Streetlamps had been lit, and couples strolled in and out of their spotlight. In the distance, a church bell tolled the hour, which was nine o'clock. It was nearly April, but the air still carried the winter's chill, and Casanova decided he must shut the window before he caught cold.

He was bothered by the Contessa. Not because of her vulgar overtures to him, but because he felt they had met before, but could not remember where or when.

Casanova was pleased by the dinner spread, especially since he did not have to pay for it. He was on holiday, but as a guest of an old Duke he had once encountered in Venice. The Duke had prevailed upon him to take his holiday in Trieste. Casanova had accepted the invitation, which promised fine accommodations and entertainment while he helped the Duke organize his extensive collection of pornography.

A mustachioed waiter appeared with an offer of dessert with hot chocolate. Everyone was eager to indulge in this delicacy, and soon a silver urn and Dresden china cups were brought before them. Enjoying the tantalizing aroma of the sweet chocolate, Casanova indulged in observing his fellow guests.

The Contessa did not have the airs of a born and bred aristocrat, but a professional, perhaps a *cortegena honesta*, an elite courtesan.

The cleric was quick to grab a cup of chocolate and took a sip, closing his eyes to savor its flavor. The Reverend Blackstone wore his collar as if he were unused to it and Casanova could tell by the Reverend's mannerisms, he was a man of the city rather than a country parsonage. Casanova imagined this fake pastor had dark dealings in Trieste and could possibly be a spy.

Contessa must have been having similar thoughts, but she was less introspective about her speculations, "Tell me, Mr. Blackstone, why have you come to Trieste? Surely there are no Church of England establishments for you to visit here?"

The Reverend did not reveal much in his answer. "You are correct. It is not on a clerical matter, but to visit a former colleague."

"Oh?" persisted the Contessa, "is your friend a smuggler, or perhaps a spy? Trieste is a known rendezvous spot for those who have secrets to trade or contraband to sell."

The Reverend gave her the most indulgent smile and asked, "And how is it that you, Contessa, would know of such things?"

Her titter of laughter was meant to deflect further questions. "What else is any woman of intelligence to do? We track the scent of scandal like bloodhounds, hoping it will enliven our dreary lives."

"How monotonous for you, if your imagination runs wild upon acquaintance with a simple parson." From the self-satisfied look on the Reverend's face, he seemed to be enjoying the lady's failure to get anything more out of him.

In Casanova's estimation, both the Reverend and the Contessa were hiding their identities, but what of the young couple?

The groom wore no ring, and the bride kept her ring finger from view. The youth seemed frisky and could not seem to stand still, while the girl's eyes flitted about as if it was her first time away from home. Casanova imagined they were childhood sweethearts escaping arranged marriages designed to separate them.

He decided to keep a protective eye on the couple, especially since the Contessa seemed a little too interested in them. She seemed to focus on the young lovers as if they were her prey.

Casanova sought to distract her and gave her the lewdest look he could muster.

Any woman would be flattered by this look, and the Contessa was no exception. She gave him an equally lustful smile and winked at him. He had been holding his breath, but when she turned to the waiter and asked for more chocolate, he exhaled.

"Some more chocolate for you too, my dears," offered the Contessa, and the two young people nodded. She beckoned to the waiter, and the gemstones on her fingers flashed with the reflection of the candlelight. Those rings! Now he remembered where he had seen this woman before. In recognizing her and her jewels, her intentions became clear.

The waiter returned with the last pot of hot chocolate and poured it for each of them. Casanova stretched out his arms and legs and yawned dramatically. "It is late, and the journey has been tiring."

Before he could rise, the Contessa put a hand on his arm and said, "Wait, let us finish our chocolate and enjoy the warmth of the fire for a few last moments. We have enjoyed each other's company for so long, and we may never see each other again."

Casanova leaned in closer to the Contessa and, putting a hand over one of hers, whispered, "Some of us may have other ways to warm our beds."

The Contessa's lips curved into a smile, but she licked her lips before passing a cup of chocolate to Niccolo. Before the young man could drink his, Casanova interrupted him, and asked, "I had been admiring your hat, Niccolo. Perhaps as a gesture of our new association you can let me try it on? I would like to have a similar one made if it suits me."

"Oh, I left it in our room. Shall I go and fetch it?" He put down his cup and was rising when the Contessa stopped him.

"I am sure it is not necessary." She waved at the young man to sit down. "I am certain it can wait until morning, can it not, Monsieur Casanova?"

Casanova smiled, not answering. The young woman rose. "I can go."

The Contessa twisted her rings and anger flashed momentarily in her eyes. "No, I insist. We must all finish our chocolate first."

Casanova waved his hands and acquiesced. "It can wait until tomorrow. The Contessa is most considerate, for if you were to leave now, your chocolate would become cold. The flavor is not the same then, is it?"

So they drank. The Reverend had pushed aside his empty cup, and the young couple were wiping their lips with napkins, when, the Contessa gave a gasp, and with a frozen look and bulging eyes, she leaned forward and fell face down onto the table.

Casanova was not surprised when the Reverend, after examining her, announced, "She is dead."

THE WAITER WAS WRINGING HIS hands, but the Reverend took charge, instructing him to find the proprietor and advising them all to leave the table. Casanova admired the false cleric's brisk efficiency.

As a cluster of officials hovered around the body, the Reverend slipped away. Swabbing his face with his handkerchief, he surprised Casanova with his observation. "Well, there is one dearly departed that will not be greatly mourned."

"You knew the 'Contessa'?" Casanova asked.

"I recognized her, though she has changed since she has posed for this." Like a magician, the Reverend flourished a card with a painted image from his sleeve.

Casanova raised his eyebrows. "Yes, it is she. Are you a collector?"

The Reverend smiled. "More of a purveyor. The Duke has quite a collection, which is why I have come to Trieste."

Casanova nodded. "You wear a good disguise for such pursuits. If you are stopped, no one will search you, and if they find any of your—er, goods—they would be likely to let it go. I have masqueraded as a cleric myself."

The Reverend stuffed the handkerchief and the picture into his sleeve and nodded. "No doubt we have much in common, including our destination. You are to catalogue the Duke's exotic collection, and I am to purchase from it. I will bid you goodnight, then, for I am certain we shall meet again soon."

IT WAS TIME TO DEAL with the young couple.

White-faced, they clung to each other by the fire. Despite its warmth, they were shivering, and tears were trickling down both of their cheeks.

"Young ladies, it is time to end the charade," Casanova said to the couple, who cringed at his words.

The young lady gave a loud sniff and wiped tears from her face. "Nicci, stay silent, and nothing will happen to us."

"The Contessa knew who you were, so you might as well share your story," said Casanova, "after all, I want to help you, while she was determined to kill you." He paused and was gratified at their gasps. "Well, perhaps not both of you, but certainly Nicci."

Nicci moaned, but his companion raised a hand meant to stop a confession. Nicci ignored her and said, "Monsieur, you are a believer in true love, and you make no judgement about who we give our hearts to, no?"

Casanova glanced from one to the other, and nodded. "You do love each other, that is obvious. But your masquerade is equally obvious."

Nicci blinked, trying to keep tears at bay, "Do you think the others noticed?"

"I am certain of it, which is why the Contessa met her end."

Nicci's hand covered her mouth to suppress a cry. Casanova's voice was firm. "Come with me. We should not discuss this here." Taking each by the arm, he guided them out of the dining room.

The way was clear as the three of them climbed the stairway. The proprietor had assigned his famous visitor to a large cozy chamber with the fire lit, and the bedclothes turned back. Casanova looked wistfully at the bed, but launched himself into the comfortable-looking chair beside the fire. The young couple, or rather the two young ladies, stood before him, heads lowered as if they were errant children, which in fact, they were.

"Well?"

Two tear-stained faces looked up at him, but one of them displayed defiance instead of shame. "We refuse to be separated. It is why we ran away—together. There is no shame in that, is there?"

"Not at all. I would have done the very same, " he admitted. "Did you know the woman who called herself 'Contessa'?

The two shook their heads. "We could never have met a woman like *her*," said Nicci, and then noticing his raised eyebrows, she explained. "Our families live in a castle outside of Umbria, though Beatrice's family owns the castle, and my family manages the vineyards. It is remote, and there are few guests who come to visit, and those mostly come to sample the wine."

"Until the Comte," said Beatrice, her nostrils flaring, "who was seeking more than my father's fine wine. He asked—no, demanded—me as his bride."

"Demanded?"

"My father owed a debt, and this man claimed he had the right to collect it. With last year's blight on part of the vineyard, the yield was not as it once was. My father could not pay the amount that had come due."

"So he traded his daughter instead," said Nicci, scowling.

"He had no choice," said Beatrice, and added, "but the grooms did not go after us, and he did not hinder our escape."

Their story was as he had suspected; he had heard it so many times before. He had also encountered the dead woman before, in a similar scenario. "Please, tell me the name of this Comte who pressed your father for your hand?"

"The Comte di Montevigliano."

Casanova felt exonerated. He had identified the false countess accurately. It was time he lifted the veil for his two young friends. "The usual accomplice of our false Contessa."

Two pretty mouths formed nearly perfect circles, and two sets of eyebrows were raised as high as they could go. Simultaneously they exclaimed, but in different phrases.

"False Contessa."

"Accomplice."

He gestured for them to be seated and, like obedient children, they perched together on a hassock nearby.

"At first, I did not recognize her, for she had changed her appearance. But when I caught sight of those rings, which are unique, it reminded me. It was in Venice, in the palazzo of a noble acquaintance. There was a young lady, the daughter of our host, who was quite accomplished at playing the spinet. She had been tutored by a young musician, also of my acquaintance. There was a performance, attended by this Comte di Montevigliano and a lady introduced as his step-sister. This time she was not a countess, but merely called Senora Allegra. Though she dressed tastefully, I did think her jewelry was vulgar, particularly the many large rings she wore, with their flashing gemstones. Not quite the thing for a woman of noble birth."

Beatrice brightened. "They *were* quite vulgar."

Casanova nodded. "But it was when she handed over the cup of chocolate that memory flashed clear. The rings, the very same I recalled seeing on the hands of the Comte's sister as she poured wine for the musician."

"And?" prompted Nicci, who had been unable to remain seated any longer.

"The young man suddenly rolled his eyes, and pitched forward, dead. Much like the lady tonight."

"She poisoned him!"

Casanova raised a warning finger. "He was poisoned, of that there was no doubt. In Venice, it is not uncommon for a guest to expire in such a manner. In the case of the musician, he had been known to engage in liaisons with many a married woman and betrothed young girl, so there were plenty of suspects. But I had caught a strange look on that woman's face as she poured the wine for the hapless man. Her nostrils were pinched with excitement, and she licked her lips. The very same thing the 'Contessa' did tonight, although when she noticed my observation, she covered it nicely by remarking on her love of chocolate."

"The chocolate was poisoned?" asked Nicci, as she abruptly sat down, "and she handed it to me."

"Then how is it that it was the Contessa who died?" asked Beatrice.

Casanova tented his fingers and smiled. "I can provide an easy answer. It was I who switched the cups."

Both young ladies started and raised a hand to their open mouths. "You . . . you . . . poisoned her?"

Casanova gave a sad smile. "No, my dears, she poisoned herself. Rings such as those of the false Contessa are easy to come by in Venice, long known as the capital of poison. The gaudy jewels cover repositories of poisons, easily accessed when pouring drinks."

"But how did you know which cup held the poison?"

Casanova enlightened them. "I am more known for my amorous adventures than for my observations. One day, I shall write my memoirs, and it shall be more evident. I had noticed a small chip in the gold trim on the cup the Contessa raised for Nicci. I created the distraction by asking after your hat and switched the cups."

"But why did she want to poison Nicci?"

"Your father had never seen the Comte before he arrived at your home, eh? As much as the lady is a false Contessa, so too is this Comte. The pair frequent the salons and casinos looking for old men with young daughters who would welcome a match with the 'Comte.' In Venice, the father undertook to verify the credentials of the Comte and his sister, and they disappeared. This duo learned of your father's debt from the real Comte, who had used it as a stake in gambling with them. They saw to it that they won the stake, and so began their plan to not just collect on the debt, but to capture the entire estate through marriage with Beatrice."

"But we got away," said Nicci.

"And the Contessa was dispatched after you to remove Nicci, the Comte's rival. She must have followed you from Umbria. Thankfully, her story ends in Trieste."

"But why did she wait until we arrived here in Trieste?" asked Beatrice.

"A distant city, where the Comte could easily claim you were his errant wife without being challenged. Then a quick ceremony and he whisks you back to the castle, where he now takes residence and charge of the vineyard. It is certain you and your father would not have survived for very long after that."

"Ghastly," said Nicci.

"Wait, do you anticipate the Comte's arrival?" Beatrice paled and grabbed his arm.

"It is a possibility," admitted Casanova, "though I would expect it would not be until tomorrow. For tonight, you two should be safe. Besides, he will not get far by challenging the famous Giacomo Casanova. The authorities do not suspect poison and the Contessa's death shall be deemed an unfortunate attack of the heart. If the Comte appears, I shall call him out as a fraud. Now perhaps we should retire for the evening. It has been such a long day. "

"We could not possibly go to sleep. Please let us spend the night here, with you."

Casanova's eyes took in the creaminess of skin, the flutter of long lashes and the trembling full lips of the two young women. He sighed, "If you insist."

He felt most welcome at The Continental.

Fire with Fire

Geneviève Goggin

THE SMOKE DESCENDS INTO THE valley like a raging river and Livia Sinclair must decide—evacuate, as she's been directed, or stay to find the missing man. Her mask is hardly taking the edge off and her eyes sting. The first lick of flames crests Copper Mountain. If the wind shifts to an easterly, Sea-to-Sky Park will be next on the fire's agenda to burn down BC's coastal mountains.

The radio crackles for the third time. "Come *in* Sinclair, what's your 10-20?" She can picture Atwater, the local police commander, his face purple with rage at being ignored by a lowly park biologist. She'd better answer before she finds herself knee-deep in probation hearings.

"I'm in C-loop. One camper is still unaccounted for—Chuck Armstrong, according to the registry."

"Time to go. 10-24. I repeat, 10-24. Do you copy?"

She copies, all right—Assignment Complete—barked at her in Atwater's classic way. She knows the type, was married to one for nineteen years. But a tourist is in the backcountry about to experience more adventure than he bargained for.

"He owes five bucks for last night's ice delivery. Revenue generation is management's priority, so . . ." Poking the bear isn't going to help, but she can't stop herself. Atwater gets under her skin.

"Livia Sinclair, get back to Incident Command Post. *Now.*" A different voice—Stephen Blackwell, the new park superintendent. Livia will face a heap of paperwork if she doesn't go back. Why risk everything for some guy who doesn't listen when he's told to stay put and wait for evacuation instructions? His sister, Denice, made it out fine, didn't even put up a fight. If Livia channeled Dr. Chang, he'd ask her if she's digging in her heels only because men are telling her what to do. They are *not* your ex, he'd say. Livia is not the person she was then.

"10-4. On my way back. Over and out."

Help me. I didn't mean it. Please let me go.

LIVIA WHIPS DOWN THE ROAD over ruts, dried and packed from the hottest spring on record. She's nauseous. The smoke is to blame. Not only the smoke—something else is making her unsteady. She's spent the last two years in therapy learning to follow her instincts. Now, one edict from on high, and she's running in the opposite direction.

When she arrives at the office, Felix—the one ranger who has her back when she speaks truth to power—accompanies her to the superintendent's office, where Atwater is still loitering. He should stick to his lane and evacuate the town. Yet, Blackwell tolerates his interference in park jurisdiction. No, he doesn't just tolerate police presence—the two men are tight for reasons Livia doesn't understand. As though to reaffirm their alliance, the park top dog pats the cop on the back, like some secret code.

"Livia, full report please," the superintendent says.

"Like I said over the radio, the whole campground is evacuated, except the one dude, but I've been ordered to let him die."

Felix shoots her a look. He's always trying to save her from herself, and she loves him for it, but enough is enough. Blackwell ignores Livia's outburst, reserving his wrath for later, no doubt. The man doesn't take kindly to being questioned publicly, or privately, for that matter.

The crew gathers around the table, and they pore over the huge map printed on the plotter for last year's mock emergency exercise. It was all theoretical then, but now, it's a question of life and death. Or in the case of Chuck Armstrong, death.

The superintendent taps the map. "Felix, you and the other rangers will load evacuees on the boats at the marina. The maintenance crew will go with Commander Atwater to help with the train evacuation in town." He flicks his hand toward the door like he's shooing flies out of the room.

"Livia, you're on the highway with the other biologists. Your job is to stop Vancouver weekend warriors from trying to drive through to Whistler. Good luck with that."

Highway. Great. She's being punished.

I can't breathe. Somebody help me. Please, I don't want to die . . .

LIVIA HEADS TO THE BASEMENT for traffic cones and high-viz vests. She's about to round the corner to the storage lockers when whispers stop her in her tracks. She inches forward, careful not to let her gear belt rattle.

"Should we search for him?" It's Commander Atwater, in his unmistakable husky voice Livia suspects is an act to make up for his diminutive stature.

"Livia looked," says the superintendent. What the hell is he on about? She didn't check past the confines of the campground.

"Plus," the superintendent adds, "he's a piece of shit."

"But he swears it wasn't him." Atwater's voice goes up an octave.

"You know damn well what guys like him are like. Greasy little man looking to cash in on a fungus and trashing everything in sight to get it."

The two men go quiet. Did they hear her? Livia backs away and slips into the locker room. She leans over the sink and pushes down the urge to puke. They gave her orders. Anything else is above her pay grade. A quick call to the camper's sister, and then she'll let it go.

I promise I won't go again. I just wanted to see if it was true. Please . . .

* * *

"I'VE BEEN WAITING FOR YOU people to call about my brother. The cop's ghosting me." Denice clears her throat. Livia waits, leaving room for the answer to her question about why they were camping. She learned that trick from watching her study animals—if you wait, they get used to you and show who they are.

"He wanted a quiet campout to celebrate my so-called graduation from eating-disorder school. Some present." She emits a guttural sound somewhere between a chuckle and a sob. "Please find him. He's the only family I've got."

"We're searching for him." Livia is a skilled liar. Had to be to survive her marriage. "Did your brother mention anything about a special mushroom?"

"He's always on about a cure to make me stop gorging. Last year, it was ground shark cartilage."

Livia waits again. Silence. More is coming, she knows it.

"Chuck means well, but what I need is for him to leave me be. But our parents left him in charge of the money, so . . ."

A tightness in her throat throws Livia off. Why do women let men— *beloved* men—tell them how they should exist?

I couldn't sit back and watch. I needed to try. Let me go!

LIVIA STANDS AT THE ROAD barricade with the other poor suckers stuck on highway duty. The boss was right about one thing; people are fervent about their 'right' to get places. Some are persistent *and* assholes—a winning combination.

"We're evacuating the region because of an uncontrolled forest fire," Livia tells a silver-haired man in a Lexus LX that costs more than her annual salary. "Please turn around." She's on autopilot, repeating the same obvious message over and over.

"Just heading to Whistler for business," says the guy behind the wheel, in the way men of a certain age declare their intentions as fact. "I won't stop on my way through." His concession, such as it is.

"Nope," Livia says. She's run out of polite public servant patience. "You won't be stopping, because you won't be going through."

That wipes the charming smile off his face.

"You don't have to be a bag about it."

"Apparently I do." Now she's done it—crossed the line. This is a crisis, no time to argue with privilege.

He revs his engine like he's going to burst through the barrier. Then he complies. He's so pissed, his three-point turn becomes a seven-pointer. In a final show of fury, he flips her the bird and peels out, tires screeching, horn blaring. Livia waves him goodbye. Good boy.

She shouldn't care about saving jerks like him, but she does. Because it's her job. Isn't it their job to save everyone? Why were Atwater and Blackwell skulking around, talking about Chuck Armstrong like he's a dead man walking? But she has her orders, the chain of command and all that bullshit.

How many times has she done as she's told—by her dad, her ex, her boss, all of them men—only to hurt others, to lose a bit of herself? Too bloody many. She won't stand by and do nothing. Not anymore.

"Guys, I'm going back to find the camper. Cover me."

I'm going to die. I'm dying! Please, someone . . . anyone . . . I'll stop.

LIVIA HAS AN IDEA WHERE to look for the tourist. She finds the GPS pin she'd set last year on a hike to the chanterelle patch east of C-loop. A Google search would have given him a starting point, but he'd have to be clueless to think others haven't already picked over the area.

Going up is risky—the winds and fire have a secret pact to surprise her at every turn. She wishes she'd grabbed more PPE. All she has is her helmet, goggles, and mask. No Kevlar clothes for her. Whatever. If she doesn't find Chuck, she'll go back to road rage central. In and out in an hour.

Trudging up the almost imperceptible path, Livia wonders if Dr. Chang was full of it. Maybe she has a God complex and *should* be following directions like a conforming little government worker-bee. What if she gets stuck up here?

The trail narrows and she loses the way. She backtracks and finds trampled moss—he must be up here. The sky darkens. Thickening smoke hugs the mountain. Livia stops. Here it comes—the dreaded easterly. The intensity of the heat ratchets up a notch. It's because she's hiking up the gully at full tilt. It's *not* the fire. Can't be. She checks her GPS to make sure she's still pointing toward the chanterelles. Almost there.

I won't take the mushrooms . . . I promise. . . HELP!

"ANYBODY UP HERE?" LIVIA BLARES her bear horn as she walks around the chanterelle clearing. The rumor of a new miracle diet mushroom has brought all kinds of shady characters looking for it, illegally harvesting everything else along the way. Livia's looked everywhere for it multiple times—no luck.

A gust makes the trees creak. Piercing crackles join the cacophony—the fire is near. She shuts her eyes and catches her breath, but her heart won't slow.

That's when she hears it. A moan. She turns around, trying to determine the origin. A cough comes from the opening beyond the hemlock stand, and she runs toward it. There. Slumped against a tree. She reaches the slouched figure and kneels over the semi-conscious man. His hands are cuffed around a towering red alder. What the hell? These are not sex-toy cuffs. They're standard issue, the kind both the police and the rangers use.

"Wake up. Snap out of it. Do you have the key?" It's a ridiculous question, but it's all she's got. Spontaneous explosions go off as the parched woods ignite in patches all around her. Although she's heard of this phenomenon, nothing's prepared her for the panic as the inferno closes in.

"Who did this to you?" Chuck doesn't respond, doesn't stir. Livia jerks at the handcuffs. They won't give. She tries to squeeze his massive hand through the hole, but it's one thumb-width too thick to slip through. She drops the limp arm, and something falls from his hand. A tiny brown mushroom she's never seen before. Could it be the enigmatic fungus causing a stir in the nutraceutical world? She pockets it to examine under a microscope later. If there *is* a later.

No time. Either she leaves him, or she pulls out her field knife and releases him from the cuffs. . . and from his thumb.

I'm sorry . . .

BEEPS AND HISSES FILL THE room. The pungent blend of disinfectant and flowers sets Livia into a coughing fit, and she yanks the tubes from her nostrils.

"Steady, Liv." He's here. Felix is always there when you need him, when *she* needs him. She forces her eyes open through gummy ointment.

"How is he?" Livia's voice is rough like a smoker's.

"I'm in awe that you used the firefighter's carry to drag the guy down the mountain," Felix says.

"Is he OK?"

He shakes his head. "I'm sorry. Smoke inhalation."

Livia closes her eyes, closes her heart. Felix puts a hand on her bandaged arm.

"The mushroom?" she asks.

"I have it. I didn't tell anyone." He pauses. "The superintendent's been arrested. Atwater threw him under the bus after we got your picture of the handcuff's serial number. And Atwater's under review. All thanks to you."

"A man died, thanks to me."

Felix knows better than to contradict her.

* * *

LIVIA SITS AT A COLD fire pit. The campfire ban is still on, but she's seen enough fire to last her a lifetime, even as the fall chill seeps into her bones. Denice passes her a s'more she's made over the Coleman flame. It's Livia's first vacation all year, and she's never stayed in her own park's campground before.

"Camping trip, Take Two," Denice says. "I miss Chuck, you know. But without him, I'm finally free." She says no more and eats her fourth s'more. At this rate, they'll both be on sugar highs for hours.

When it gets dark, and mushrooms have faded into the night, Livia will grab the telemetry gear and show Denice the bats. Misunderstood, vilified creatures. Beautiful as they are.

I can breathe. I am who I am. Livia and Dr. Chang say so. It's not my fault the superintendent didn't report his cuffs missing.

Two if by Sea

Linda Ryea Richard

"Luanne, open up!" My sister's urgent shout, accompanied by her pounding on the cabin door, jolted me from my stupor.

"Lucinda?" Groggy and struggling with nausea, I fumbled to open the lock. "What in heaven's name? Are you alright?"

"It's gone," Lucinda moaned as she burst into our stateroom, stumbling to regain her balance as the Caribbean Princess rolled beneath us. "I don't know how it happened. One minute it was there and then . . . I can't believe I lost it."

I stared at her, dumbfounded. I didn't have a clue what she had lost—except maybe her mind.

Lucinda's face was deathly pale, her grip clammy as she grabbed my arm. Her nails dug into my wrist as she gave it a good shake. "You need to help me search for it."

"Search for what?" I wrenched myself loose and rubbed the crescent-shaped marks she'd left behind.

"Greta's gorgeous ruby and diamond bracelet I wore tonight. The white gold cuff with those dazzling red Burmese rubies? You could buy a small nation with what that thing's worth. Oh, why didn't I listen to Greta? She said not to breathe on it, let alone touch it . . ."

"Greta?" Greta Baumgartner, who works at my sister's realty agency, had an on-again, off-again friendship with Lucinda. The last I knew, they were on the outs. "Why would she let you borrow her jewelry?"

"Well, she doesn't exactly know about it. That's why you need to help me look," she begged, her frantic gaze darting about the compact room.

"You stole the bracelet?"

"Borrowed." She gave me a not-so-gentle shove. "C'mon, get dressed."

I grumbled as I wriggled back into the sundress I'd worn that day. Why I'd let my sister rope me into this trip was a mystery. I'd had doubts about it from the minute she'd burst into my kitchen, waving the ocean liner's brochure under my nose. But, as Lucinda eagerly pointed out, it wasn't every day she snagged "Realtor of the Year" and scored two free cruise vouchers. With my husband, Bud, away on a long-planned fishing trip to Maine, relaxing on deck while sipping complimentary cocktails sounded lovely. Then I thought about how queasy I can get kayaking our Vermont lakes when the wind comes up.

"These big ships all have stabilizers." My twin sister's retort made me feel like a dumb homebody. "A couple tabs of Dramamine, and you'll be right as rain."

Baloney. I'd been green as a frog since we hit open water. You'd think, after sixty years, I'd be less gullible. And despite being Lucinda's twin, you might expect our personalities to be more alike. But nope, not a chance. The only thing we share is our outward appearance. Mama says when we were first born, the only way to tell us apart was the birthmark on my neck. Bud says it came from Lucinda kicking me on her way out. He's probably right.

"Greta paid a fortune for that showstopper," Lucinda wailed, wringing her hands. "I just have to find it!"

I willed my unsettled stomach to cooperate as she tugged me along the winding corridors toward the elevator. "What were you thinking?" I demanded between panted breaths. "You had no business taking that bracelet."

"Borrowing," she repeated. "Besides, Greta rarely wears it. She keeps it in my office safe because she doesn't trust her cleaning lady."

"Doesn't she have a safety deposit box?"

Lucinda looked at me, puzzled. "Why pay for that when I have a perfectly good vault? Besides, we borrow each other's things all the time. I still haven't gotten back the pearl earrings I lent her for the realty gala."

"Pearls aren't on the same level as diamonds and rubies," I pointed out.

"No, but I thought I could slip it back undetected. Greta would be none the wiser."

I stopped in my tracks, my jaw dropping. "You honestly thought that would work? When has anything ever gotten past Greta?"

Lucinda waved me off and led me into the elevator. She fussed with her hair in the mirrored walls, the same walls that showed my green gills. "When do you last remember wearing the bracelet?" I asked.

"At the Starlight Supper Club," she said. "The cuff kept snagging my shawl when I cracked open my lobster. I definitely had it on during the floor show, too."

A wave of self-pity shot through me. "There was a floor show?"

"Was there ever! It's too bad you decided to turn in early, Luanne. You would have loved seeing all those talented dancers in their glittering costumes. It was like a *Dancing with the Stars* episode on the ship!"

"I wasn't sleeping," I mumbled. "I was dry heaving in the bathroom."

"Well, whatever you were doing, it's a shame you missed it. The lobster was to die for."

I bit my tongue, deciding further sniping wouldn't help. The sooner we found that bracelet, the sooner I could crawl back into bed and pray for a quick death. "Did you check under the table? It may have fallen onto the floor."

She shook her head. "I tried but couldn't see very well in the dark. And I didn't want the others getting the wrong idea."

"It couldn't hurt to check again. Which table were you at?"

"The same one as yesterday." She sighed. "I hate assigned seating. We have nothing in common with those oddballs they paired us with."

I pictured the fellow passengers we'd shared meals with the last few evenings. Reginald and Muffy Winthrop, whose pompous Boston accents grated on my last nerve. Adrian Bellini, a self-proclaimed ladies' man, whose suffocating cologne aggravated my nausea. And sweet old Edna Bailey, who was blowing every dime of her late husband's insurance payout on a once-in-a-lifetime sea voyage.

We picked up the pace, Lucinda striding toward the ornate two-story lounge on Deck 4. Glancing down at my loose cotton sundress and flip-flops, I felt ridiculously out of place. Well, so be it. Figuring out what happened to Greta's bracelet was more important. If we didn't recover that piece before the ship returned to Miami, Lucinda would be up to her neck in serious hot water.

At the entrance, her head swiveled left and right like a surveillance camera as she assessed each passenger. The Winthrops were mamboing across the dance floor. Adrian Bellini, the smooth-talking charmer, stood at the bar, his eyes scanning the room for potential targets. Mrs. Bailey sat alone at the table, her gaze distant as she sipped her wine, seemingly lost in thought.

"I wouldn't put it past those hoity-toity Winthrops to swipe my bracelet," Lucinda said with a glare in their direction.

Greta's bracelet, I silently corrected. Aloud, I said, "With their fortune? I doubt Mrs. Winthrop needs or even wants more jewelry. She probably has more expensive baubles than Princess Kate."

"In your dreams," Lucinda scoffed. "Did you see that gaudy necklace she's wearing? Those gems are as fake as her husband's toupee."

I peered closer at the giant stones draped across Muffy's chest. They did dazzle. But Lucinda rolled her eyes derisively.

"Oh, c'mon, Luanne. Wake up and smell the coffee. Their pretend accent didn't fool you, did it? And what kind of name is Muffy, anyway?" she huffed. "It sounds like something you'd name your cat."

It was just like Lucinda to fling around wild accusations without any proof. More likely, my featherbrained sister had visited the loo, removed the bracelet to wash up, and absentmindedly left it behind. It wouldn't be the first time. Bud had torn apart the pipes under our sink a few months ago to retrieve one of her rings.

"Wait here," she directed, casting a pitying glance at my wrinkled dress. She swirled her lace shawl around her bare shoulders and sashayed across the lounge in her crimson silk jumpsuit, stilettos clicking a path in Edna Bailey's direction.

From my relegated spot near the entry, I watched her chat with the silver-haired woman. Edna fingered the lapel of the same wool jacket she had worn last night as she listened to whatever nonsense Lucinda was spewing. I'd thought at the time that the garment was heavier than I'd want to wear, and decided that since Edna was a toothpick, she probably felt cold in the air-conditioned space. When my sister lifted the pristine tablecloth to brazenly peer underneath, Edna responded with astonishment—eyebrows rocketing upwards, lips frozen in a startled O.

Should I rescue poor Edna? I was still mulling it over when Adrian

Bellini stepped away from the bar. He swiped one hand through his slicked-back hair before sauntering in Lucinda's direction. Oh, no. We had more important things to do than deal with that letch. I raised one hand to catch my sister's attention. When that didn't work, I started waving my arms like I was directing a plane to the gate. That did the trick. Lucinda barreled back to the entryway, practically knocking people out of her way.

"Don't look now," I said, "but Adrian Bellini is heading this way."

We both gave subtle glances in the playboy's direction. He moved stealthily through the crowd like a predatory lion, staring at us as if we were injured antelope ripe for the picking.

"Ugh, so sleazy," Lucinda said with an eye roll. "He looks like a gigolo in those gold chains and silk shirts. Probably makes a living scamming lonely widows out of their savings. Act natural and follow my lead."

"Good evening, ladies." Adrian's voice was oily smooth. His gaze lingered a moment too long on the chunky gold braid draped across Lucinda's collarbone. "I'm so glad you decided to rejoin the festivities. It's Melinda, isn't it?"

"Lucinda," she corrected. "And my sister, Luanne."

"I prefer Annie," I said.

"Annie," he repeated before turning to Lucinda. "And should I call you Lucy?"

She grimaced in response.

"Lucinda it is." Bellini reached his arm around her in an overly familiar gesture. "It's a shame to have two such beautiful women standing here alone. Come join me for a cocktail."

Before Lucinda could react, I shoved his hand off and stepped forward, planting myself as a barrier between them. "No, thank you. We were leaving."

His dark eyes flashed briefly before that smug smile reappeared. "Why would you want to do that? Good music, great company—"

"Look, Romeo," I said. "We're not interested in having drinks with you tonight—or any other night. Now, do yourself a favor and move on."

Bellini reeled back, unaccustomed to rejection. I watched him regain his composure before conceding defeat and slinking off.

Lucinda tilted her head, a smile playing on her lips. "Well, looks like meek little Annie Taisley finally grew herself a backbone."

I knew Lucinda was just teasing, but I also detected a measure of pride in her voice. Even as kids, when I truly was "Little Annie Taisley," my bold twin had taken on the role of protector. I'd been a timid child, too afraid to stand up to the freckle-faced bully next door. But not Lucinda. When she'd caught sight of him chasing me with a garter snake, hellfire blazed in my sister's eyes. She'd stuck Dad's baseball bat under Billy Jenkins' freckled nose and threatened to pound his shiny red bike into scrap metal if he so much as looked my way again.

Now, as the dark-haired man disappeared into the crowd, a swell of self-satisfaction rose in my chest. I'd stood my ground without Lucinda's help. Empowered, I pointed to our right. "How about the ladies' room? Did you go in there tonight?"

Lucinda shrugged but led me down the softly lit hall. A gentle piano melody floated from embedded ceiling speakers as we pushed through the door. A woman with a cloud of red curls stood at a sink, eyes closed as she swayed to the music.

Lucinda's gaze narrowed on the glint of metal about her wrist. "Hold it right there!" she proclaimed, holding up one hand theatrically.

The woman appeared stunned. "P-pardon me?"

"Your left arm. Show it to me."

"I don't understand. Why—"

Lucinda grabbed the woman's arm, making her whimper in fright. As soap bottles toppled and water dripped onto the tile floor, my sister brought her face close to the bracelet, squinting. "Well, hell," she said, realizing her mistake. "It's a medical alert bracelet."

Mortified, I shoved Lucinda aside. While she checked the stall she'd used earlier, I helped steady the shaken woman. "Please forgive my sister. She lost a valuable piece of jewelry this evening and is upset." At this, I threw a pointed glare in Lucinda's direction.

"I . . . I tried to explain," the woman stammered. "I have allergies."

"You practically scared that poor woman to death!" I chastised Lucinda as we beat a hasty retreat.

"Oh please, she'll live," Lucinda said. "Unless she eats shellfish. Then it's a crapshoot."

"Okay, think back," I said, raising my voice to carry over the swell of the music from the lounge. "Where else did you go this evening? Did you visit the bar?"

"No, I drank champagne." She pointed to the elaborate golden sculpture to our right, stacked with rows of glistening crystal flutes arranged in a glittering pyramid. A sommelier, looking sharp in his black tuxedo, replenished the pyramid to keep it pristine. With a flick of his wrist, he popped the cork on a magnum and deftly poured the bubbling golden fizz into two flutes. Lucinda paused mid-step and, polite as a minister, asked me, "Would you like some?"

I choked down the bile rising in my throat. "I don't think so."

"Listen." She poked me with her elbow. "I have a plan to get the bracelet back."

I had a bad feeling about this. "What kind of plan?"

Lucinda leaned in and whispered her idea into my ear with a knowing smile.

"Are you insane?" I rocked back on my heels. "That's never going to work. Besides, you don't even know whether the bracelet was lost or stolen. Someone might find it and turn it in. You did report it to the Ship Security Officer, didn't you?"

"Do you think I'm an idiot? That's the first thing I did when I noticed it was gone. The SSO took down the details but didn't seem hopeful of it turning up. Now, get moving."

"Lucinda," I protested weakly. "I *really* don't want to do this. I don't feel well."

"Take some more Dramamine."

I dragged myself back to our stateroom, feeling I was pulling the ship's anchor behind me with every exhausted step. After changing into a slinky black dress, I opened the small velvet box Lucinda had stashed among her unmentionables. I shook my head, gazing at the sparkling centerpiece she facetiously dubbed "The Rock." Pure zirconia, of course, but no one could tell the difference from a distance.

One final glance in the mirror and my spirits sank. Below my neck, I looked good; from my pasty face up—death warmed over. Definitely not Lucinda's vision for bait. I took a fortifying breath before teetering back to the lounge in my toe-pinching heels. Time to find my scheming sister.

As planned, Lucinda stood chatting with the Winthrops, the incident in the restroom long since forgotten. She tapped one foot in time to the music as the older couple glided back toward the dance floor.

"The ring's too big," I complained, joining her.

"Doesn't matter. Just wave it around so everyone can see it."

I reluctantly raised my hand, while praying that the loose ring didn't fly off. "This is stupid."

"It'll work," Lucinda assured. "We're going to catch that sticky-fingered crook red-handed, and when we do, I hope the captain throws him in the brig."

I scanned the room while making a show of readjusting the jeweled comb I'd shoved into my messy updo. My gaze caught on a tall, broad-shouldered man hovering near the stage, keenly surveying the crowd. "Is that the SSO?" I whispered to Lucinda.

"Did you find your bracelet, dear?"

I spun around at the unexpected voice. Unfortunately, so did Lucinda. Our heads cracked together with a dull clunk, sending a wave of dizziness through me. The room spun as I lost my balance, arms windmilling as my heels skidded from under me. I crashed into the glittering champagne tower like a human wrecking ball.

The flutes shattering on the parquet dance floor drowned my screech of alarm. I landed flat on my back amid puddles of bubbly, my dress soaked and my pride destroyed. Though my ears were ringing, I swear the crowd gave a collective gasp.

"Lord love a duck." Lucinda exclaimed as more of the tart bubbly dripped onto my face. "Are you okay?"

My nose wrinkled at the overwhelming yeasty stench. I coughed and wheezed while carefully struggling to sit upright amidst the shards of glass. Some vacation this had turned out to be. Not only was I seasick, but now I had an aching back and throbbing head. And I blamed Lucinda for every bit of it.

"You poor dear." Edna fussed over me, dabbing my drenched, bedraggled dress with a handful of linen napkins. "Just look at you; you're a mess."

As she leaned toward me, the old dear's wool jacket gaped open. My eyes widened when I spotted the compartments cleverly stitched into the garment's inner lining. Poking from one was a loop of a pearl necklace. Another contained a man's pocket watch. Why, that piece looked like the family heirloom Reginald Winthrop had been wearing last night. And that glint of gold. Was it Greta's missing bracelet?

Oh. My. God. Sweet Edna Bailey was a pickpocket!

The security officer clamped a hand around Edna's thin arm. Lucinda snatched the gold cuff from the jacket's inner lining. My sister's eyes blazed with triumph as she held the bracelet aloft, the Burmese rubies glowing like fiery embers in the chandelier light.

Tilting her head to one side, she smiled at me, still sprawled on the floor in a sea of sticky champagne. "Well, what do you know, Luanne?" she said smugly. "I captured the thief. I told you my plan would work."

Classic Lucinda. I hate it when she gloats.

Mimosas, Mansions, and a Kidnapped Maltese

Bonnie Finn

"Should we have another mimosa?" I asked my friend Quinn.

"We'd be foolish not to." She pushed her hair out of her eyes. "But we should order something to eat too."

Although we were both blonde, Quinn's hair was straight and silky, while mine was curly and far too often frizzy. We both wore a size 8, but Quinn looked like she walked right out of a fashion magazine. I tended to look like I had just rolled out of bed.

We had decided to vacation in Newport, Rhode Island, to celebrate the publication of my third mystery book, and were sitting by the pool at the Blue Door Resort. We'd had nothing but sun for the past two days with temperatures in the mid-eighties during the day and seventies at night.

Beaches, Gilded Age mansions, delicious seafood. What's not to love?

Everything about Newport itself has been fantastic. For privacy, the cottages were situated so that one couldn't see any others. Despite the available air conditioning, we kept our windows open at night to hear the waves while falling asleep. Apparently, the woman in the cottage nearest ours kept her windows open too, and she brought her dog. And it barks. Yips, really. Usually, we're both dog lovers, although I prefer cats. I have nothing against dogs unless they disturb my beauty sleep, which this one has done for the past two nights.

I waved our waiter over and asked for another round of mimosas and a pastry basket.

"Right away," he said. "My name is Mike, and I'm pleased to serve you today. What brings you ladies to Newport?"

"Abbie just had her third book published, and we're celebrating," Quinn said.

"Congratulations," Mike said. "What do you write?"

"Mysteries," I replied. "My pen name is Abbie Dubois."

"Oh my god," he squealed. "You're THAT Abbie Dubois? I *love* your books. I've got both of them."

"Thanks so much. If you bring them in, I'd be happy to sign them for you."

Loud voices interrupted the peace of the pool. I noticed a teenager—maybe seventeen, with a bad case of acne—a few tables from ours. He was with his parents.

"This place is so boring," he complained loudly. "There's nothing to do. I told you I wanted to go to Cabo, not stupid Newport."

"Dammit, Sam, be quiet." The father banged his fist on the table. "At least try and act as if you're enjoying this trip. It's costing me a fortune."

"I don't care how much money you spent. I'm still bored," the kid said. "At least in Cabo, I could drink."

"If you can come up with the money to go to Cabo, we'll go."

"How much? I'll use my trust fund."

"It would be fifty thousand for all of us to go, and you're not allowed to go into your trust fund until you're twenty-five. And I'll raise that age to thirty if you don't behave."

The kid rolled his eyes and sighed dramatically, but the threat quieted him. Mike brought us another round of mimosas, a basket of muffins, croissants, and Danish, and a large bowl of cut-up fruit.

I nodded toward the entrance. "Do you see who just walked in?"

"Oh, my goodness," Quinn said. "Isn't that the woman in the cottage next to ours?"

"And her little dog, too." Mike imitated the wicked witch in The Wizard of Oz.

The tall, regal-looking woman wore a white caftan and large dark glasses. Her white hair was perfectly coiffed, her makeup flawless. She held a pink jeweled leash with a sweet-looking Maltese scurrying beside her. Even from this distance, I could see the elaborate pink rhinestone collar and the pink bow on top of the dog's fluffy head. One of the hotel staff followed behind her, carrying a hot-pink dog bed. As the woman sat in a chaise lounge near us, the staff member placed the bed at the woman's feet.

Mike leaned in and whispered, "That's Mrs. Carlyle. She's a regular. Comes every few months and brings Coco, the wonder dog, with her every time."

Quinn selected a lemon poppyseed muffin from the basket. "I didn't think the hotel allowed pets."

"Normally, we don't," Mike said. "But Mrs. Carlyle is an exception. She's richer than Zeus, even by Newport's standards. I call Coco the wonder dog, because it makes me wonder why the rich do what they do. She insists on imported bottled water for the dog, and the staff has to walk Coco and pick up her messes. The dog and Mrs. Carlyle both get spa treatments every afternoon. She even has our chef make her homemade dog biscuits. Not only that, but she never closes her bedroom window because 'Coco likes fresh air.' She just adjusts the thermostat to keep the cottage comfortable. What a waste. Whenever she sleeps, she takes out her hearing aids, so *she* never hears the dog barking its head off. Everyone on staff hates her."

"That dog is treated better than most people," I said.

"You said it," Mike replied. "It doesn't matter that the little beast barks that infuriating bark. She's even bitten some staff members. We smile and nod and take whatever abuse Mrs. Caryle doles out because she tips well, not to mention we'd get fired if we didn't."

He went over to Mrs. Carlyle, giving the pooch a wide berth.

"I guess complaining about the dog's barking won't do any good," Quinn said.

"Doesn't sound like it." I took a bite of a chocolate croissant. "And it doesn't sound like Mike and the rest of the staff like the little ankle-biter much, either."

I glanced up to see Mike again, looking peeved. As he passed our chairs, he whispered, "That damn woman and her damn dog will be the death of me. I have to go downtown and get Coco breakfast from a restaurant. Downtown Newport is crawling with tourists. It's going to take hours."

"Poor Mike, I wouldn't want to be in his position." I sipped my mimosa and watched a middle-aged man sporting a pencil-thin mustache approach Mrs. Carlyle.

He bent down to pet Coco, who nipped at him. He pulled his hand away before she made contact.

"She's just as cute as can be," he said. "And how is Coco Chanel Carlyle, my favorite Maltese, today?"

"Wishing, like her owner, not to be disturbed." Mrs. Carlyle picked up a book—the universal sign for "go away."

"I'm so sorry, Mrs. Carlyle. I'm just a sucker for cute little puppies." He placed a business card on her table. "It's so good to see you here again. Now, if there's anything you need, anything at all, you just let me know, and I'll come running."

He finally took the not-so-veiled hint and headed back to the main building.

"I wonder what she would have done if he hadn't gone." Quinn popped the remainder of her muffin into her mouth.

"Probably order the staff to behead him."

"Do you lovely ladies need anything else?" Mike was adorable, but he had the unnerving habit of seeming to appear out of nowhere. "I wanted to check in with you to make sure you're all set before I go."

"This was perfect," Quinn said. "Thanks."

"Mike, who was that man talking to Mrs. Carlyle just now?"

"That's Victor Lockwood. He's our head of security, although you'd think his job was to suck up to Mrs. Carlyle and that mangy mutt."

After finishing breakfast, we decided to visit one of the mansions. We followed the winding path to our cottage, changed, and called an Uber to take us to The Marble House. We spent a delightful afternoon touring the "summer cottage" William Vanderbilt built in the late 1800s.

Upon our return to the hotel lobby, we spotted Mrs. Carlyle weeping uncontrollably. Standing next to her, Mr. Oliver, the hotel manager, patted her shoulder.

"Coco means everything to me," she sobbed. "She's my *baby*. You simply must find her. Where is that blasted security man? He's been hounding me all week, probably looking for a tip. But now that I need him, where is he?"

Quinn and I exchanged glances.

Mrs. Carlyle spotted us and hurried over. "You were sitting next to us this morning. Have you seen my little Coco?"

"No, we haven't," I replied. "We've been gone most of the afternoon."

"We'll let you know if we see her," Quinn said.

Mrs. Carlyle thanked us and accosted the next arrivals to learn if they'd seen her fur baby.

"Do you want to go out somewhere for dinner or eat in one of the restaurants here?" Quinn asked.

"Let's try the restaurant in the main lodge. I peeked at the menu, and they have a lobster mac and cheese I'm dying to try."

We changed and followed the maze-like path to the restaurant. To our surprise, Mike was once again our waiter.

"Do you work twenty-four hours a day?" I asked.

"I'm covering for Carrie, one of our massage therapists. Coco Chanel bit her this afternoon during her massage. Carrie refuses to come back to work until Mrs. Carlyle and her dog leave."

"I don't blame her in the least," Quinn said.

"This was obviously before the pup went missing," I said. "When exactly did Mrs. Carlyle notice she was gone?"

"They have the same routine every day," Mike said. "After lunch here, they go to the spa, and then return to their cottage for a nap. When Mrs. Carlyle woke up, the dog was gone and sitting in that pink dog bed was a ransom note for fifty-thousand dollars. She's to leave the money in her cottage tomorrow and then head out somewhere for the afternoon. She told our manager, who called an emergency staff meeting."

"Hmmm," I said.

Quinn looked at me and shook her head. "I know that look, and it has never meant anything good. What are you up to?"

"Mike, how long have you worked here?"

"I've been here since we opened six years ago."

"So, you must know the staff pretty well. Do you think Carrie could have taken Coco?"

"Possible, but I don't think so. After I took her to the hospital to have the bite taken care of, I dropped her at her apartment. I found out about the dog the moment I got back. I stopped at Starbuck's on my way, so I suppose she *could* have snatched the dog while I was there. Starbucks was unusually busy, but still . . ."

"What about the other staff?"

"Maybe," Mike said. "On the one hand, Mrs. Carlyle's a pain in the wazoo, but she tips us all well when she leaves. On the other hand, who knows what someone might do if they really needed money?"

"Speaking of needing money," Quinn said. "How about that kid who was whining about going to Cabo?"

"Good thought," I said. "It might just be a coincidence that his father challenged him to come up with the same fifty grand that the ransom note demanded. Mike, where could he stash the dog so no one can hear it?"

"No one could hear it in any of the cottages provided the windows are closed and the A/C is on. And the parents are staying in a different cottage than their son. If the kid gave the dog a tranquilizer, that could keep her quiet."

That seemed a stretch to me, but then again, the dog had disappeared while Mrs. Carlyle was sleeping, and that sounded like something a kid might pull off. "What about the security guy? How long has he been working here?"

"It's Victor Lockwood's first season."

"There's something about him I don't like," I said. "He's too smarmy. Are there a lot of crimes here at the resort?"

"We've had a few thefts here the past month or so—nothing major, some jewelry left at one of the tables when a guest went swimming. AirPods. Petty cash. Nothing more serious than that."

"Are you working tomorrow?" I asked.

"Yeah, I'm on all week."

"Come find us in the morning if you want to help us on an adventure."

"I'm in!"

"Abbie," Quinn said. "What are you planning?"

"I'm not a hundred percent sure yet, but I'm working on it."

The next morning, I outlined my plan to Quinn, who was dubious, but game. We went to the pool and staked out a table. We'd barely sat down before Mike appeared, bubbling with excitement.

"You'll never guess what's happened," he whispered. "I just brought Mrs. Carlyle to the bank where she withdrew fifty thousand in cash."

"I have a brilliant idea that just might catch a dog-napper," I said. "We persuade Mrs. Carlyle to let me hide in her cottage. Whoever comes into the cottage after she leaves is the dog-napper."

"I don't know, Abbie," Quinn said. "This isn't one of your books. It could be dangerous."

"I'll bring my pepper spray," I said. "It'll be fine."

Mike suggested we use our cell phones to keep in contact.

"We'll need to be quiet, so text only," I said. "No calls. Now we need to get Mrs. Carlyle on board."

"I doubt it'll take much," Quinn said. "She sounds desperate to get Coco back. But how do you get into her cottage without being seen?"

"I can help with that," Mike said. "At lunchtime, I'll bring lunch to her cottage. We'll let it be known that she's too upset to eat in the restaurant like she usually does. We have a big service cart with a shelf on the bottom where you can hide. I'll cover the cart with a tablecloth and bring her lunch and you into the cottage. Nobody will suspect a thing."

"You're a genius," I said. "Now, let's go convince Mrs. Carlyle."

Five minutes later, Mike, Quinn, and I knocked on Mrs. Carlyle's cottage door.

Quinn was right—it didn't take long to convince Mrs. Carlyle to let me hide in her cottage and wait for the dog-napper. Not only did she want Coco back, but she wanted to draw and quarter whoever had taken her pet.

"Let's go over it one more time," I said. "Mike will bring your lunch to your cottage in one of those service carts at 11:30, with me hiding on the bottom shelf. Mrs. Carlyle will leave thirty minutes later and go to our cottage, where she will hang out with Quinn. That way, it looks like the cottage is empty.

"Mike will go back to work to avoid any suspicion and keep an eye on as many people as he can, staff and guests. If he sees or hears anything suspicious, he'll text us to let us know. I'll hide in the bathroom and wait for whoever has Coco to come get the ransom money. When they do, I'll text both of you, and you'll call for help."

I looked at the others to see if there were any questions.

Mike did. "What will you do if they see you? You're not a cop. You could get hurt."

"Whoever took Coco is just out for a quick buck. They're not going to look in the bathroom. They're just going to take the money and run. I doubt they're dangerous. And remember, I have my pepper spray."

We went our separate ways, Quinn to the pool, and Mike led me to a utility closet to hide in while he prepared the service cart. Ten minutes later, Mike returned.

The cart was much smaller than I expected. "Are you sure I can fit under here?"

"Only one way to find out," Mike said.

Glad I wore shorts, I crawled onto the shelf at the bottom of the cart and curled up in the cramped space.

"Hold on tight," Mike said.

Even with his warning, I almost fell off the cart as it bounced along the path to Mrs. Carlyle's cottage. Each bump, pebble, and turn sent shooting pain up my legs. Several painful minutes later, I heard a knock and Mike's voice saying, "Mrs. Carlyle, I've brought your lunch,"

The bump over the threshold was a particularly nasty one, rattling my teeth. I could hear the clinking sound of cutlery and dishes as Mike set the table for Mrs. Carlyle. Finally, he lifted the tablecloth. I took the easy way and rolled over onto the floor—not exactly elegant, but at least I was free.

"I brought you something to eat, too," Mike said. "You need to keep up your strength for the afternoon's sleuthing."

Mike left, and Mrs. Carlyle and I ate in silence. She gently spooned her gazpacho as I wolfed down a turkey club with fries. On the dot of noon, she retrieved a robin's-egg-blue Chanel bag from her bedroom and deposited it on the living room floor, as the thief had demanded. "Thank you for doing this." And then she left.

I was tempted to open it, to see all that money, but thought better of it and sat on the tub's edge, playing games on my phone, texting Quinn and Mike. With the door shut and the A/C on, the bathroom became an ice chest. At 2:15, I heard a thud from the bedroom. I sat quietly shivering, barely breathing, wondering what was going on in the next room. I strained to hear over the low hum of the A/C, catching only barely perceptible, dull noises.

The bravado I felt with Quinn and Mike was gone, and I realized I was foolish to think I could do this. I texted Quinn and Mike, "Someone's here."

Mike texted back, "I'm calling for help."

I called Quinn's number and muted the phone so she could hear me, but no one could hear her. I pressed my ear against the door, hoping to hear something, anything. *Is he still out there? Has he gone? Where's the help Mike promised?*

Hearing nothing, a sick feeling knotted my stomach. The dognapper *had* gotten away with it. Suddenly, I heard a loud thump just outside the door, and then a crash, followed by a muffled curse. Still no Mike. Heart thumping wildly, I cracked the bathroom door and peeked into the bedroom. A figure lay on the patterned rug, the food cart toppled on its side.

The figure looked up, and I found myself staring at a hoodie-wearing Victor Lockwood. I'm not sure who was more surprised, him or me.

"What are you doing in Mrs. Carlyle's cottage?" he demanded.

"I might ask you the same thing," I replied, with more bluff than bluster. The line to Quinn was still open, and I quickly lowered my hand so he wouldn't notice. The pepper spray was on the tank of the toilet, out of reach.

"I'm the head of security," he said. "I'm investigating the kidnapping of Mrs. Carlyle's dog. You obviously have her dog, and you're here to pick up the ransom money."

"I'm here to catch you in the act," I said. "You're the dog-napper. You have Coco."

"Don't be absurd," Lockwood said.

"Then why do you have the bag with the ransom money under your arm?"

"I'm calling the police," he sneered, pulling a pistol from his pocket and aiming it at me. "Who do you think they'll believe? Some mystery writer or the man entrusted with hotel security?"

So much for my theory that whoever took Coco wouldn't be dangerous. Just then, the hotel manager rushed into the room, followed closely by Mike.

"I have this under control, Mr. Oliver," Lockwood told the manager. "She was grabbing the reward money. She must have Mrs. Carlyle's dog stashed somewhere."

"He's lying," I shouted.

Mr. Oliver looked back and forth, not knowing who to believe, but I could tell he leaned toward believing Lockwood's lies.

"Look," I said. "He has the ransom money under his arm."

"Because I just took it from her," Lockwood said. "Keep her here, and I'll go to the main lodge and call the police."

"Don't let him go," I shouted. "I know he took Coco."

"It's true, Mr. Oliver," Mike declared. "Abbie was hiding in the cottage to catch the dognapper."

Lockwood edged toward the door, the money bag still under his arm. Another step, and he'd be out of the cottage. The hotel manager still looked uncertain about who to believe.

Lockwood's hand was on the doorknob now. Once he was out of the cottage, we'd never catch him. I was next to the table and our lunch dishes were still laid out. I grabbed a plate and threw it, frisbee style. It nailed him right in the middle of his back. He went down like a sack of potatoes.

It took a while for Mike and me to explain, all the while Lockwood proclaiming his innocence.

"THIEF," a voice shouted. Mrs. Carlyle and Quinn stood in the open doorway, the missing pooch cradled in Mrs. Carlyle's arms.

"We found Coco in your security man's apartment." Mrs. Carlyle shot daggers at the manager.

"Abbie called me," Quinn said. "As soon as we heard his voice, we knew it was Lockwood. Mike told us where he lives. It's just a few streets away.

"He stole my precious baby to get the ransom money."

As the police led Lockwood away, we could hear him yelling about his innocence. Quinn and I chose to spend what was left of the afternoon by the pool, enjoying the warm sun. Mr. Oliver came by with a tray of mimosas.

"Mrs. Carlyle took Coco home so her veterinarian can check her out. She paid your resort bill in full and left instructions that anything you want is on her for the rest of your stay."

We thanked Mr. Oliver, and after he left, shared a high-five.

"What do you think we should do?" Quinn asked.

I raised my mimosa. "Have more of that lobster mac and cheese and sleep peacefully with the windows open."

Blood on the White Rose

Sharon P. Lynn

Angie Banks grabbed Matt Riley's shoulder, but he shook her off and finished buckling the child into the back seat of his car. Breathless after chasing him up a steep, snow-covered hill, Angie wheezed as her lungs tightened.

She wanted to shout, "What are you doing?" but words were beyond her.

Five-year-old Joy looked past Matt. "Are you okay, Angie?"

Angie placed a hand on her chest and nodded.

Matt turned and his forehead creased. "*Breskva*, breathe." He closed the door and grabbed Angie's shoulders; his thighs pressed gently into her lower body. The normally intimate moment instead felt like a gentle restraint.

She wanted him to explain the sudden race, but for that she needed air. "What . . . is . . . going—?" She mouthed the words between coughs.

"Later. Breathe."

Matt pulled her meds pouch from her bag, shook the canister, connected the spacer. "Here." He folded her hands around the inhaler.

Sucking the medicine into her lungs, Angie tried to breathe through fear triggered by Matt's uphill dash and the exertion-generated asthma attack. When she lowered the inhaler, Matt handed her an opened water bottle and led her toward sheltering firs in front of his car.

She swirled the water in her mouth, spit it onto the snow. Swish, spit, swish, spit. She always did it three times. She'd made a game of it with Joy, practicing so the child wouldn't be frightened if they were alone when Angie had an attack.

Not trusting her voice, she stamped her foot and glared. Matt responded by guiding her to the passenger door and wrapping her in his arms.

"Be quiet, *Breskva*. Let this pass." He pushed a tendril of her pale red hair behind her ear. Her hair's color had inspired his nickname for her, the Croatian word for peach.

The pain in her chest was lessening. She choked out a demand. "What's going on?"

"There's no time to explain."

"Why not?"

He sighed, folded himself over her, bent his head to hers. In the shadow of the trees, an onlooker would see a pair of lovers, not a silenced argument.

"We have to get out of here."

Here was Plitvice Lakes National Park in Croatia, the second stop on the trip they'd been sharing with Joy's parents. The month-long winter journey was the only time Tod and Vanetta Lynch included their daughter, Joy, and her nanny, Angie, in their travels. Even then, Angie and Joy were on their own, a challenge for Angie, who didn't speak Bulgarian, Slovak or Russian.

When she told Matt about this trip, he'd insisted on joining them in Croatia, to introduce them to his family.

As she calmed her breathing, Angie wondered what Matt couldn't explain.

Minutes before, they'd been strolling on a boardwalk in the 74,000-acre park on the UNESCO World Heritage List. Snow and ice covered the forest where water flowed through limestone karst, coursed over ninety waterfalls into natural dams and lakes, creating a fairytale backdrop for photos. When Matt's phone died from taking so many pictures, she'd given hers to him.

As Matt framed the vista around them, screams rose from below. Angie grabbed Joy and held her close.

"Wait here." Matt rushed downhill, disappearing behind firs obscuring the trail.

"What's wrong?" Joy asked.

"I don't know, sweetie." Angie crouched, blocking Joy's view with her body.

"Let's go see." Joy squirmed to get by.

"No. Matt will tell us when he gets back."

Angie was unaware of the runner until his elbow clipped her arm as he sped uphill. She pulled Joy closer and watched until the man disappeared. He hadn't even waved an apology.

"Look. That waterfall isn't frozen yet." Angie's attempt at distraction earned a pout from Joy. Before she could try a new tactic, Matt sprinted up the path, grabbed Joy, and raced away with the child in his arms.

"Somebody's hurt," he called over his shoulder. "Let's get out of the way before the medics get here. Ready for an adventure, Joyful?"

"Yes!"

"Wait!" Angie had shouted before taking off after them. Tempting "Joyful" with adventures, calling her by his nickname for her, were Matt's usual tricks to capture the child's attention. Most of the time, it was all in fun. Was this?

Now, locked in Matt's arms, Angie studied the anxious expression in his familiar sapphire eyes, resisted finger-combing the curl of wavy black hair falling over his forehead. When his chilly fingers gently brushed her cheek, she pushed them away.

"Explain." Her reedy voice didn't disguise her anger. She coughed.

"No talking." His order was sharp. "Breathe."

She took slow breaths; her eyes locked on his.

Matt ducked and peeked through the car window, smiled, and gave Joy a thumbs-up. Straightening, he whispered in Angie's ear. "A bunch of women were screaming over a man who was bleeding. Some guy was going through his pockets. He took off when I got there."

Angie's stomach clenched. "A runner?"

"Dressed like one."

"He passed us."

"Did he hurt you?"

"No."

"I told the women to call 112 and stay until help arrives. We should go."

Angie pushed Matt aside. "We can't just leave without telling the Lynches."

Matt tightened his grip. "Yes, we *must*. Let's go."

Angie's strength was no match for Matt's. She'd never be able to wrest the girl away from him.

No one else was in the parking lot. Even if she screamed, even if people came to her aid, they'd believe him. He knew the language. He belonged.

"Trust me." Matt opened the door, steered her into the seat, and reached across to buckle her belt, just as he had Joy's.

"We can't leave before you talk to the police." Angie whispered to keep Joy from hearing.

"The others will do that, *Breskva*." His breath was soft against her cheek. "We need to leave." He closed the door.

From the back seat, Joy asked, "Are you okay now?"

Angie smiled weakly at Joy. "Yeah. I shouldn't have run up the hill."

"Where are we going?" Joy asked as Matt headed toward the exit.

"It's a surprise." He pulled over to let an ambulance and police car pass.

"You still have my phone. I should call Vanetta," Angie said.

Matt patted his pockets. "I'm sorry. I think I dropped it running up the hill. We'll replace it later." Hiding his face like a coach on camera, he mouthed, "Don't scare Joyful."

Angie brushed a tear from her cheek, hoping no one had seen it. She had to stay strong for Joy. Mechanically, she replaced her meds in her shoulder bag. Somehow, she had to get word to Vanetta. Figure out how to get Joy back to her parents. Her fingers brushed the slim edge of her tablet inside the padded pocket of her bag. She needed Wi-Fi.

She barely heard Matt tell Joy Croatian folk tales on their drive through the mountains, as she tried to work out the reason for his sudden secretiveness. Angie knew little about the Balkan nation on the Adriatic, but Matt spent childhood summers and still spent Christmas holidays with family near Zagreb. She'd thought his presence on the trip would be a blessing.

Angie had been excited when the Lynches agreed to her request to include him. She'd introduced Matt to them three years before when he'd bumped into Angie and Joy at the library. Still, Tod had to cajole Vanetta. "It will feel more like a vacation for the girls if Matt keeps them company. And we won't have to feel guilty about spending time with our research."

Vanetta had smiled stiffly and retreated to her study. "Fine."

Angie didn't believe the Lynches ever felt guilty about ignoring Joy. Tod was a history professor in his mid sixties, and Vanetta, nearly forty, a novelist who taught occasional creative writing classes. They put work first, and were gone often, sometimes for long stretches. They rarely spent time with their daughter.

Angie had been looking on the campus newspaper site for sophomore-year housing. When she'd seen the Lynches' ad for a live-in caregiver for their newborn, it seemed perfect. Taking the job extended her time at the university, but she'd finished her early childhood degree this past summer. She couldn't imagine leaving Joy now.

Matt's job as a corporate pilot kept him away as much as the Lynches, but when he was home, he practically lived with Angie and Joy in a mother-in-law suite behind the house. Adventures with Matt had made the trio Joy's surrogate family.

But Matt's familiarity with Croatia was fast turning into a disadvantage. He'd just isolated her and Joy in a place where she had no resources.

Squinting as a glint of early winter sunset hit her eyes, Angie noticed a sawmill on a forested road. A few miles later, in a village of side-by-side houses lining a narrow, winding street, Matt pulled into a parking lot.

"Ta da!" He gestured toward a small restaurant and inn.

"Where are we?" Joy asked.

"Ravna Gora, best little town in Croatia." Matt's grin was proud. "And *Bijela Ruža*, the White Rose."

He jumped from the car and unbuckled Joy. "Come meet my family."

Angie followed them up the steps and through a windowed porch with tables and benches. A wood sleigh decorated for Christmas stood in a corner. Beyond the threshold, Matt greeted a woman in a dimly lit reception area. She beamed and hurried around the counter to hug him. Angie heard her name and Joy's before Matt switched from Croatian to English.

"This is my Aunt Marija," Matt said. "She and my Uncle Ivan own this place."

"It's so good to meet Matt's friends." Marija hugged Joy, then Angie. "We weren't expecting you until tomorrow."

"Plans changed. I hope it's all right," Matt said.

Matt hadn't shared his plans to meet his family with Angie. Why hadn't he told her before they left? And why had he shown up a day early?

"Of course. I'll call Elena and Niko. They can bring the kids to dinner tonight. Ivan will be home from work soon."

"I'll get the luggage," Matt said.

Angie grabbed Matt's arm. "We can't stay here. Vanetta—"

He touched her lips with his finger. "Relax. I told the Lynches before we left Split." Matt tipped her chin up and kissed her. With his lips still brushing hers, he whispered, "It's okay."

No, it wasn't.

"We want you to stay." Marija smiled, misunderstanding Angie's hesitance. "Matt is family. You are family. Come." She held out a hand to Joy.

Angie smiled politely and followed Marija and Joy upstairs to a bunk room with four twin beds and a small private bath.

"It's family style," Marija said. "Matt said it would be best. Come down when you're ready."

"I need to go," Joy said, bouncing from foot to foot.

"Then go." Angie waved her to the bathroom, sat on a bed, and retrieved her tablet. Yes, there was guest Wi-Fi. Angie sent a quick email to tell Vanetta where they were. Moments later, after a "thumbs up" reply, Angie took her first deep breath in hours.

After a meal of soup, *sarma*–a cabbage roll–and dessert, Ivan, on zither, and Niko, on *bugarija*, a guitar, played traditional music while the children danced. Between songs, the adults shared more wine and told stories about Matt's childhood visits. When Elena announced it was time to get their kids home, Angie was surprised to see it was after nine.

"Can I play with them again tomorrow?" Joy asked as Angie settled her into bed.

"We'll see," Angie said.

"Where's Matt?"

"Right here." He leaned against the door frame. "I came for story time."

Angie snuggled with Joy and read a short fairy tale.

At its end, Matt rose from a stool near the door. "Kiss good night?"

Joy hugged him. "This is a *great* adventure."

"I'm glad you like it."

"You need to sleep now." Angie watched the child's gaze drift to the bit of sky framed by lace-edged curtains.

Matt tugged Angie into the hall, flicking the light, and closing the door behind him. Picking up the brandy glasses he'd left on a low table in the hall, he handed one to Angie and clinked his gently against hers. "A toast to adventures?"

She looked at him through eyes drowsy from dinner and drinks, took a sip, and collapsed on a couch near the table.

"Whoa. That's strong," she said.

"Plum brandy. Traditional drink."

"But it's nice." She sipped again, letting the warmth melting through her nurture an uncommon bravado. "You owe me explanations."

Matt sat next to her. "I have a lot to tell you." He touched a finger to her parting lips. "Just wait. And promise you won't tell anyone what I'm about to say."

She saw concern—or maybe pleading?—in his eyes. Was he afraid of her reaction? But she had no choice if she wanted answers. She nodded.

"The short version is, well, our meeting three years ago wasn't accidental." He swallowed his remaining brandy and put his glass aside. "I'm with the FBI, and I was told to, um, befriend you. To get close to the Lynches."

"FBI?" Wary, she pulled away. "Befriend?"

"The Lynches are spies. They came to Croatia to defect to Russia."

"That's crazy." Angie's thoughts roiled. The Lynches defectors? Matt an agent?

Matt pulled a vibrating phone from his pocket. He swore as he read a text. "We need to leave." He rose and pulled Angie to her feet.

"Why?"

"Vanetta is on her way here."

"How do you know?"

"We're tracking them." He answered her unspoken questions. "That last night we were in Split, I bugged their luggage. My local contact just texted. But I don't know how they know we're here." He turned Angie toward the bedroom. "Let's get Joy."

She reversed in his arms and pushed against his chest. "They know because I told Vanetta."

Matt's eyes narrowed. "Why?"

"She's Joy's mother."

Matt shook his head. "It doesn't matter now. Police are on the way. We have to leave, and I have to warn my family."

Before Angie could argue, a voice behind them demanded, "Where's my daughter?" Vanetta and a man stepped around a glass partition at the landing. Angie recognized the man's clothes; he was this morning's runner.

Angie moved forward. "She's asleep. Where's Tod?"

"He's . . . hurt. We need to go to the hospital in Zagreb." Vanetta glanced at the man. "Alexei will drive us."

"There's no need to wake her." Matt stepped in front of Angie. "Tell me which hospital and we'll bring her in the morning."

"No. I want her now."

"Vanetta, what's going on?" Angie asked, still feeling the brandy-boosted bravery.

Alexei pulled a knife from his pocket. "It's none of your business. Bring the girl."

Vanetta sighed and spoke sharply in Russian, scowling at Alexei.

Matt pushed Angie toward the bedroom, then like a soccer player, slide-tackled Alexei, knocking him off his feet and propelling them through the glass and down the stairwell. Thuds and grunts followed their descent. Ivan's shout rose from below.

"What's all the noise?" Joy stood in the open door, blinking in the hall light. Discordant sirens screeched in the distance.

Angie felt her chest tighten as she crouched and pulled Joy close.

"Joy, baby, come to momma." Vanetta, arms outstretched, stepped forward.

Joy rubbed her eyes and looked from her mother to Angie. "Is momma coming on our adventure?"

"Don't . . . know." Angie's voice was failing.

"You're coming with me." Vanetta grabbed the child.

"No!" Joy circled Angie's neck with her arms, squeezing tightly.

Angie struggled to loosen Joy's chokehold.

"Come here." Vanetta clutched her daughter.

"I want Angie."

Angie scooted backwards, pulling everyone through the open door. Her inhaler was behind them in the bedroom. She needed to breathe so she could talk to Vanetta.

"Angie!" Joy screamed. "Angie!"

"Come here!" Vanetta tugged, and Joy squirmed.

Angie grasped Joy's small carry-on and swung it as hard as she could, knocking Vanetta off balance and onto the floor. Angie straddled Vanetta's back, pinning her down. The woman screamed and flailed beneath her. Angie nudged Joy toward the far wall and whispered, "Inhaler."

Joy found the medical pouch. As they reached toward each other, Vanetta bucked and tossed Angie aside. Angie's head cracked against the footboard of the nearest bed. Joy screamed again as Vanetta lunged for her. Angie ignored the pain, pushed herself upright, catching Vanetta in the gut. Vanetta let go of Joy and the women wrestled, tumbling back toward the doorway. Angie's hand connected with the stool, and she swung it hard at Vanetta's head.

At the blow, Vanetta collapsed soundlessly. Angie stared at the unmoving form and prayed she hadn't killed her. Blood tinged Vanetta's hair.

Angie scooted backward, gasping, and saw Joy peeking out from behind the bed frame, holding the bag with her inhaler.

Joy scrambled onto Angie's lap, crying. "Are you okay, Angie?"

Angie nodded, wrapped an arm around Joy, opened the bag, and awkwardly prepared her inhaler and raised it to her lips.

Joy scrambled off and dug through the bag to find the water bottle Angie always carried. Handing it to her, she pulled a collapsible cup from Angie's medical kit, opened it, and held it out so Angie could swish and spit.

Angie's breathing returned to normal, but her head throbbed. Gradually, the noises below diminished. She hugged Joy, rocking her and hoping the tearful child would fall asleep despite her silent mother lying near them.

Angie jumped as a shadow covered Vanetta, but exhaled when she saw Matt. A police officer and a couple of medics accompanied him.

"It's all right now," he whispered, stepping over Vanetta and crouching next to Angie and Joy.

Angie winced when Matt stroked her hair and touched the bump.

"You need a medic."

"I'm fine."

"No, you're not." He spoke to the medics in Croatian, nodding at their responses.

"Is she . . . ?" Angie glanced toward Vanetta.

"She'll be okay." Matt lifted Joy and sat on the bed with her. "They want to check you and Joy."

"What happened?" Joy snuggled in Matt's embrace, gently touching a bandage on his forearm.

"A lot, but I'm fine. Everything will be fine."

Angie hoisted herself to the bed and Matt slid next to her.

They watched as the medics tended to Vanetta, placed her on a stretcher, and took her away.

The police officer and Matt spoke in Croatian until the woman medic returned to examine Joy, then Angie. She pulled an instant cold pack from her bag, activated it, and applied it to Angie's head, lifting Angie's hand to hold it in place.

Matt translated. "She doesn't think you have a concussion, but she wants me to check on you tonight and get you to a clinic tomorrow." He hugged Joy. "And she wants you to get some sleep, Joyful." He rose and tucked the child back into bed. "We're going out in the hall so Officer Marić can talk to Angie."

Joy grabbed Angie's hand. "Don't close the door."

"I'll leave it open a crack." She bent to kiss her. "Close your eyes, sweetie."

Angie answered questions about everything from the runner in the park to her fight with Vanetta. When the officer left, Angie checked on Joy before asking Matt, "How's Vanetta?"

"She'll be okay, but it could be quite a while before Joy sees her again."

"Why?"

"Because Tod was the man in the park. He died there."

Angie's eyes widened. "What happened?"

"Tod wanted to take Joy back to the U.S. Vanetta disagreed."

She would be in custody during the murder investigation, he said, then, most likely, stand trial with the Russian. After years, maybe decades, in prison, Vanetta would return to the U.S. to face espionage charges.

Angie gasped. "What about Joy?"

"I think we'll be able to take her home in a few days."

She glared at Matt. "What '*we*'? You lied to me for three years. I don't even know you."

"I'm sorry, *Breskva*. I never lied about how I feel." Matt grabbed Angie's shoulders.

"You never told me what you were doing."

"I couldn't."

"Right, you 'befriended' me. So, now you move on to the next assignment? Someone else like me?"

"There's nobody like you, *Breskva*." He pulled her against his chest.

The long night had drained Angie, and she struggled to pick through its mental and emotional rubble. She deeply loved Joy. She still wanted to love Matt. She let him hold her and gave in to tears.

Later, Angie felt Matt's nudge and saw Joy race across the hall, bathed in pink dawn light. She scrambled between them.

"Are we still on our adventure?"

"You bet, Joyful." Matt kissed her hair.

Angie hugged Joy and whispered as the child settled into her lap. "And it's a big one."

DEER CRACKERS

SHIZUKA OTAKE

"I HATE THIS." I PRESS my face against the window.

Until an hour ago, it was perfect fall weather. Now, the wind whips through the trees, strewing reddened Japanese maple leaves across the moss garden.

"It'll stop by morning. Don't worry." Mika taps her shoulder against mine.

Tomorrow's the last day of the eleventh-grade trip—three nights and four days in Kyoto and Nara. We've seen too many temples, an archive, a swordsmith, and other historical places. We were supposed to go to Nara Park in the morning. All I want is to go there with Mika, Sho, and Hideki, my three favorite people in this world.

The last time I went there was almost three years ago when Mom and Dad were still alive. Petting one of the park's miniature deer was the highlight of that trip. Even though I live in Japan now, I haven't been back.

"Come on, Ayu." Mika grabs my hand and pulls me off the floor. "Let's lay out our futons."

"It's only eight. What about our baths?" My cousin Sachi and Chiemi, who're sharing the room with us, are in the communal bath. Mika and I wanted to wait until the post-dinner rush was over.

"Let's claim our space."

She slides open the closet door and pulls out a folded futon from the top shelf. They're heavy. I keep my arms close to my body, taking small steps before dropping mine to the floor by the window. Our bags are already there. Matching purple backpacks we bought just for this trip. A small airplane charm that used to be mine dangles off the handle of Mika's bag. I gave it to her on the train.

I plop down on the futon and spread my arms like wings. The tatami mat floor smells sweet. The worn yukata, the hotel's cotton kimono, wraps around me like a blanket. I could actually go to sleep right now. If I didn't have to pee. Again. That tea they served at dinner should come with a warning.

In the hall bathroom, I step out of my cloth slippers and into the plastic bathroom ones. I hear rustling from one of the other stalls, so I press the *otohime* when I pee. The gadget's rushing water sound doesn't mask everything. A girl's retching in the other stall. Gross. She takes a ragged breath. She probably drank too much. Some kids hit the vending machines after dinner and bought beer.

I open my stall and come face to face with Sachi. Her small eyes are red, her face flushed. I know she hasn't been drinking. She's been purging. "Are you okay?"

"I don't feel well." She gargles and spits. When she washes her hands, chipped blue nail polish glitters in the water.

I hand her a paper towel. "You were sick last week too." Twice.

She twists her hands in her yukata. With her delicate frame and pointy face, she looks like a distressed fox. I don't want to corner her, but no one else in the family will say anything. Not my aunt. Definitely not my uncle. "Did you make yourself throw up?"

"No!" She pulls back like I've slapped her.

"I'm worried about you. You could really screw up your throat." I stare at her and wait her out. She's never been good with silence.

"I just got too full." She holds her hands out in a circle in front of her stomach. Her forearms look like chicken wings. "I didn't mean to throw up."

Her bulimia's escalating and I don't know what to do. "Maybe you should talk to your mom. She could help you find someone."

"Like a therapist? I'm not crazy!"

Nice. She knows I have online sessions with my therapist back in New York. She stomps down the hallway to our room with me following. Chiemi's back from the bath, and I decide it's a good time for me and Mika to leave.

* * *

AFTER MIKA AND I SWEAT it out in the bath, we stop by the vending machines in the lobby. I pick up two Pocari Sweat sports drinks—one with sugar for me and one without. Bitch or not, Sachi needs electrolytes.

Back in the room, someone has pushed our futons aside. Sachi's sitting at the coffee table, a half-empty bottle of sparkling water in front of her. Chiemi's duffel bag is tipped upside down, its contents spewed across the floor. She's sifting through her clothes.

"What's going on?" Mika asks.

Chiemi shakes out a sweater. "Have you seen my cosmetic pouch?" The infamous Chanel pouch. Her parents gave it to her on her birthday and Chiemi adores it.

"When's the last time you saw it?" I ask.

"After dinner. I used a makeup wipe before the bath. I left the pouch here." She sniffs, fighting back tears. "I've looked everywhere for it."

"Not everywhere." Sachi pushes herself up and walks over to the window, where Mika and I left our knapsacks. "And you and Mika were here alone."

"You think we took it? Fine!" I unzip my bag and tip it over. Underwear, clothes, a Ziploc of toiletries, a bag of shrimp chips, and lychee candies pour onto the floor. No black cosmetic bag.

Sachi's mouth drops open in an oh. Why is she so shocked?

"Maybe it wasn't you." She grabs Mika's bag.

"Sachi, stop!" Chiemi says.

Too late. Sachi unzips the bag and throws everything out. A white case that says *underwear*, a gray one that says *clothes*, toiletries in a clear case. And a black leather pouch. With the gold Chanel logo.

"See!" Sachi's face is gleeful.

"I didn't take it," Mika says. "I have no idea what it's doing in there."

Flecks of blue glitter dot the leather. I pick up the pouch. It smells like expensive cream, leather, and something faintly sour.

"Chiemi, did you leave the room after me and Mika?" I ask.

"Just to get Sachi a drink." She points to the sparkling water on the coffee table.

"So, *you* were in the room alone, Sachi. You could have put that pouch in Mika's bag."

"You're crazy! Why would I do that?" Sachi crosses her arms. A tiny muscle juts out on the side of her chin.

I look at the identical knapsacks tossed on the floor. And think about Sachi's stunned look when she saw the contents of my bag. It wasn't Mika she'd been after. It was me. She'd mixed up our bags. The airplane charm, which I'd had forever, must have confused her. Sachi and I have been drifting apart since I joined karate club instead of drama club with her. But this is beyond.

I show Chiemi the pouch. "See the corner right by the bottom of the zipper? There's glitter. Like Sachi's nail polish."

"I was wearing the same color. I took it off before my bath." She extends her right arm out to me. There's a trace of polish on the base of her thumbnail.

Fair enough. I have an idea and raise the pouch to my nose and sniff. "It also smells a little like puke."

She grabs the pouch from me and brings it to her face. "I just think it needs to be aired out. Sachi wouldn't take it. That makes no sense. And I don't see why she would want to get you or Mika into trouble."

"Do you think Mika took it?" I ask.

Chiemi looks from Sachi to Mika. In the few months I've known her, I've never seen her in an awkward situation. Maybe those don't happen to pretty people like her.

"I can't wait to tell Mom about this." Sachi flicks the corners of her mouth up into a smile that looks sweet. Unless you know her. "She's not going to like you being friends with a thief."

That's what this is about. She thought I was going to tell Aunt Kyoko about her bulimia. So she decided to create something to hold over me. And now she can't go back.

She flits to the door. "I'm going to go tell Ms. Shimizu what happened."

* * *

"I WANT TO KILL HER," Hideki says.

"Shh. Not so loud," I say, although no one's listening in. I messaged Hideki as soon as Sachi left. Five minutes later, Hideki, Mika, Sho, and I are in the hallway outside the banquet room. Someone's vacuuming inside and staff carry out dirty plates.

"You should tell Ms. Shimizu everything you just told me. About Sachi puking up her dinner and the glitter on the bag and the smell and everything." His spiky hair seems to quiver with anger. The neckline of his yukata gapes, and I'm tempted to slip my hand in to touch his back. I need to focus. I'm not here to make out with my boyfriend. This is a council of war.

"I could, but it would screw things up at home."

"Your aunt wouldn't appreciate it if you got Sachi in trouble." Sho says. He understands that appearances are sometimes the only thing that matters. As the town mayor's son, people notice everything he does.

"Wouldn't your aunt believe you?" Mika asks.

"My aunt won't even admit Sachi has an eating disorder. Can you imagine what she would say if I accused Sachi of being a thief? Or of playing tricks on me?" I grip my thighs. A few months ago, when I had to move to Japan, my aunt said she hoped it would work out. Meaning that if it doesn't, she'll send me away.

Mika presses a hand against her chest. "I'll tell Ms. Shimizu what happened. That way it's my word against Sachi's."

I can't let that happen. Even if Ms. Shimizu believes her, Sachi can make life hell. Chiemi will stick up for her best friend. This could end up on Mika's school record.

Hideki stands in one liquid movement.

"Where are you going?" Sho says.

"To Ms. Shimizu's. I'll fix this. I'll message you later."

I press myself off the floor. "We're going with you." Hideki can be dangerous when people mess with his friends.

* * *

MS. SHIMIZU ANSWERS HER DOOR in the hotel's yukata and a padded jacket. She tells us she expected to see Mika, not a crowd. Ms. Suzuki, the teacher sharing the suite, heads downstairs to give us privacy. Mika, Sho, Hideki, and I squeeze together on a sofa like passengers on a crowded train. It doesn't take Mika long to tell Ms. Shimizu what happened.

"I don't know what to do about this. I'm not saying I don't believe you, Mika. And it's true that Sachi was in the room alone." Without makeup, Ms. Shimizu looks too young to be our teacher. Faint freckles dot her nose. "Either way, this is a serious incident. I'll have to talk to the principal when we get back."

I feel Mika shaking next to me and take her hand. Could I get the school to administer a lie detector test? Would that even work? Sachi's so self-centered, she could probably make herself believe whatever she wanted.

"*I* stole it," Hideki says.

I grab his leg. "What are you doing? Ms. Shimizu, he didn't—"

"You know Chiemi and Sho used to go out, right? She dumped him, and she's been a real bitch to him. So I went into the room and stole that pouch." Hideki flashes a grin.

"And how did it end up in Mika's bag?" Ms. Shimizu crosses her arms and leans across the table. "You were going to put the blame on your friend?" She's not buying this. Not at all.

My pulse is pounding so hard, I'm sure everyone can hear it. I squeeze Mika's hand for courage. Aunt Kyoko is going to kill me. But Hideki got in trouble before protecting me, and he could get expelled over this. "Hideki's lying," I say. It's my first offense, so they won't expel me. Will they? I bow my head so my eyes won't give away my lie. "I stole it. Then, I heard someone coming, panicked, and shoved it in Mika's bag. I'm sorry."

Are we going to get kicked out? Both Hideki and me?

"Ms. Shimizu." Sho's voice shakes. "They're both lying." He tucks his hands into his yukata sleeves. "Chiemi and I argued. I was mad at her, so I took the pouch and—"

"You heard someone coming and panicked. I'm starting to see a pattern."

I can't believe Sho is doing this. If this gets out, his dad's reputation could get trashed.

"Do you believe me?" he asks.

Ms. Shimizu presses her hands against the sides of her face. "I need to think about this. I'll let you know what I've decided tomorrow."

Is this going to work? All of us admitting to a crime none of us committed.

MY HOODED JACKET IS MOSTLY keeping me dry in the morning's light rain. The ground is soft, and the air smells like pine. Also, like flour and rice bran. Like deer crackers.

The teachers announced three options for the day. One was the Buddhist Museum. Which sounds about as much fun as watching laundry spin. Only two kids chose that. Most of our grade picked option two—the Art Museum. Mika, Hideki, Sho, and I made it here to Nara park.

We step onto the path and deer rush us like paparazzi swarming celebrities. I hold out a cracker and two deer push each other. The stockier one gets in front and snatches the cracker out of my hand. I open four packs and the boldest of the deer plow through them in seconds. Offering my empty hands, I make the no-more sign, and the deer look for their next prey.

I tiptoe to a tiny deer that stands back from the others. She gives me a wet glance and inches closer. I take out my last pack of crackers, which I saved for her.

After breakfast, Ms. Shimizu took me and Mika aside. We stood under the eaves, getting damp from the rain. "What you and Hideki and Sho did last night was reckless," she said. "You could have all gotten into serious trouble with the school."

I couldn't argue with her. And I knew it was better to stay quiet.

"Mika, I know you didn't take that pouch. I'm not going to bring this up with the principal." Ms. Shimizu glanced around, as if making sure no one was listening in on us. "Now all of you have to put this incident behind you."

"Of course." Mika bowed lightly. "Thank you."

Now that she was off the hook, I wanted more. "You think Sachi's innocent?"

"I can't take sides with my students." She crossed her arms against the wind. "Whatever Sachi did or didn't do will stay with her."

"It's not fair."

"You sound very American, Ayu." Miss Shimizu shook her head. "You must let it go."

The deer bleats. I open my hand and she takes a cracker with her small teeth. She pulls back and I drop my gaze. She noses the side of my face. When I lift my hand, she lets me touch her soft neck. I know she's just doing it because she wants another snack. But that's enough. She reminds me of the last time I was here with my parents. When we were together and didn't want anything more.

Now, my friends are with me in this rainy park. Mika laughing. Sho and Hideki racing to see who can feed more snacks to the deer first. We're here. Together. That's more than enough.

DEAD MAN'S REUNION

VENITA BONDS

DR. HARPY ROBICHEAUX BRAKED FOR an alligator stretched across the narrow dirt road. With a thrust of its tail, the beast launched itself into the black water. Thanks to the gators, deer, and heavy fog in Maurepas Swamp, she'd be lucky to reach Robicheaux Fish Camp by midnight. Her Cajun daddy would be waitin' on a hot coal. Never mind that she'd driven straight through from Houston after seeing patients all day.

Three months ago, Hurricane Katrina had left thousands of bodies in her wake, including two of her relatives. Great-uncle Gustav de Gaulle deserved to be dead, but Cousin Lucien had died while searching for survivors. A gator hunter found Lucien's mangled airboat hung up in a cypress tree near New Orleans. All that remained of the heroic young attorney in the blood-spattered airboat was his left ring finger and a boot shredded by alligator teeth. It was a horrifying end to her favorite cousin; she hoped the crash had killed him before the gator attacked.

Harpy wheeled her Jeep Wrangler into the fish camp and parked beside a swamp buggy. Zydeco music blasted from the two-story lodge on the foggy lakeshore. The *fais do-do*—a Cajun dance party—was in full swing. It didn't seem right to hold a family reunion so soon after the tragedy.

Looking as gray and paunchy as a possum, her daddy was waiting under a yard lamp. Pascal Robicheaux hurried to embrace the tall brunette. "*Quoi ça dit?* Did you have car trouble, *chère?*" he demanded in Cajun French. "What took you so long?"

"Houston's three hundred miles away," she replied in English. "I got here as fast as—"

"And your finger, she is broken that you couldn't dial the phone?"

"Nobody *dials* anymore, Daddy, and—"

"An antiquated but useful figure of speech."

"I accidentally left my phone charger at the hospital," she fibbed. "My battery died."

"Your usual defense. Me, I wish we still used rotary phones. They didn't have batteries."

Guilt stabbed her. "Sorry. I, um, get busy and forget to call."

"*Ça c'est bon,* I'm equally guilty," he apologized, passing his arm around her slim waist. "I've got no excuse to ignore my favorite child."

She laughed and tugged his beard. "Your *only* child."

"Then I'm doubly guilty." As they entered the lodge, he said, "Half the crowd's drunk as a left-handed bicycle on Grandmère's muscadine wine."

"Like last year, *n'est-ce pas?*"

Featuring an accordion, two fiddles, and a washboard, the Zydeco band was performing "Pop Dat Coochie" for the sweating line dancers. Harpy's eleven-year-old second cousin, Gertie, broke out of line. Squealing, the gangly auburn-haired child leaped onto Harpy's back, grabbed her French braid, and spurred her around the room like a horse.

"You're too big to ride her this year, *bébé,*" Pascal chided.

"Yeah, she ain't but a string bean," Gertie said, sliding off. "Don't they feed y'all in Texas?"

Harpy laughed. "You're a fine one to talk, runt. Go dance."

Elbowing a path to the elevated deck, Pascal settled his daughter into a rocking chair. He handed her a red Dixie cup and splashed fiery, home-distilled corn liquor into it from a quart jar. They sat breathing the November air and listening to gators harumph in the swamp, competing with the band.

Pascal leaned back and rested the jar on his round belly. "You should've come home when your great-uncle died. The papers ain't signing themselves."

Harpy nearly choked on the moonshine. Couldn't he let her relax before bringing up Gustav de Gaulle's will again? This was why she hadn't called on the drive over.

"I wish you'd quit chewing old clothes," she said in idiomatic French. "I told you, I don't want the inheritance. I'm heading back to Houston tomorrow afternoon."

"The veterans' hospital can do without you for a few days. You've got family business here."

"I've got patients *there*. My wounded warriors need me." Her throat tightening with disgust, she said, "Gustav betrayed men and women like them. I'm glad he's gone."

"Me, too. But I'm thankful your mama and aunt can't hear you, *chère*." He crossed himself. "God rest their souls."

"I'm thankful they didn't know what their uncle did, or not even God could rest their souls."

The childless bachelor had intended to pass his fortune to his twin nieces. When they flipped their airboat two decades ago, Gustav transferred the bequest to Lucien and Harpy. Strange that Lucien had perished the same way their mothers had.

Stranger still was Gustav's decision to leave them in the will after last year's blow-up. While visiting her aged great-uncle at his Lake Pontchartrain estate, Harpy discovered a damning ledger from World War II. When she confronted him with the evidence of his crimes, Gustav shoved his German-made Walther P38 into her face and tossed the documents into the fire. Cousin Lucien had sworn to have him arrested for war crimes, but without the evidence, the FBI did nothing about it.

Pascal broke into her memories. "You've gotta quit milling the dog's tail."

"What's that mean?"

"You're procrastinating."

"I didn't ask for this." She sipped moonshine and gasped as liquid fire coursed into her stomach. "Lawsy, this stuff's got twenty fights to the gallon."

He raised the quart jar. "Yeah, let's drink to Lucien. He loved my 'shine."

As she clinked her cup against the jar, she said, "It's weird that he and Gustav died only two weeks apart."

Pascal drained the jar, belched, and said, "If it were anyone but those two, I'd agree. But your playboy cousin liked challenging Madame Fate, and Gustav outright mocked her."

His allegation puzzled her. "Lucien lived on the edge, yes, but how did Gustav mock fate? He had a stroke."

"Wasn't he asking for one, clearing hurricane debris? Frederick found him in the garden."

She stared at him in astonishment. The Creole gardener's claim made no sense. "Why would a rich ninety-five-year-old do manual labor? That was Frederick's job."

He shrugged. "That's what Frederick said. He's heartsick. They were together forty years."

She narrowed her eyes in suspicion. "What did *he* inherit?"

"He'll get the garden cottage, two acres, and a stipend. He says Gustav would've wanted him to keep tending the grounds."

What a pitiful inheritance for a long-term partner. Twelve years Gustav's junior, Frederick had enjoyed a lavish lifestyle. Had he known Gustav planned to shortchange him? Harpy let the silence stretch out.

Pascal screwed the lid off a second jar. "I know what you're insinuating, *chère*, but the coroner ruled his death a stroke."

"Under those circumstances? I'd love to see the autopsy report."

"*Tcch*, the body went missing before the autopsy."

Harpy felt her mouth drop open.

"Don't look at me like that. The morgue had too many bodies to process after Katrina."

She tossed back the moonshine. Gasping for breath, she stood and lurched against a post. "I bet Frederick stole it so they couldn't prove he killed the old sinner."

"You're drunk. Sit down before you fall."

She raised her empty cup. "Thanks to your rot-gut, I'm drunk enough to see a way out. Good ol' Freddy deserves a reward. I'll sign the estate over to him."

Pascal stared into his corn liquor as though reading tea leaves. "The will makes no provision for that. You're the last of Gustav's bloodline. If you refuse to sign, the State will take it. Frederick will get nothing. Is that fair?"

Lucien should have resolved this mess after the FBI refused to act, she thought. He'd been a financial lawyer, for heaven's sake.

Scowling, she said, "Daddy, I can't take blood money."

He stood and cupped her chin. "I get that, but I fear you'll end up in court on some IRS tax charge. Is that what you want?"

Her brain reeling from stress and alcohol, Harpy said, "All I want is to go to bed."

"**WHATCHA GONNA DO WITH THE** money, Harpy? Everybody's talking about it."

Harpy pulled a washrag off her eyes and saw an auburn ponytail dangling from the top bunk. It belonged to Cousin Gertie. She'd demanded they share Cabin 3, and then insisted on burning the kerosene lamp, hence the washrag. The child swung down like a monkey and landed on her.

"*Tonnere mes chiens,*" Harpy swore, shoving her off. "Get back in your own bed."

"Not until you spill."

"I'm not taking it. There's blood on all his sh—stuff."

"You were gonna say *shit.*" Gertie's brown eyes burned with fiendish delight. "I wanna hear about the blood."

"You're morbid. And too young to understand."

"I'm not a baby. I gig frogs and help Papa butcher gators. What'd Gustav do?"

Harpy gave up. "You swear to let me sleep if I tell you?"

Smiling, Gertie crossed her heart.

"He was an art dealer in New Orleans," she said. "He went to Paris right before World War II."

"Dumbass."

"*Conniving* dumbass. He intended to buy stolen art. When Paris fell, he cut a deal with the Nazis."

"What kind of deal?"

Her heart pounded as she visualized the ledger. "They paid him to spy on the French Resistance. People died. Soldiers. Civilians. Kids like you."

Gertie stopped smiling.

"He used the loot to buy the mansion on Lake Pontchartrain. That was only one of his many investments."

"Why didn't they put that son-of-a-biscuit in jail?"

"Nobody knew what he'd done until I found the evidence. Lucien called the FBI, but—"

Gertie bolted upright, pointing at the window. "Who dat?"

Harpy sat up to look. "It's only fog."

"Fog with a beard and zombie eyeballs?" She hiccupped and giggled.

In sudden suspicion, Harpy demanded, "Did you get into Grandmère's punchbowl?"

"Accidentally."

"Go sleep it off, you pie-eyed pelican."

Gertie cut her a sly grin. "If you swear to take me to the mansion. Grandmère says it's haunted."

"Grandmère loves to scare little girls with her Hoodoo nonsense. We're not going."

"Afraid a zombie will get you?"

Harpy pinched her. "There's a crawfish boil tomorrow. And Wurlitzer's wrestling a monster gator."

Gertie twirled a finger in the air. "Big whoopie."

"And your mama says I get you into trouble at every reunion."

"Mama don't have to know."

"I guaran-damn-tee you she'd find out. We're not going."

Gertie opened Harpy's purse and dug out a phone charger. She dangled it in Harpy's face. "I heard you tell your daddy you left this in Houston."

"You little spy!" Harpy tried to grab it.

Gertie scampered up the ladder to the top bunk. "'Liar, liar, pants on fire.' That's what Pascal's gonna say when I show it to him."

"This is extortion, you baby devil."

"This is *negotiation*. Want me to charge your phone?"

THEY SLIPPED OUT OF CAMP at dawn. Hungover and sleep-deprived, Harpy could barely navigate the hurricane-stricken back roads. The pine forests looked like dragons had blasted them, but their destruction was nothing compared to the human devastation. Thousands dead. Families displaced. Lives changed forever.

A family sat outside a wrecked school bus, the mother cooking over an oil drum. The children waved at their passing Jeep. Harpy thought of Gustav's will. While it was wrong to accept blood money, as a physician, she was obliged to help suffering people. She'd talk to Pascal about using the money for charity.

They reached the Greek Revival mansion two hours later. Chunks of roof were missing, the windows boarded, the front door bolted. Gertie slapped mosquitoes swarming her bare legs. "I'm gettin' et up."

"C'mon. Watch out for snakes."

They clambered over downed trees into the garden. Although Frederick's cottage had survived, Hurricane Katrina had knocked down the power pole and uprooted every tree.

"Dammit to dogs," Gertie swore. "The storm did a number on the place."

Harpy mopped her face with her T-shirt. "And somebody did a number on Gustav. He wasn't working out here."

Rain began falling as they picked their way to Frederick's cottage. The door was open, but no one was inside. How strange to leave the house exposed to rats and snakes. Worried that the elderly man was sick or injured, Harpy led Gertie to the boarded-up mansion.

No one responded when they pounded on the door. Pulling a picket out of a broken wrought-iron fence, Harpy used it to pry the plywood off a kitchen window. Since the sash was locked, she had to smash the dirty panes to peek inside.

"Frederick, it's Gustav's great-niece." Hearing nothing but echoes in the dark house, she fished out her penlight.

"Sweet," Gertie said. "If a zombie gal crawls out of a closet, you can check her pupils . . . if she still has eyeballs."

"Put your tongue in your pocket, you morbid child."

Gertie crumpled to the ground and clutched Harpy's legs. "Zombie gal's gonna put *your* tongue in her pocket."

"You wanna go sit in the Jeep, zombie gal?"

"And let you fight the living dead by your lonesome?"

Living dead. The words hit Harpy like ice water. She wondered what had happened to Gustav's body. Had the Nazi collaborator become a zombie? Maybe he'd shuffled out of the morgue and returned to the mansion. This was Louisiana, after all.

Gertie snatched the penlight, making her jump. "Boost me through the window. I'll open the door for you."

When Harpy hesitated, she said, "So, you *are* scared of zombies."

"No, I'm scared your mama will kill me if you get cut."

"I'll be careful."

Once inside, they followed the penlight's thin beam through murky rooms that stank of mildew and putrefying rodents. Water dripped from the ceilings and pooled on the floor. They kept hollering for Frederick.

"Race you!" Gertie galloped up a dark staircase.

Cussing, Harpy stumbled after her. Just as she reached the gallery, Gertie jumped out of a doorway. "Zombie gal's fixin' to eat you!"

Harpy nearly fell downstairs. "I ought to open up a can of whup-ass," she snapped. "You scared me half to death."

They heard a shout from downstairs and then a thud. Gertie pasted herself to her cousin. "It's a zombie, *n'est-ce pas?*"

"No, it must be Frederick." They rushed downstairs and found him sprawled face down in the kitchen. Harpy thrust her phone at Gertie. "He's had a fall. Call 911."

Supporting his neck, the doctor carefully logrolled the white-haired Creole. He was unconscious. Blood streamed from a gash on his wrinkled, walnut-brown forehead. Harpy stripped off her shirt, folded it into a tight rectangle, and applied light pressure to the wound.

"Frederick, open your eyes," she said.

From behind her, a deep voice rasped, "You want him seeing you in that black brassiere?"

A bearded man was pressing Gertie against him, covering her mouth with his left hand. Harpy saw a stump where his ring finger had been. While little trace remained of the successful attorney in the ragged swamp rat, Harpy had no trouble recognizing the Walther P38 he'd jammed against Gertie's skull. Her brown eyes wide, Gertie stood still as a heron.

Harpy reached for the picket. "Let her go, Lucien!"

"Don't—I'll shoot her in the head. Push that pigsticker over here."

She skittered it across the tiles. He kicked it behind him. "I'd planned to nab y'all at camp, but then I heard her blackmailing you."

So, Gertie *had* seen Lucien's face in the window. Harpy wished she'd believed her. "Turn her loose, dammit."

"No can do. She's insurance. You're gonna sign the will over to me."

"I'll be happy to, right after you let her go. I don't want the inheritance."

"Nobody gives up a fortune without a fight," he scoffed. "That's why me and Gertie's goin' for a ride."

"No way. This is about you and me."

"And the New Orleans Mafia."

She blinked in surprise. "What's the Mob have to do with us?"

"I lawyered for 'em. Thanks to the unholy trinity—bad investments, slow horses, and fast women—I needed money." He chuckled ruefully. "The don found out I skimmed two million bucks out of his legal defense fund."

You're crazy, she thought. "They cut your finger off?"

He shook his head. "Losing one finger beat getting cut up for crab bait. I had to play dead."

Lawsy, he'd amputated his finger and faked his death. A man that desperate would have no trouble killing a child. She had to de-escalate the stand-off and free Gertie.

Lowering her voice, she said, "You were mighty clever, leaving your finger and that chewed-up boot. Bleeding all over the boat sealed the deal. We were sure a gator ate you. I wish you'd told me you were in trouble. I could've helped you."

He laughed. "Helped me? You're the goody two-shoes that pissed off the old man. He swore he'd leave the estate to Frederick if we squealed."

Harpy realized he'd lied about going to the FBI. And he hadn't waited for Gustav to die of old age.

Gertie squirmed. Lucien slipped his maimed hand to her skinny neck and snapped her head back and forth. "Be still, brat."

"Cut it out, Lucien," Harpy cried. "You'll get nothing if you hurt her."

He shifted his grip to Gertie's ponytail. "You and the kid are gonna help me disappear."

Frederick moaned and opened his eyes. Lucien flashed the injured gardener a cruel smile. "I smothered your sugar-daddy and dragged his ass outside. I bet you bawled like a little girl when you saw your rake in his hand."

Frederick reared up. "I'll kill you!"

Lucien ground the pistol into Gertie's temple. "You'll be wearin' her brains, dandy-boy."

Harpy eased the old man back down. Lucien returned his attention to her. "I knew Pascal wouldn't cancel the reunion, so I laid low 'til you showed up."

Gertie started whimpering. White-faced, the child looked close to fainting. A plan took shape in Harpy's mind. Curling her fingers around the bloody compress, she repositioned it on Frederick's brow.

"Here's what we'll do," Lucien said. "You keep the mansion and give me the liquid assets—cash, gold, jewels, stocks."

She nodded. "Deal. Now let her go."

"Not 'til it's done, and I'm on a plane." He planted a kiss on Gertie's head. "Wanna live in the swamp with Cousin Lucien a while?"

Gertie mule-kicked his knee. "Want me to gig you like a bullfrog?"

Lucien stumbled backwards. Before he could regain his balance, Harpy leaped up and screamed, "Hey, zombie gal, put your tongue in your pocket!"

Gertie went boneless. Caught off-guard, Lucien tried to catch her as she slipped from his grasp. Harpy threw the bloody compress at his face. The pistol cracked like thunder.

Harpy screamed, thinking he'd shot the child. A second later, she realized Gertie had escaped. Adrenaline surged through her veins as she stared into the smoking gun muzzle. Her limbs shook. Her vision tunneled. Becoming aware of burning pain in her left arm, she crumpled to the floor.

"You heifer, don't you die before I get my money!" Lucien hollered, shaking the gun at her. An instant later, he shrieked in agonized surprise and fell. The pistol slid across the tiles. Gertie stood over him, gripping the iron picket she'd stabbed into his back. Screaming, he tried to get his hands behind himself to pull out the spear.

The child jumped clear of him and grabbed Harpy. "Are you gonna die?"

"And let a zombie gal eat me?" Harpy mumbled, trembling and cold. "No freakin' way."

Frederick knelt and examined her arm. "It's only grazed, *bébé.* You're shocky, though. Gertie, fetch towels from the cupboard. Wrap her arm and then hold her feet in the air. I'll check that bullfrog you gigged."

He picked up Gustav's pistol and crouched over Lucien. His hand quivering, he pressed the muzzle between the wounded man's eyes. Lucien's shrieks turned to snorts of terror.

"Please don't kill me! Please, Frederick."

Harpy and Gertie stared in horror, waiting for the gunshot.

The pistol wavered, and then Frederick slowly rose. "You're not worth four horseshoes on a dog, you murdering coward. You won't be faking your death when they give you the needle."

Tears mingling with the blood on his furrowed cheeks, Frederick shuffled out of the room.

Gertie whooshed out her breath. She wrapped Harpy's arm, covered her chest with kitchen towels, and elevated her legs. "You gonna faint?"

"Not if I keep cussin'. Did you call 911?"

"I will in a sec." Her brows drew together. "Mama's gonna kill you for gettin' me in trouble again."

Harpy laughed despite her pain. "Tell her we'll throw the family reunion somewhere tame next year, like Biloxi."

"Biloxi has hurricanes. And floods. And probably zombies."

Lucien moaned, "Is an ambulance coming?"

Gertie showed her teeth in a savage smile. "Shut up or I'll bite you, you son-of-a-biscuit."

"No biting, zombie gal," Harpy said. "Dial 911 before our stupid cousin bleeds to death."

"Dial?"

"It's an antiquated but useful figure of speech."

Harpy closed her eyes and pictured the rotary phones she'd buy for herself and her daddy. No more dead batteries. No more being too busy to call. Together, they'd decide how to give away her inheritance.

ABOUT THE AUTHORS

Mary Adler writes the Oliver Wright WWII Mysteries set in northern California, her home, where she creates habitat for pollinators and admits to being in a co-dependent relationship with her two rescue dogs from Mexico. She is active in Sisters in Crime and the Short Mystery Fiction Society. Her latest short stories appear in *Bethlehem Writers Roundtable* and Malice Domestic's *Mystery Most Devious*. Find out more at MaryAdlerWrites.com.

Allison Baxter has taught high school English as a Second Language for 29 years. She has published short fiction and nonfiction pieces. Her most recent publications include short fiction, "Anamnesis," in *The Examined Life Journal: University of Iowa Carver College of Medicine*, a mystery, "On Ice," in *Mystery Magazine*, and flash fiction, "Faith," published in *Meaningful Conflicts: The Art of Friction, an Off Campus Writers' Workshop Anthology*. She is the secretary of Sisters in Crime Chicagoland and lives with her family and Max, a basset doodle who is so cute that no one cares when he eats their slippers.

Venita Bonds is a Registered Nurse and author of four historical romance novels. A former Longridge Writers Group instructor and technical writer for an intelligence agency, she is a copy editor for *The Astro Restoration Project* and *Killer Nashville Magazine*. She pens health-related articles for *The Lions Club News*. Her Southern folk tales have appeared in *The Saturday Evening Post*, *The No Sleep Podcast*, and *The Huntsville Historical Review*. She currently writes paranormal mysteries set in Louisiana. Her "Southern Folks and Ghosts" blog can be found at www.venitabonds.com.

Susan Daly writes short crime fiction as her way of crusading for social justice. Her stories have appeared in a surprising number of anthologies, and "A Death at the Parsonage" won the Arthur Ellis Award for best short story from the Crime Writers of Canada. She lives in Toronto and hangs out with Sisters in Crime, Crime Writers of Canada, and other known criminal types. She can be tracked down at www.susandaly.com.

Mary Dutta is the winner of the New England Crime Bake Al Blanchard Award for her short story "The Wonderworker," which appears in *Masthead: Best New England Crime Stories*. Her work can also be found in numerous anthologies including the Anthony-nominated *Land of 10,000 Thrills: Bouchercon Anthology 2022*. She is a member of Sisters in Crime and the Short Mystery Fiction Society. Visit her at marydutta.com and enjoy her blog at Writers Who Kill.

Since winning the Bethlehem Writers Roundtable Short Story Award in 2014, **Tracy Falenwolfe**'s stories have appeared in over two dozen publications including *Woman's World, Black Cat Mystery Magazine, Black Cat Weekly, Mystery Magazine, Spinetingler Magazine, Flash Bang Mysteries, Crimson Streets*, and several *Chicken Soup for the Soul* volumes. She is a member of Sisters in Crime, Mystery Writers of America, and the Short Mystery Fiction Society. Find her at www.tracyfalenwolfe.com.

Kate Fellowes is the author of six mysteries, including "A Menacing Brew," which was a featured title in *First for Women* magazine. Her short works have appeared in many anthologies, and periodicals including *Victoria, Woman's World, Brides*, and *Romantic Homes*. Winner of the San Diego Public Library's Matchbook Short Story contest, she met the challenge to craft a mystery just fifty words long. A founding member of the Wisconsin Chapter of Sisters in Crime, her working life has revolved around words— editor of the student newspaper, reporter for the local press, cataloger in her hometown library. She blogs at http://katefellowes.wordpress.com.

Bonnie Finn's love for mysteries began with Trixie Belden and Nancy Drew, devouring both series as a kid. Those childhood favorites sparked a passion for creating her own tales of intrigue fueled by two simple words: "What if?" Originally from Rhode Island, she moved to Vermont after falling in love with a funky, rustic log cabin nestled deep in the woods. There, she lives with her long-time partner, John, and their sweet Yellow Lab/Golden Retriever mix, Abbie. Surrounded by colorful maples and rolling hills, she is currently writing a ghostly, cozy mystery set in Vermont, with her pooch lounging nearby.

Geneviève Goggin is the author of creative non-fiction and made-up stories appearing in *Flash Fiction Magazine*, *The Short Story Show*, *Friday Flash Fiction*, *WIRED*, *101 Words*, and others. Her stories have been included in anthologies and have won or been short-listed for contests, including the Federation of BC Writers 2023 literary contest. She is mining her career in national parks to write her first mystery novel set in the coastal wilds near Vancouver, Canada, where she lives. Find her at www.genevievegoggin.com.

Margaret S. Hamilton wrote "Voices in the Caves" after a trip to southwestern France. She has published over thirty short stories including "Pickup at the Main Street Diner" in *Put Out the Lights and Cry*. Her debut amateur sleuth mystery, *What the Artist Left Behind*, is on submission. She is a member of Sisters in Crime and Mystery Writers of America and blogs monthly on Writers Who Kill. She lives in Cincinnati with her husband and two standard poodles. https://margaretshamilton.com.

Still sane(ish) after 27 years of teaching high school English, **Vinnie Hansen** has retired and plays keyboards with ukulele groups in Santa Cruz, California, where she lives with her husband and the requisite cat. She also writes crime fiction. A Claymore and a Silver Falchion finalist, Vinnie is the author of the Carol Sabala mystery series, the novels *Lostart Street* and *One Gun*, as well as over sixty published short works. Level Best Books will re-issue *One Gun* in 2024 and publish her new suspense novel, *Crime Writer*, in 2025.

Born in Jamaica and raised in Atlanta, **Ann Michelle Harris** is a lawyer by day who writes crime, romantic suspense, and fantasy. She is a Maggie finalist, a double finalist in the Pages From the Heart contest, and a finalist for the Eleanor Taylor Bland Award from Sisters in Crime. Her short story "Changeling" is featured in the grifter crime anthology *Hook, Line, and Sinker.* Her YA fantasy novel *North* debuts in January, 2025. She is a member of Sisters in Crime, Atlanta Writers Club, and Georgia Romance Writers. Find her at annmichelleharris.com.

Beth Irish is a health sciences librarian who writes professionally for information science, medical, and consumer health publications, but has always dreamt of writing a mystery. After attending her first *Murderous March* conference, she found her kindred spirits in the Mavens of Mayhem, Upper Hudson Chapter of Sisters in Crime. She joined SinC, the Guppy Chapter, and the Mavens in 2021. She's served as the Mavens' president as she writes her first cozy mystery.

Erin Jori began her writing career as a journalist covering high school sports for her local newspaper. Her interest in crime writing took root while working as a production assistant at *Court TV.* A content marketer by day, she recently completed her first suspense novel and is revising a second. Erin lives in Chicago with her husband and daughter.

Sharon P. Lynn is a midwestern writer with a background in small town journalism, seasoned with academic writing, poetry, and public relations. She is a Guppy steerer, treasurer of Wisconsin Sisters in Crime, and past board member of SinC Chicagoland. She is also a member of Mystery Writers of America and is a recent finalist of the Midwest Region's Hugh Holton Award. Find her at sharonplynn.com.

For 20 years, as a producer for the *America's Most Wanted* TV show, **Cindy Martin** traveled the world chasing down fugitives and interviewing law enforcement and victim's families. Her short stories include "Malice Challenge" [*Paradise is Deadly* (2023)], "Grave News" [*Notorious in North Texas Anthology* (2024)], and "Key to the Past" [*Crimes in the Old*

Dominion Anthology]. Cindy is a member of Sisters in Crime, Mystery Writers of America, and International Thriller Writers. When Cindy isn't writing her debut thriller, she's teaching killer fitness classes. She lives in South Florida with her husband, three daughters, two cats and two dogs.

Sally Milliken's short stories have appeared in the wedding anthology *Malice, Matrimony and Murder* and the online magazine *Stone's Throw*, but her published credits began in *Hook, Line, and Sinker: the 7th Guppy Anthology* for which she is eternally grateful. She also is the 2023 winner of the Golden Donut Award of the Writers' Police Academy, and she won the First Prize in the Bethlehem Writers Group 2023 Short Story Contest. She is working on her first novel, a historical mystery set in 1882 and based in coastal Massachusetts, where she lives with her family. Visit her at sallymillikenauthor.com.

Lisbeth Mizula, happy Guppy and member of SINC, has written and performed her own stand-up comedy material, published short fiction in local and national publications, and collected wins in writing contests. She has a horror/romance novella in the editing stage and is currently working on a humorous mystery set in Good Deeds, Texas—the small bay town where good deeds are legally required of all residents every Tuesday, the only acceptable excuses being jail, institutions, or death. Lisbeth lives with her husband, brother, and a dog named Noodle.

Shizuka Otake is a writer born in New York City. In her twenties, she lived in Tokyo for four years, and now wishes she had a magic door between the two cities. She loves mystery novels, Japanese TV, and traveling—a.k.a. prowling bookstores and eating. Shizuka writes about identity and the need to find home. In 2022, she won Sisters in Crime's Eleanor Taylor Bland Crime Fiction Writers of Color Award.

Mystery and suspense author **Cynthia Rice** is a physician living in the Milwaukee area and a proud member of Mystery Writers of America and Sisters in Crime. Her debut novel *The Last Broken Girl* was released on June 3rd, 2024; the novel won the 2023 Claymore Award in the category of suspense. When she is not working on her next novel, Cynthia keeps busy reading, traveling, and playing mediocre tennis and golf. She lives with her two cats, Clarice (NOT named for *Silence of the Lambs*) and Porkchop.

Linda Ryea Richard's love affair with the written word began before she could read. Fearing another round of "Hickory Dickory Dock," adults would flee when the toddler approached, clutching her book of nursery rhymes. In high school, she entertained readers with a weekly newspaper column. Linda then spent four decades as an educator and judicial administrator, collecting stories that now fuel her fiction. "Two If By Sea" introduces Lucinda and Luanne, feisty identical twins from her novel-in-progress. Linda resides on a picturesque Vermont lake with her husband and a Miniature Schnauzer, the latter who harbors delusions of being a Doberman.

KM Rockwood draws on a varied background for her stories, including as a special education teacher in inner city and alternative schools. In addition, she has worked as a laborer in manufacturing facilities and supervised an inmate work crew in a large state prison. She is currently retired. Published works include the Jesse Damon Crime Novel series (Wildside) and numerous short stories.

Nina Wachsman is a former art director and illustrator who studied under Maurice Sendak at Parsons School of Design. She has published stories in mystery and horror magazines and anthologies, and *The Gallery of Beauties*, her debut novel, was nominated for an Agatha and a Silver Falchion. Its sequel, *The Courtesan's Secret* received a 5-star recommendation from the Historical Fiction Company, and the third book in the series will be published by Level Best Books in September 2024.

www.ingramcontent.com/pod-product-compliance
Lightning Source LLC
Chambersburg PA
CBHW071251190726

48292CB00007B/2500